Warbow

The Saga of Roland Inness

Book 2

Wayne Grant

To Mary—you were the first grownup to read these books and to believe I might actually be a writer. Your excitement is half the fun.

Contents

Map

The Saga of Roland Inness

The Sprite

The wind came out of the north, not quite a gale, but a rare summer gust of chill air that sent spindrift flying from the tops of the waves. The *Sprite* ran before it—south toward Iberia. She was a sailing cog out of Dover with a single square mainsail that was drawn taut as a bowstring. That morning she had left the relative shallows of the English Channel behind and entered the Bay of Biscay. All sight of land was lost as the sea shifted from grey-green to a deep, cobalt blue. The swells grew as the bottom fell away.

On deck, sheltered from the following wind by the small raised sterncastle, sat two young men—one tall and dark-haired, the other fair and compactly built with a thatch of ruddy hair. The latter gnawed happily on a hard biscuit. The former looked near death.

"Roland, ye should try one of these. It might settle the stomach," said Declan O'Duinne, thrusting his half-eaten breakfast under his friend's nose.

His companion only groaned in response. The thought of anything in his stomach at that moment was enough to bring on a new, black wave of nausea. Roland Inness had set foot on a boat for the first time just three mornings before in Dover. Then, the notion of a sea voyage seemed full of adventure and excitement—and thus it had been as the vessel crept down the coast in calm waters.

But this constant rising and falling of the small ship since losing sight of the shore left him unsure of his legs and less sure of his gut. He'd spent the fourth morning on board hanging over

1

the wooden rail trying to coax what little remained in his empty stomach to come forth. He longed to be back on solid English soil, but events in the greater world had conspired to place him on this pitching deck.

It was July in the year 1190 and Richard, the newly crowned King, had joined the great Crusade to retake Jerusalem from the Muslims. He had charged Sir Roger de Laval with the task of scouting out the situation in the Holy Land in advance of his arrival with the English army. On his mission, Sir Roger was to present himself as simply another knight come to join the Crusade. In that guise he was to act as Richard's eyes and ears.

His squires were duty-bound to be at his side. To Roland and Declan, it seemed a grand adventure, brimming with opportunities for glory. Certainly they would face great peril in the Holy Land, but great honour would surely come to those who rescued Jerusalem from the Saracens. Still, the Holy Land was more than three months away by sea and, as the boy once more scrambled to the rail, he felt certain he would never reach there alive. Roland Inness was seasick—and a sorry sight to behold.

Master Henry Sparks, the ship's commander and a sailor of long experience, stuck his head over the railing of the sterncastle and looked at the young squires below. For a man with such a round frame, he moved with incredible agility about the deck—never seeming to lose his balance or stumble over the chaos of supplies lashed everywhere. He was a man of near perpetual good cheer and was in a buoyant mood as he kept one hand firmly on the steering oar and surveyed his passengers.

"Got a bit of the rolly-pollies, me lad?" He shouted this at Roland with more amusement than concern.

"He's been throwin' up everything he's et in July, Master Sparks," Declan offered happily, "and he's working on bringin' up June!"

"Ah, 'tis sad," the Master shouted over the rising wind. "I've seen stout men beg to cut their own throats rather than endure another hour of this constant pitching—to and fro, to and fro."

Roland could endure no more and heaved toward the rushing blue sea below. Nothing but bile came forth and the boy wished he had something—*anything*—left to expel. He wiped his mouth with the sleeve of his tunic and thought for a moment how easy it would be to just slip over the rail and into the water. He couldn't swim a stroke and his misery would be quickly over. Instead, he staggered back to his position under the sterncastle.

The two squires had taken up quarters in the scant shelter there. Roland sank against the rolled-up blankets that were part of the travelling kit Lady Catherine de Laval had prepared for them. Deep in the bundle he felt the length of hard yew that was his longbow. Idly, he ran his hand into the folds and gripped the weapon that he had crafted with his own hands. The feel of it was always comforting.

Beneath his head he could feel several hard objects wrapped in a second blanket. One was the dagger he took so long ago from the assassin Ivo Brun and the other was the only gift he had ever received—a silver amulet embossed with a spreading yew tree. It was given him by Lady Millicent de Laval, Sir Roger's daughter and only child, to remind him of home. He was fifteen years old, and these were the sum of his possessions.

"Take heart, lad," the Master called from above. "By midday this little squall will have passed and the sea will quiet a bit. Before we pass the Pillars of Hercules, you will be used to the motion—such that solid ground will seem strange to walk upon!"

The sick boy leaned forward and held his head in his hands. His fellow squire edged away, afraid that at any moment a new eruption might issue forth from his friend. Declan O'Duinne was Irish and perhaps a year older than the young man at his side. He had been commended into the service of Sir Roger de Laval during one of the late King Henry's campaigns to subdue his troublesome Irish kinsmen. Sir Roger had bested the boy's father in battle, but spared him for the sake of his courage.

This boy was no hostage or prisoner taken by a conqueror. His father had bidden him serve the big Norman knight and the boy accepted that service willingly. Being squire to a soldier of Sir Roger's prowess was an honourable station—and perhaps profitable in the end, though his master seemed to have no care for wealth himself. Declan O'Duinne was as ready for adventure as any lad of sixteen, but he made no bones over his fervent hope that glory might come with a bit of treasure attached to it.

Looking across the short deck of the vessel, past stacks of provisions and the scurrying crew, Declan saw his master sheltering under the forecastle. An oiled tarp was secured beneath the raised tower and at each rail, forming a reasonable bulwark against the weather. Under this shelter, Sir Roger had established rude quarters near his great warhorse, Bucephalus. The huge animal was secured in a makeshift paddock in the hold, but such was his size that he could lift his massive head through a hatchway and rest it on the deck above. The big knight was absently running his hands through the horse's mane as he spoke to the man sitting next to him.

His companion was a smaller man, but broad of build and muscular-looking, despite the shapeless monk's robe he wore. The two were engaged in an animated conversation. It had been thus for most of the short voyage and the squire wondered what the two men discussed. Declan knew little of this Father Augustine, who was known to his flock as Friar Tuck, save that he had come from the Midlands of England and played some role in helping his fellow squire flee Derbyshire for poaching a deer—and other crimes that couldn't be spoken of.

The monk was more than friendly enough, but there was something about him that both alarmed and comforted the Irish boy. Tuck was a Knight Templar, which should have marked him as a fanatical warrior for the Christian cause, but there was little in his carriage or speech to suggest anything but a man of the mildest character. Declan could not quite sort out these competing impressions, but he was certain that he preferred the monk be with them rather than against them.

Amidships, the Irish boy saw a man as thin as a ferret walking on one of the two narrow catwalks that ran along the cog's bulwarks and connected the raised decks fore and aft. He tossed a weighted line ahead of the plunging *Sprite*. This he had done all the previous day as they had beat down the English Channel—calling out soundings that varied but little. Early on the fourth day, as the land disappeared over the horizon, the soundings showed the bottom falling away. Now he held up the knotted end of the played-out line for the Master Spark's inspection.

"No bottom, sir."

"Very well, Boda. Secure the line. We'll not need it 'till Spain comes over the horizon."

"Aye, sir." The man that Sparks called Boda retrieved the sounding line, coiling it expertly between the palm of his right hand and his right elbow. He stowed the line in a bag tied to a peg on the mast. Completing his task, he moved with the confident ease of a veteran sailor over the plunging deck toward the bow.

From the beginning, there was something about Boda's manner that Declan did not like. He had seen the man shoot them dark looks on several occasions since setting sail from Dover. He nudged Roland and nodded toward the sailor.

"That man Boda—he's been watching us careful—and it's not out of love I'm tellin' ye. He looks like a black-hearted villain, with those ratty little eyes always dartin' about."

Roland had also seen the man staring at them on more than one occasion and wondered what interest he could have in two squires. Whatever his character might be, he was, at the least, unsightly. His body was as gnarled as a piece of driftwood and he was missing his teeth in the front. His skin seemed to have the texture and colour of a tanned hide.

"He bears watching, Dec, but I'm hardly up to it. I'll trust you to keep an eye."

"Oh, that I will," the Irish boy replied grimly. "Trust me on that."

***

True to Master Sparks' word, the wind died as the morning progressed and the sea began to calm a bit. A pale sun could be seen through a thin overcast. For Roland, the slacking of the wind and waves was a godsend. For the first time in hours he could think of something besides the misery in his belly. The boy leaned on his friend to rise, but the Irish boy jerked away. Roland could almost grin at Declan's reaction.

"I'll not spew on you, Dec. In fact, I think I may live. Where can I get a piece of that biscuit?"

Declan relaxed a bit and tossed his friend one of the hard crumbly disks that passed for victuals on this voyage.

Roland chewed aimlessly on the morsel, then pulled himself up and climbed to the deck of the sterncastle where Master Sparks kept a weather eye on all that transpired on the *Sprite*. The ship's master beamed at his new arrival.

"See! I told ye, ye'd be in the pink by noontide, lad. Here...man the oar a bit." He turned the heavy oak steering arm over to the boy, who grabbed it with both hands and braced himself against the push and tug of the sea. Sparks clasped his hands behind his back and surveyed the horizon. As far as could be seen in any direction was the blue sea.

"So Master Inness, no land in sight. Some find that troubling—do you?"

Roland glanced about at the featureless expanse of blue.

"Aye, sir—a bit. Seems a body could get easily lost out here."

Master Sparks chuckled and shook his head.

"Aye, Master Inness, ye can indeed if yer not careful. Other shipmasters prefer to stick near the shore of France on the voyage down to Iberia. I call 'em 'coasters.' For some it's fear and for some it's ignorance—for it more than doubles the distance." The man shook his head and frowned. "Now I prefer this landless horizon and care not to slink along the coast of France. Can you feature why?"

Roland thought for a long moment.

"Do ye dislike the Franks, sir?" Sparks erupted in a booming laugh.

"Har! That's close enough to the truth! By Neptune's beard, I cannot stand the Franks. They are a perfidious race— but that's not the *principal* reason I shun their shore."

Roland waited patiently for the *Sprite*'s fat little master to continue. After a brief pause for dramatic effect, he spoke.

"Far more ships come to misfortune upon the land than upon the sea, lad. Reefs, shoals, rocks of all kinds inhabit the waters of a lee shore, not to mention the odd lot of local pirates. Nay, the sight of land is nothing for a man to take comfort in— if he trusts his vessel. 'Tis nothing but trouble, but out here," he swept his arm broadly across the southern horizon, "there's naught to put a great gapin' hole in your bottom! 'Tis the way I like it."

"What about the monsters and serpents that are said to inhabit the deep waters?" the boy asked.

"Never saw a one," the master shrugged his shoulders, "unless ye count the great whales as monsters, but they do us no harm."

Roland made a mental note to ask the master what a whale was, but was more interested at the moment in how Sparks could find his way on this featureless sea.

"How do ye know which way to steer out here, away from any landmark?" the boy asked. "In the woods near my home, I knew every tree and rock. By those I could guide myself, but on the sea there is nothing."

"Ah, but there ye're wrong, boy," the man replied. "Attend careful now, for this is a deep mystery. We can judge our direction fairly well by night by using the North Star. Ye know the one I mean?"

Roland nodded. His father had taught him years before that one star stayed fixed above the northern horizon, while all the others danced around it in a great circle across the sky.

His father... The sudden, sharp sting of tears surprised Roland. He quickly turned aside so Sparks would not see. This memory of his father had come to him unbidden, but very clear. They were standing together in the small field near the rude hut that was their home high on the flanks of Kinder Scout mountain. It was a winter night and the furrows of the field were frozen hard. Rolf Inness stretched his arm up toward the heavens.

"There, son—just above the tall pine. See the seven stars of the Plough? Follow them up to the last one in the handle, the bright one there. That's your guide at night. It will always point true."

7

The boy kept his head turned toward the bow so Sparks would not see his brimming eyes. It had been less than a year since his father's death, and the rawness of the pain lingered. That spring, driven by famine, Roland had taken a deer on the Earl of Derby's land with his longbow. Longbows in the hands of peasants were a threat to their Norman overlords and when the kill was discovered, a manhunt was launched.

Roland fled, but Rolf Inness paid for the boy's crime with his life—put to death on the orders of William de Ferrers, the Earl's son. In his grief and rage, the boy had cut down three of the murderers with his bow—though not de Ferrers. That nobleman fled in a blind panic from his ambush.

Roland's boyhood ended that day and he became a fugitive, only narrowly escaping the wrath of de Ferrers and his men in the weeks that followed. As he tried to gather himself and control this sudden flow of emotions, Roland saw his master across the way chuckling at something Friar Tuck had said. *Tuck.* He would likely have died in the forests of Derbyshire if Friar Tuck had not stumbled upon him and again in London when the monk had saved him from the blade of the de Ferrers' assassin, Ivo Brun.

He had much to thank the man for but it was the large, balding knight laughing at the forecastle that had saved him from the life of an outlaw—or worse. A chance meeting on the road to York had been his salvation. Sir Roger de Laval had taken him in and made him a squire. It was a miracle for which he thanked God in prayer each night.

Dry-eyed now, Roland turned back to Sparks. The ship's master was staring at him and the boy realized that he hadn't answered the man's question.

"Aye, Master Sparks, my father taught me to use the stars—but what of the day? How then do you steer?"

Sparks chuckled good-naturedly. "You're a curious lad, aren't ye? It's a virtue I prize and rarely see! Daylight *is* a different matter. The sun is some small help, but not so reliable. Depending on the season, its path changes. And if clouds prevail, day or night, these signs are all useless." The man paused to let the boy ponder this nettlesome problem.

Warbow

"For a real guide, by dark or light, you need one of these!" He drew a square box from a small chest and carefully set it on the deck of the sterncastle. He raised a hinged wooden lid to reveal that it held liquid—and in the liquid floated a curious object. Roland peered into the box. On close inspection, it had the vague shape of a fish. Master Sparks used one hand to turn the fish's tail toward the rudder. Almost instantly, it swung back around until the head again faced the stern of the ship.

"The head always points back toward England!" the boy exclaimed.

"Not quite, lad. It points that way at present, because England is north. This is a lodestone, passed down to me by me father who got it from some misbegotten Italian. The magic of it is the fish's head always points to the north."

Roland had heard of such a device from his grandsire, the old Viking for whom he was named. His Norse ancestors had used the stars and knowledge of tides as well as the flight of seabirds to guide them, but they knew of this pointing instrument from their far travels.

"How does it know north?"

"That's the mystery, and I cannot tell. But it always knows, no matter clouds or fog or brightest day. It always knows. With this I can steer true south from the mouth of the Channel and be sure I will strike Iberia in five days, if the wind holds as it now does."

"How can you tell it will take five days to reach land, sir?"

Sparks threw back his head and laughed. "Full of questions aren't we? I hardly expected that when ye were pukin' over the rail!" He clapped Roland on the shoulder and took the heavy steering oar back in his large hands. "It's a long voyage Master Inness and if you've a mind, I can teach ye what I know of navigation—all in good time."

The boy nodded as he walked to the forward rail of the stern castle. *He could wait.* He watched Sir Roger, sitting with his long legs dangling into the hold, scratching the nose of his grey warhorse. His master had taught him that patience was a necessary virtue for one of his station and that even revenge must wait its time. It was one of many lessons he had learned from the Norman.

The day would come when he would take his revenge for the murder of his father, but for now another debt had come due and he must follow his knight into war. He had heard the call for Crusade from the King's own lips, but the Holy Land still seemed far away and Jerusalem the stuff of legends. His cause was watching the back of Sir Roger de Laval, whether near to home or in far-off lands. This was his duty to the man who had saved him—and a promise he had made to the Lady de Laval.

He did not intend to fail them.

Iberia

"Land ahead, Master Sparks!"

Roland sat bolt upright at the cry that came from the watch on the forecastle. *Land.* He may have come to terms with the sea over the past nine days, but was no less anxious to be back upon solid earth. Declan O'Duinne was slower to react, but he too was stirring.

"Come on you sluggard," Roland said as he dragged his fellow squire from his bed roll. The two scrambled forward, past where Sir Roger and Friar Tuck still slept, and up to the small platform that was the forecastle. A pale sun was rising through thin clouds to the east and Roland strained to catch a first glimpse of the great Iberian Peninsula. He could see nothing through the thin morning mists.

"Declan...can you see anything?"

"Not a thing—but then yer the one famous for the sharp eyes as I recall. Great hunter and tracker and all that. Can ye not see something as big as Spain?"

"Afraid not. I think I need trees and rocks about to be of any use at all. Seeing some speck in this watery waste is beyond...wait! There!" he pointed to the right of the bow. "Something is showing—just a little bump above the horizon!"

"That'd be the Torre de Hercules."

The voice was Boda's, and it startled the two boys.

"'Tis a great tower o' stone, built by the old Romans to warn away ships from the headlands."

Roland nodded toward the man. This was the first time since the voyage began that the gnarled old sailor had exchanged more than a suspicious glance with the boys. As if to offset this accidental civility, he gave the squire a sour look in return and resumed his watch. Declan was leaning forward over the railing and straining to see the far shore.

"There! I can see it now!" he shouted, pointing to starboard. "Spain!"

Roland was bursting with questions and Boda wasn't talking. He grabbed Declan by the arm and dragged him back to the sterncastle where the ship's master smiled a greeting.

"Master Sparks—will we be putting in near here? Are we going ashore?" Roland's voice betrayed the eagerness of a landsman to be off a pitching deck.

"I fear not, lad—though I know 'twould be a comfort to ye. Nothing but trouble ashore in these parts." The *Sprite*'s Master scowled toward the dark shape of the Spanish coast as though it were a nest of vipers.

"But Tuck says these are Christian lands here in the north," the boy replied.

"Aye, 'tis Christian—on most days, but so be England and there's plenty of mischief there, ye'll agree? The Moors to the south would slit yer gullet in the name o' God and the Christians hereabouts would do it for a shilling. I say stick to the sea and keep a distance from the lot! We'll follow the coast, but not put in."

***

As the days passed, the weather continued to cooperate. The breeze was steady out of the northeast and Master Sparks kept the *Sprite* headed due south on a broad reach. Roland had almost completely overcome his seasickness and wondered if he had been cured or if the malady was only in retreat until the swells grew high once more.

Sir Roger tried to keep his two squires busy with grooming Bucephalus and mucking out the big warhorse's stall under the forecastle. The boys didn't mind, for it gave them an opportunity to overhear what their master and Friar Tuck were discussing.

"We'll be drawing near to Lisbon in a day or so and I've advised Master Sparks to steer clear, though I know he would like to take on provisions," said the monk.

"And what harm lies in Lisbon, Father?"

"Ah, more than meets the eye," Tuck replied. "The city fell to the Christians forty years ago when a party of Dutch knights travelling to the last crusade happened along and took the place by storm. 'Twas the last real Christian victory along this coast, though I hear the Spanish press the Moors in the north. Our Christian cousins haven't been able to push very far inland or much further south, but they haven't forgotten how useful passing Crusaders can be. I know of the bishop here and he would demand that you, as a matter of tradition and courtesy, strike a blow at the Saracens."

Sir Roger de Laval snorted as he sat sharpening a dagger on a whetstone. He didn't know much about this slightly round, but sturdy friar before setting sail—only that he had helped Roland Inness get out of Derbyshire just ahead of the Earl of Derby's men and that he was a member of the Knights Templar.

This order of military monks was known throughout Europe and far beyond for their skill and courage in battle and a fanatic loyalty to their cause. The order had been formed to protect Christian pilgrims visiting the sacred sites in the Holy Land, but in only a hundred years the Templars had become a force to be reckoned with, both in war and politics. It had not taken the veteran soldier long to confirm that this jovial monk was as schooled in the art of war as he—and far better schooled in the ways of the world they were entering.

"I've no quarrel with these blasted Moors of Spain. As you say, they've been here for centuries and will no doubt be here for centuries more. If they were camped in Cheshire, why I'd smite them day and night, but they are not. Seems to me to be the problem of the Portuguese and the Spanish."

"Aye, 'tis their problem," said Tuck, "but should we put in there, they will make it our problem as well."

"I'm on a mission for King Richard, and I'll be damned if some local potentate should try and hinder me!" the knight protested.

"But you cannot say so," Tuck reminded him. "Lisbon is the last Christian port for hundreds of miles. It is on the frontier with the Muslim world and crawling with spies from all sides. If any learn of our mission, we will encounter far more than a diversion, I fear. And Roger, heed you, it is the Christians more than the Moors we need to fear on this journey. Not all love our King and many would do more than hinder us if they knew your charge."

"Yes, yes..." the big knight nodded in exasperation. "I like it not that we fly a false flag, Father, but I take your point."

Roland listened to this exchange with rapt attention, until the massive nose of Bucephalus nudged him roughly on the shoulder. He realized that he had been brushing the same spot on the horse's flank for many minutes. To the boy, Lisbon sounded less like a distraction than a grand adventure, but he had to trust the judgment of Tuck. It had not failed him yet.

That night the wind blew the few scattered clouds away, leaving the sky ablaze with stars. The squires lay on their bedrolls gazing upwards. Roland looked back over the stern of the *Sprite* and quickly picked out the North Star where his father had taught him to look. Beneath his head he felt the familiar shapes of his hidden possessions. He turned and, reaching between the folds, curled his hand about the round silver amulet that had been the gift of Sir Roger's daughter.

Roland wondered what Millicent de Laval was doing back at the small castle on the wild border with Wales. The summer past he had tracked her into the forbidding Clocaenog forest when she was captured by Welsh raiders. She, in turn, had saved him in their desperate flight from that dark place. From that, a bond had been forged between the two. He remained a peasant squire and she the daughter of his master, but there was something there akin to friendship.

Millie de Laval was a formidable young woman—he could no longer think of her as a little girl. She had given him the amulet the day they parted. She said it would remind him of home and bring him good luck. He knew she was at least half right—he would not forget her or Shipbrook. He closed his eyes and began to drift off.

He prayed she was right about the good luck.

The Summons

The sun was just beginning to dip below the trees to the west of the small castle at Shipbrook. It was more than an hour until sunset, but Lady Catherine de Laval was worried. Her daughter had not returned from her afternoon ride, and while this was not unusual, it unnerved the woman. Less than a year had passed since the girl was seized by the Welsh warlord Bleddyn and spirited away over the border to the wilderness of the Clocaenog forest. Had it not been for Roland Inness and his longbow, she might still be there, or be dead, and young Inness was now long gone over the sea following her husband.

Roger de Laval was a man who always made her feel safe, made her feel like nothing could really touch their family. But while he brought the girl home from Wales unharmed, the incident had shaken her like none before. And now Roger had been gone for months and with him his squires, Roland and Declan. Shipbrook seemed empty without them and it played upon her nerves. She paced along the western wall walk of the small fortress she loved and looked to the west—looked for her daughter.

"She'll be along, Catherine." The man who joined her on the west wall of the castle was a Welshman himself, but one the de Laval's trusted above all men. Sir Alwyn Madawc was Sir Roger's Master at Arms and oldest friend—her friend too.

"I have two of my best men shadowing her. And besides, if I know my own kind, the raiders will still be squabbling as to who will be leader since our lad Roland killed the last one.

15

They'll have no time to be making trouble on this side of the border, at least for a while."

"Alwyn, I know I am taking too much counsel of my fears, but you know how close we came to losing her." Lady Catherine turned as she spoke, fixing him with that steady gaze that discomfited many.

"Aye, Catherine, we were caught napping. We all thought the raiders were too bloodied by their last venture into our lands to come again so soon. We will never make that mistake again. I have patrols out morning and evening watching the ford. Millie is safe as long as she stays to our land—and while she may be a handful for her mother, she has yet to cross me on an issue like this!" The knight grinned and it transformed his scarred face from fearsome to almost gentle.

"You don't miss much, do you, old friend?" the lady replied. "I seem to be the only one these days who cannot talk some sense into the girl!"

Sir Alwyn continued to grin broadly. "Give it time, Catherine. Seems I remember a young lass who was very much like that. Ran off with a Norman knight against the express commands of her own mother."

Catherine de Laval gave him a withering look, then laughed out loud. Yes, she had run off with the young soldier who was now her husband—to her mother's woe. Roger de Laval was little more than a soldier of fortune back then with nothing to impress even a minor noble family. She had prospects aplenty in those days, but she knew from the beginning that he would be her man. Prospects be damned.

"You have me there, Alwyn, but next time you compare me to my mother, I will have you clapped in irons until my husband returns!"

The knight nodded his surrender, then pointed over Lady Catherine's shoulder.

"And here comes your wayward daughter now, my lady."

Catherine swung around to see Millicent on her favorite palfrey racing ahead of her two bodyguards who were hopelessly overmatched, both in the quality of their mounts and in their skill as riders. Few could match Millicent de Laval in the latter. Lady Catherine could see, even at a distance, that her daughter had a look of pure joy on her face as she raced toward the small west gate of Shipbrook.

In but a few moments, she heard the sharp clatter of hooves on the cobbles below as her only child arrived back safely to their fortress. Her keepers were still half a mile from the gate. Lady Catherine nodded to Sir Alwyn and made her way to the central courtyard where the Lady Millicent was already handing over her lathered mount to a groom. The girl saw her mother approach, and while her face was still flushed with the excitement of the race, her posture stiffened.

"Well ridden," Lady Catherine called out with a smile, and her daughter's tense frame softened. In many ways the girl strongly resembled the woman approaching, with the same long auburn hair and brown eyes, but at almost fourteen, she was taller than her mother and had the purposeful walk and carriage of her father.

She's more of a young woman each time I see her, Lady Catherine thought. She had grown half a foot in a year it seemed and there was no mistaking the changes in her figure. The lean girl who could outride anyone in the county would now pass for a woman. In another year there could even be suitors. The mother smiled to herself. *They would not know what they bargained for with this one.*

"Millie, supper is in an hour and we have much to discuss."

"Discuss, Mother?" the girl replied distractedly.

"Aye, daughter. We've been summoned."

Now the girl's distraction vanished.

"Summoned? Where…by whom?"

"Why to London, Millie. By the Queen."

For a moment Millicent looked puzzled. *Queen?* The King was unmarried. Then she recalled that there was a Queen in England still.

"Queen Eleanor?"

"Aye lass, the very same. She has summoned the noble ladies from every house in the Midlands as well as Cheshire to a reception in London. We are to accompany Lady Constance. The news came but an hour ago."

"We are to meet the Queen?"

"Aye."

"Why, Mother?"

"Well that is a good question, daughter. Perhaps you should ask her when you meet."

Millicent knew when her mother was teasing her. She smiled.

"Perhaps I should."

***

William de Ferrers shrugged off his wet cape as he entered the keep of Peveril Castle. Tossing it aside, it scattered the pack of hounds that camped outside the main hall. He didn't notice the fleeing dogs or the scurrying servants who knew all too well the look on the young lord's face. His mood was as dark and sullen as the fierce summer thunderstorm he had just ridden through. In a year of good and bad fortune, the wheel had turned once more.

"Fetch me the priest!" he thundered. But the priest had already heard the clattering hooves of his lord's arrival in the courtyard and appeared immediately at his side.

"My lord," he bowed. The man who stood before de Ferrers was dressed in a simple black robe, but one made of wool so finely spun that it shimmered in the light of the great hall's fireplace. He was tall, fair-haired and handsome. His hands were large, like those of a woodsman, but the golden rings on his fingers belied any notion that he was a simple friar who laboured in the priory fields. "You bring bad news." It was a statement, not a question.

"And how would you know that, *Brother* Malachy?" the young nobleman snarled as he reached for the flagon of ale a servant placed before him. The priest gave no sign that he resented the nobleman's refusal to grant him the honorific of "Father." Instead he smiled.

"Your countenance alone would tell the tale, my lord— even if I had not already heard of King Richard's generosity to his dear brother."

De Ferrers drained his cup and wondered how this churchman always seemed to know things before he did. It was unsettling. He had been informed of the King's action at court but a few days past and rode hard from London to Derbyshire only to find the news had somehow preceded him. And bitter news it was.

Richard had granted his younger brother, Prince John, the overlordship of Nottinghamshire, Cheshire, and the de Ferrers' own Earldom of Derbyshire—the three rich counties that girded the country from the centre of the island to the Irish Sea. The news had arrived from Burgundy where the King was parlaying with Philip of France. It was his final act before departing to lead the great Crusade to free Jerusalem from the Mohammedans.

With both the King and his own father, Earl Robert, departed for the Holy Land, William counted on having a free hand to rule Derbyshire as he wished and perhaps even expand his holdings. Now he would be answerable to an overlord who had no intention of leaving England to fight for the Cross. It was an unhappy complication.

"So what gossip have you heard, priest?"

"Why, the same as you, my lord. The King is gone and has bought off his brother the Prince by letting him feast on the revenue of the Midlands."

Aye, thought de Ferrers. *Richard looted their coffers to finance this bloody Crusade and his brother would likely be worse!*

"I can see this troubles you, my lord," the priest continued, "but have you given thought to the possible advantages?"

"Advantages! Have you lost your senses, priest? Where is the advantage in John *Lackland* plundering our fortune?"

"My lord," the priest continued smoothly. "You were not happy with the taxes levied by Richard, and Richard was a man with whom you could not deal. The King is a man who seeks his destiny with little help from the lords of Derbyshire. And a King who does not need you is to be feared. But John, poor John, has dreams of his own and will need help to achieve them—from men such as you, my lord."

"Dreams? What dreams does John have? Don't talk in riddles, priest."

Father Malachy wondered, for not the first time, if this young nobleman was really capable of understanding any plan more complicated than a child's puzzle.

"My lord," he said patiently, "Richard will be gone for years and is as likely as not to die in the Holy Land like so many others have done. I have received word that Emperor Barbarossa drowned in Anatolia before he even reached the Levant. Kings are not immortal. And even if he survives, do you think John will sit idly while this opportunity passes him by? There is no love lost between these brothers, no matter what gifts Richard may bestow. John wants the crown. You can be sure of that!"

William de Ferrers looked at the young priest as though seeing him for the first time. *John wants the crown.* Why had he not seen this before? And with Richard embroiled in his religious war, John could win—*would* win if enough of the nobles rallied to him. *The priest was right!* John Lackland, whom King Henry had been loath to trust with any of his key territories, would not be satisfied with but three counties, no matter how strategic. He would set his sights on the throne and all of England. But someone would need to be his right hand in the Midlands, and why not William de Ferrers? *Why not, indeed?*

The nobleman waved a hand as though brushing aside Father Malachy's view of the world. "What you say is treason. I could have you drawn, quartered and headless for these words." Malachy did not flinch, but drew very close to the young nobleman and spoke quietly.

"Aye lord, you could, but you would lose the value of my counsel—counsel that can help you achieve your destiny."

"And pray, what is my destiny, priest?"

"My lord, to be Earl of Derby is a fine thing, but I have always sensed you were destined for more. More you shall never see if Richard is king. If he survives and returns to his throne in London, he will reserve his favour for those comrades who fought beside him in France and on Crusade. Of that you can be sure. And what if you stay true to Richard and John triumphs—which well he could? It could be your head on a pike as easily as mine. Mark it my lord, all must in the end

20

choose sides. Will you stand with a man who needs you and is but a few days ride away, or with one who is hundreds of leagues away and owes you nothing?"

De Ferrers did not respond. He was already contemplating a new and glittering future unfolding in ways unthought-of but a few hours before.

***

Many hours passed before Father Malachy took leave of William de Ferrers. As the priest hurried to his own quarters in the great keep, he could barely contain his excitement. His mission here in Derbyshire was beginning to bear fruit! He thought back on all that had passed since he appeared ragged and hungry at the gate of Peveril Castle the summer before. His arrival at this grey fortress was no accident, though his timing had certainly been a stroke of good fortune.

He had found the Earl, Lord Robert, wracked with fever and near death and had produced a convincing prayer vigil at the old man's bedside. As luck would have it, the Earl recovered the very next day. It was most certainly good fortune for the Earl and the priest, but it was no miracle. For in truth, Father Malachy was no priest. Lord Robert proclaimed it a benediction from God and heaped praise and reward on the poor, pious churchman who had worked such a wonder.

William thought the priest's arrival, just as the Earl took a turn for the better, was merely fortunate timing. Nevertheless, Malachy had been richly rewarded by his father and installed as a member of the Earl's household. Thereafter, the old man sought his counsel on affairs both large and small, which the priest was only too eager to provide. William resented this intrusion into their affairs and made no secret of it, yet the priest always treated him with careful deference.

For as he came to know the old Earl, Malachy understood that Lord Robert de Ferrers would not be the vessel for his plans in Derbyshire. The old man was completely loyal to Richard and seemed to have no greater ambition than to live out his life as Earl of Derby. To advance his plans for the Midlands, the priest would need someone with bigger dreams and looser loyalties.

Thus, the Earl's household was shocked when the priest proclaimed that Lord Robert, who owed his life to divine intervention, now owed God a service—and that service was joining Pope Gregory's Crusade. The Earl could redeem his debt and assure his eternal salvation if he would depart forthwith to free the Holy City of Jerusalem from the Mohammedans. Within a fortnight the Earl had assembled a select group of loyal knights and departed to take ship in Southampton. He left his only son, William, to rule in his stead over Derbyshire.

Throughout the old man's illness, recovery and sudden departure, the young de Ferrers had taken care to behave with the proper amount of solicitude for his father's wellbeing, but it had been a struggle. For most of the past year, as his father's health hobbled the old man, William had governed Derbyshire with a strong hand, much stronger than Lord Robert's had been. The old man may have been one of the great warrior nobles of the Normans—*in his day*—but he had grown soft.

William well remembered the stinging rebukes his father had cast upon him for dealing firmly with the Danish scum who lived in the highlands. One of that race of mongrels almost took his life high on the slopes of Kinder Scout mountain with a longbow! He knew it was a Dane and would have had him proper if the old man had not called off the search. The Earl feared *angering* the peasants. He was an old fool.

Soon after those events, his father took ill and hovered near death for months—months in which William introduced discipline back into the rule of their lands. *Who cared if the peasants were angry with him as long as they feared him?* It was his first taste of real power and he liked it very much. Now, with his father's departure, he had no fear that this power would be taken away. And to his surprise, Father Malachy began to offer him counsel with the Earl barely out the castle gate.

The priest had quickly recognized that the young heir to Derbyshire was crafty, vain and ruthless, though neither brave nor prudent. He despised the man, but saw that William had the one ingredient that was key to his plans. He was *ambitious,* and therefore, a man whose allegiance could be bought. This was all he required. The rest would be easy and his master would be pleased.

***

At that moment, Father Malachy's master swung down from a magnificent black charger in front of the elaborate meeting tent set up in the heart of Burgundy where he was to parlay with his sworn enemy and fellow Crusade commander Richard of England. His herald announced his arrival.

"His Most Christian Majesty, Prince Philip, by the Grace of God, King of France."

The Pillars of Hercules

R oland and Declan hung over the rail of the *Sprite* and took in the sights as they approached the port of Lisbon. Master Sparks took the vessel in a wide, sweeping arc around the headland of Cabo Roso and steered south across the mouth of the Tagus River. The river rose in the eastern mountains of Spain and cut a path to the sea through the coastal highlands. A few miles upriver lay Lisbon.

The squires amused themselves by trying to identify the odd bits of flotsam the river sent spinning into the Atlantic as it dropped its burden into the sea. Other vessels could be seen both forward and aft of the *Sprite*, though none seemed to be approaching from the south. That way lay the lands of the enemy and it was in that direction they were bound.

As Master Sparks manoeuvred his craft through the central channel of the river, the boys could just catch a glimpse of high stone battlements far up on the north bank. On a commanding hill was a castle unlike any Roland had seen back in England. It was huge, and curled around the top of the hill like some great stony beast. This was clearly a fortress, yet beautiful in its own way.

"The Moors built the thing over a hundred years ago, and now it serves the Christian king." It was Tuck who spoke having noticed the boy's gaze. "Pretty—isn't it?"

"Aye, Father, but I'd hate to try those walls," Roland replied.

"Well, the walls of Acre are as high as that—and Jerusalem's are higher," the friar said matter-of-factly. "These places Richard has sworn to take from Saladin. The day will come, lad, when you *will* have to try such walls. Then we shall see yer timber."

Roland did not reply. He looked at the monstrous rampart of stone on the high hill and tried to imagine what it would be like to storm such a place. He could not, so there was little point in fretting over it. And soon enough the fortress receded from view. Having steered in near shore to have a look at Lisbon, Master Sparks now let the flow of the Tagus push them farther out into the blue Atlantic. Ahead lay another week or more of sailing down past the headlands of Cape St. Vincent, then southeast to the opening between the Atlantic and Mediterranean seas—the Pillars of Hercules. The sea around them was empty as they turned southward. They were in enemy waters now.

***

The *Sprite* stayed far out to sea for the run down the coast from Lisbon, save for a night-time passage near Cape St. Vincent to check their bearings. They had encountered no enemy vessels, but on the morrow they would reach the mighty strait that separated the vast Atlantic from the ancient Mediterranean Sea. Barring heavy fog, a rarity Master Sparks assured them, there would be no avoiding detection by the Saracens who controlled both sides of the waterway.

It was midnight, and with the new moon and clear weather, the stars seemed to hover just over the mast. Around the guttering light of a candle, four men gathered in the stern of the *Sprite*. In the dancing shadows just outside of the circle of light, two younger men looked on. The four huddled together and spoke in low tones, though none beyond the tiny deck could possibly hear.

"Why can we not slip through in darkness?" Sir Roger asked. He was the only one among the men who had never ventured through this narrow passage.

"Currents, winds and shoals," Master Sparks replied. "The currents are treacherous day or night and, if ye wander far off centre, ye'll haul up on a rock. Worse yet are the winds. Ye can never predict fer sure, but they tend to blow east to west after dark. If they be strong we could make no headway. In this season, we should get steady west winds once the sun rises. The Franks call the winds that come round the edge of Africa the Vendavales and if they're strong we can match the speed of the galleys that patrol these waters—barely. We need those winds, and our best chance to have 'em will come in broad daylight."

"No doubt, we'll be seen—from both shores 'fore we even enter the straits," Friar Tuck observed.

"Aye, Father," said Boda, "but these damned Moors and Berbers with their slave galleys will n'er catch the *Sprite*—not with the Vendavales at our back."

"And if they do catch us…?" This came from Sir Roger.

Boda grinned his toothless grin.

"Why you know the answer to that, me lord—we fight."

***

There was only the faintest hint of predawn light in the east when the call came back from the forward watch.

"Land ho!"

The crewman on duty practically whispered the sighting, as though a shout might arouse watchers on the far distant shore. Still, all aboard the *Sprite* heard it and moved quickly to their duty stations. The night before, Master Sparks had laid out his plan for the passage of the Pillars of Hercules and now they must each see to their duties.

Roland and Tuck were assigned to defend the sterncastle with Sir Roger and Declan guarding the forecastle. Henry Sparks was a keen observer of men and he had no doubt that both the big Norman knight and his companion, the monk, had seen their share of fighting.

He deferred to Sir Roger on the placement of his party. De Laval insisted that the Inness boy be placed aft to give him the best vantage point for using his bow. The ship's master had expressed no opinion on this matter, though he knew that a single bow on a pitching deck would be worthless against fast moving ships. Still, he was thankful that he had four extra swords at his command should they be overtaken and boarded.

26

Roland and Tuck moved quickly to their position at the first alert and the boy peered intently into the slowly-lifting gloom to the east. Gradually, as though through some wizardry, an enormous shape began to emerge from the darkness.

"Father! There!" he found himself trying to shout in a whisper just as the watch had done.

"Aye, lad. I can just see it now. Your eyes are a good deal better than my own, but that would certainly be the Rock— Gibraltar."

Roland continued to strain his eyes toward the far object. It was not just the size of this huge crag that made it so singular a sight. It was the abruptness of its presence among a puny set of hills at its flanks. He could see why the ancients looked upon it as a pillar; such was the fantastic vertical stretch of the thing.

"Whence came the name Gibraltar, Father?" the boy asked.

The monk rubbed his chin for a moment before answering.

"I cannot say for certain, but I know the Moors call it Jebel Tarik—Tarik's Mountain. Named it after old General Tarik, the first of his faith to cross over from Africa." The monk pointed off to the right, where darkness still cloaked the southern shore of the strait. "Landed right by the rock he did. Took him but a year to conquer most of Spain, the chronicles say. As for our name for it—we English have a way of taking a word that feels clumsy in our mouths and smoothing it to our tongue. I'd wager 'Jebel Tarik' has been smoothed over to 'Gibraltar' in that way." The monk shrugged. "Probably never know, my lad, and since we may all be dead by noon, it will hardly matter!" This he said with a broad smile as he slapped the boy hard on his shoulder.

Roland had grown used to Friar Tuck's gruff humour and smiled at the older man. The priest had the sleeves of his coarse brown robe rolled up and the squire could see a number of white scars among the dark hair of his forearms. Just above where the hood of the robe tied at the man's neck, he could see the very top of a shirt of mail. It was easy to forget that this genial friar was also Father Augustine, a veteran warrior of the Knights Templar.

Roland looked across the deck to the forecastle where Sir Roger and Declan stood. His fellow squire wore a sleeveless hauberk over his tunic and a steel skullcap. While Sir Roger leaned almost lazily against the high rail, Declan had unsheathed his sword and was laying about against invisible foes on all sides. Roland would have laughed out loud at this nervous flailing, but he had to admire his friend's skill with the blade. Nervous his fellow squire might be, but the sword in his hand was cutting wicked and deadly arcs.

Declan O'Duinne was a natural with the weapon. By the time they departed Shipbrook on this journey, he was pressing Sir Alwyn Madawc hard in the practice arena, and Madawc was among the most skilled swordsmen in England. Roland pitied the Saracen who took his young friend lightly.

Sir Roger's armour was more extensive, including a full hauberk of mail and a gleaming, though badly-dented helmet of steel. Over his mail shirt, he wore the black tunic of Shipbrook with the distinctive white rampant stag of the de Laval crest embroidered on the chest. This same symbol adorned the shield that leaned against the bulwark. The knight's great broadsword hung at his waist and a lethal-looking battle-axe dangled from a leather strap around his right wrist. Every inch of the man looked deadly.

Roland absently shrugged his shoulders to get used to the weight of his own mail, a parting gift from Sir Alwyn, and quickly checked the short sword that hung at his own side. He then reached for the six-foot length of yew that he had carefully placed on the deck. Deftly, he put one end of the shaft against the outside of his left ankle and, stepping over with his right leg, wedged it against his right calf. With both hands he grasped the top of the shaft and slowly began to use his weight to bend the tough wood. He grunted as he slid the bowstring into the notch. The feel of the longbow in his hand calmed him.

There was much that was uncertain in his world, but with this weapon, he felt at home. He had heard the doubt in Master Sparks' words last evening when Sir Roger had insisted on including Roland's longbow in the defensive plan, and was proud of his master's confidence. He did not intend to let him down in this, their first engagement. As he turned back, he saw Friar Tuck glancing heavenward.

"This is no good, Roland—no good at all."

"Father?"

"The weather. I'd hoped for a driving rain or at least a little fog, but alas, the sky is as clear and blue as a maiden's eye. They may have already seen us by now."

Roland did not reply. They had hoped to get well into the strait before they were seen and then outrun any pursuers. It appeared that slipping through unseen was not going to be possible and outrunning the enemy in the straits would depend on the winds and the skill of Master Sparks. Of the latter he had no qualms, but the winds seemed light and fluky as they entered the Strait.

He leaned against the rail and looked more intently toward the narrow passage that lay dead ahead. By now the mountains of Africa to the south had become visible and any observer, on either shore, would eventually sight even as small a craft as the *Sprite*.

For the next hour the ship plunged forward through cobalt seas toward the gap between the continents. Within another hour they would enter the narrowest stretch of the straits and the maximum danger. There each shore was less than two leagues away—not far for a war galley propelled by slaves. By now the sun was full up and in their eyes. The ship would be highlighted against the western horizon for any observer ashore. There could be no doubt that, by now, hostile eyes were watching them.

As if in answer to his thoughts, a cry came down from a crewman Sparks had sent aloft.

"Ship t' starboard, sir!"

Roland couldn't see it at first, but as the *Sprite* climbed a swell it came into view—a war galley—bearing north from the coast of Morocco.

"Ah...the Berbers are first out of the gate." Tuck nudged the boy at his side. "The Andalucians won't let a prize like us go that easily! Look to the north."

Almost as the monk spoke a second cry came down from above.

"Ship t' port, sir!"

Another galley had emerged from the morning mists on the Iberian side of the strait and was making for them as well. Though farther off, the Moorish galley was heading for an intercept halfway into the strait. If the Berbers let the *Sprite* slip by, the Moors might still catch them!

"Father, what's a Berber?" Roland found himself asking nervously.

"Ah, the Berber is but an undiluted Moor, lad. They are a mountain people, and like most mountain people, a hard lot. To those who crossed the strait with General Tarik, Spain must have been like an earthly paradise compared to their barren hills. So they stayed. And like all soldiers, some married local girls, some took up trades. They and their offspring built a great civilization."

"Great, Father?"

"Aye, Roland. I knew a Jewish scholar who once served the Caliph in Cordoba. The wonders he spoke of surpass most of what I have seen in our own Christian lands. Art, science, building—they excel in all of these. When first the Berbers came, they burned with their faith, but the generations that have known only the beauty and luxury of Spain have become scholars and poets while the Berbers who remained behind have stayed hard. Make no mistake though, Roland. The Moors may be more refined, but they are still fierce warriors. Every generation or so there is a new invasion from Africa and new Berber blood renews the fighting spirit of the Moors. I'd as soon avoid them all, but that does not look possible!"

Roland saw that the first galley was now but a mile or so away—close enough to see the flash of the oars as they lifted in unison from the sea. This must have been what it was like for the English in centuries past when they saw the approach of the Viking longships!

The steady advance of the galley was nerve-wracking, but the blood of his Viking forebears ran in his veins. Roland walked over to the leather quiver he had secured to the railing and withdrew three arrows. There were perhaps forty of the projectiles in the case and as many more tied in a bundle just below the sterncastle.

He examined the first three carefully. Each was the length of his outstretched arm and made of stiff ash. Goose quills supplied the fletching and the steel heads had come from the armoury of the Earl of Chester. Some of these arrowheads were thin triangles, with the point and edges honed to razor sharpness on a smith's grindstone. Others were tipped with a much longer and heavier iron spike—a bodkin point that was designed to pierce mail and armour. He would use each according to need.

He prayed that Master Sparks could somehow use his skills at the helm to see them through untouched, but that now seemed unlikely. If he was destined to have his first pitched battle here of all places, he wished the slaves in those galleys would pull harder and get on with it! The tension of waiting was unbearable.

Now a new sound could be faintly heard over the crash of wave and the crack of wind on the sails. At first Roland thought it was thunder, but the sky was dead clear. He looked at Tuck, who winked at him as though he had a sly secret to reveal.

"Hear the drums, lad? They come from the galley yonder. It keeps the poor slaves at the oars pulling as one. As they get nearer you'll hear the rhythm change—faster and faster yet. If they've taken proper care to feed and water the slaves, they can make those craft practically lift out of the water. It'll take a proper wind to outrun 'em."

He listened to the steady cadence across the shrinking distance. It sounded like some great beast striding toward them. It sounded like death. The wind continued steady, but light. Master Sparks was nudging the *Sprite* a touch to port, whether to avoid the nearer galley coming from the south or to find a more favourable wind, he knew naught. His tinkering with their bearing seemed to gain them little in their race through the strait.

The few crewmen not engaged in adjusting the sails at their master's commands hauled out long and wicked-looking pikes from the hold below. These would be used to both fend off any vessel trying to tie up to the *Sprite* and to skewer any boarders.

Boda was in charge of the pikemen. Under his quiet commands, the sailors completed their preparations and sat about the deck or leaned on their pikes. Such was their calm that they might as well have been splicing a length of hemp rope.

Roland's senses seemed to be more alive than usual. He caught a whiff of horse dung from the hold below and saw the great head of Bucephalus resting on the deck beneath the forecastle. The warhorse's nostrils were flared and his ears were pinned back. The horse knew what was coming.

"*Stand ready!*" the booming voice of Sir Roger de Laval sounded across the deck. Roland looked up and was astonished to see that while he had been musing, the southern galley had pulled to within two hundred yards of their starboard side and was closing fast.

"They've got the speed, but I swear Sparks has made them misjudge the angle. They'll pass just astern of us and have to come about to give chase!" Tuck threw a thick arm around Roland's neck as he watched the approach of the enemy. He turned to the ship's master and raised his sword in an elaborate salute. "There are no sailors like the English, Sir!" he shouted.

"None indeed, Father...None indeed." Sparks returned, never taking his eyes off the horizon.

As the Berber galley plunged toward them, time seemed to slow. Roland stepped to the low railing of the sterncastle only a few feet from where Master Sparks held the steering oar. He braced his left knee in the angle between the support post and the rail and planted his right foot to the rear. Slowly he began to block out the sounds and distractions around him and simply felt the motion of the *Sprite* as she ploughed through the swells. He gave brief thanks to God that he no longer was made ill by the motion as he gave himself over to its rhythm.

He could hear excited shouting above the pounding of the drums coming from the galley. The Berbers knew that they had missed their prey on the first pass and were frantically trying to shift direction to fall in behind the fleeing English ship. Roland could not see the forty slaves who laboured below decks to propel the ten oars on each side of the craft, but the contingent of warriors above decks was frightening.

Fully fifty fighting men swarmed about the galley, their weapons gleaming and winking in the reflected morning sunlight. Roland had never seen such an exotic sight. These men were dressed in similar robes, but of many different colours. Most sported a small turban tightly wound about the head and brandished long curved scimitars. He had heard that Muslim warriors fancied the curved slashing sword and he saw that it was true. There were also some armed with spears and about a dozen clustered near the front armed with short bows. These would be his first order of business.

The vessels now closed once more to within two hundred yards of each other as the galley swung around to take up the pursuit. An overanxious bowman on the enemy craft let fly a shaft that hardly cleared half the distance to the *Sprite*. His companions shouted and mocked his effort. Suddenly, one of the archers saw the boy at the stern of the *Sprite* with his longbow upraised. He gestured toward Roland and began shouting loudly to his fellows, who quickly gathered round, laughing and pointing at their single foe.

"Bit-tawfīq!" The man shouted this across the water accompanied by elaborate gestures. Then he turned and ceremoniously shook his rump in the boy's direction.

Tuck came up behind the boy to observe the proceedings.

"He just wished you good luck—I believe he is inviting you to take your best shot, Master Inness. I suggest you grant his request."

Roland nodded and exhaled slowly, gauging the distance and pitch of the deck. He waited until the stern paused at the highest point in a swell and released the shaft. It leapt effortlessly across the closing distance between the boats. Roland heard the cry—a mixture of shock and pain—before he realized what had happened. A dozen archers stood stunned beside their comrade and beheld—an arrow protruding from his hindquarters.

The crew of the *Sprite* erupted in cheers.

"Excellent shooting, my boy!" Master Sparks shouted above the roar. "Didn't think ye had it in ye."

From the forecastle, Roland heard a whoop he knew belonged to Declan and saw Sir Roger flash him a clinched fist and a vast grin. The boy leaned close to Tuck and whispered for the monk's ears only.

"Lucky shot, father."

Tuck winked at the boy and whispered back.

"I expect it was, but very timely. See if you can do another! I'll keep the arrows coming."

As Roland nocked his second arrow, he saw that the Berber galley was now directly astern of the *Sprite*, its oarsmen pulling for all they were worth. The drumbeat had increased its pace noticeably. Clustered in the very prow of the galley an angry nest of Berber archers shook their fists at the stern of their prey and waited until they could pull within range of their own bows.

Roland aimed carefully for the man in the very front of this group and let fly another shaft, but the *Sprite* chose that instant to roll slightly to port and his arrow struck a spearman in the shoulder instead. Friar Tuck pressed a third arrow into his hand and he drew, paused and released. He did not see where this shaft struck, but a scream came from the bowels of the ship and for a moment, one of the oars on its starboard side missed a stroke. He'd struck one of the slaves!

The boy turned to the priest beside with a stricken look.

"God forgive me, Father, I've struck an innocent man."

The burly monk took the boy by both shoulders and looked deep into his eyes.

"Who knows if he is innocent or not, lad? Now is not the time to ponder it. We need your bow or we will soon be dead—or taken as a replacement for the man you just struck. You must think on this later. Now—shoot!"

Roland whirled around and drew the longbow once more. The Berber galley had moved to within fifty yards of their stern. Even with the motion of the sea, he could hardly miss hitting someone on the crowded deck. He sighted on a particularly colourful swordsman who was straddling the port railing and brandishing his scimitar at him. In an instant the man was struck full in the chest and plunged silently into the sea.

The galley came on. The *Sprite* was now within range of their short bows and they loosed their first volley. A dozen shafts fell among the ship's company, but only one struck a glancing blow that drew blood. The sailor merely tied a rag around the wound and stood at his station.

The boy fell into a steady rhythm. Nock, draw, aim, release. Again and again—as fast as Tuck could supply arrows. Many were striking home, but there were just too many targets. As the galley drew even with the slower cog, the effectiveness of their archers was improving. As Roland dropped to the deck to avoid a volley of arrows sent his way, he saw Tuck lying flat beside him. Looking forward, he saw Declan crouched by the rail. Sir Roger raised his shield and was absently fending off a steady stream of arrows.

The Berbers had a good view of the knight now and, as the most imposing figure on the deck of the *Sprite,* he drew the attention of the archers. Untroubled, the big Norman fended off the barrage, as arrows shattered and rebounded off the shield.

A few feet away, Henry Sparks squatted on his haunches to present a more difficult angle to their foes. He still held the rudder firmly in his big hands as he tried to coax more speed from his ship. He looked briefly astern and then back to the Berber galley that was angling in toward the *Sprite* on the starboard side. The Vendavales wind that he had hoped for had not come. *Bad luck.*

The galley pulled a little ahead of the *Sprite* as it narrowed the gap between the ships. Roland could see the deck swarming with armed men and could even see some of the slaves at their oars in the hold below. Sparks had told them what to expect. The galley would soon ship oars to allow for manoeuvring close to their target. Then grappling hooks would be hurled over the railings to lash the vessels together.

Once joined, it would be a battle for survival between the crews. Roland took a quick look forward and to the port side. To his dismay, he saw the galley of the Moors approaching rapidly about a mile away. He had only a moment to worry about this new threat when he heard Sir Roger roar from the forecastle.

"Prepare for boarders!"

The Berbers shipped oars and suddenly the air was filled with flying grappling hooks. Some fell short and some did not catch, but several did. Roland saw Boda leap forward and cut the line to one with his sabre. A second crewman moved to slice a taut line near him when he took a thrown spear in his leg and fell screaming to the deck. Despite the crew's efforts there were soon too many lines binding the ships and the galley drew quickly alongside.

From the Berbers came a strange warbling battle cry that made the hair on his neck rise, even as he continued to rain death on them with his longbow. There was no mistaking their leader. He was a particularly fierce-looking warrior who was urging his men forward. He alone among the crew of the galley carried a shield and it saved him at that moment. Some warrior's intuition alerted him just as Roland released a shaft at his heart. He was barely able to get the shield up in time and was astonished to see the arrow penetrate the iron by a full six inches.

He looked directly at the boy and grinned. Shouting a final command he led a swarm of attackers up the side of the *Sprite*. The crew sent many of them to their deaths with their pikes, but many more followed. Roland saw Tuck move quickly to the ladder that led from the sterncastle to the deck below. He disappeared into a tangle of men and steel.

Roland saw that he had only one arrow left in his quiver. He placed his longbow carefully on the deck, drew his sword and plunged after the monk.

Gauntlet

The deck of the *Sprite* had become a killing ground with men slashing and thrusting at each other in a desperate effort to gain the advantage. The English crew formed a small hedgehog of pikes at each end of the deck and were fighting for their lives. No man faltered or fled, but men were falling even as they dispatched an equal number of the Berbers screaming and moaning into the hold. Roland could hardly breathe as he looked upon this scene of horror and confusion. He forced himself to follow Tuck to the ladder that led to the chaos below.

"Boy!" Roland turned to see Master Sparks tossing his head frantically to the right. As he turned toward the starboard side, he saw a Berber pulling himself over the railing of the sterncastle. If he got to the ship's master, all would truly be lost.

Roland leapt toward the man with his sword on guard as Sir Alwyn had taught him through endless hours of drill. The Berber thought the sterncastle was clear of defenders and barely had time to parry the boy's unexpected attack. His long curved scimitar rang as it swung down to deflect Roland's blade. The boy let it happen, but did not check his charge. He drove his shoulder into the man's chest and saw him topple backwards over the railing. The splash made no sound in the din of battle as he fell between the two ensnarled ships and disappeared into the sea.

"Well done, Master Inness!" Sparks shouted above the din. "Keep 'em off me a bit longer and we may still win free!"

Roland leapt to obey, silently thanking heaven he would not have to descend into the carnage on the deck below. He stationed himself near the starboard side so he could observe any approach to the sterncastle. Two more Berbers sought to get at the *Sprite*'s master, but abandoned the effort when they saw the squire waiting at the railing with drawn sword.

Below, the crew was slowly being pressed back until half the deck was in the possession of the Berbers. Roland could see that more warriors were making their way up the side of the *Sprite* to join their comrades. It was a grim picture. Then, he lifted his eyes to the forecastle and saw a sight that would remain forever clear in his memory—Sir Roger de Laval in his full battle fury.

The big knight leapt from the forecastle to the small catwalk on the port side. In his wake came Declan O'Duinne, sword at the ready. Below, the hold was crammed with provisions for the voyage, which were stacked to within a foot of the deck. The knight stepped down upon the bags of grain and barrels of water and picked his way across toward the starboard side.

The Berbers saw him coming and their war cries grew wilder. All vied for the honour of dispatching this infidel. Several threw spears that Sir Roger brushed aside with his shield as though they were mosquitoes. Two warriors leapt into the hold and swarmed toward him. The big Norman barely broke stride as he raised the axe above his head and brought it sweeping forward and down. The force of the blow sent the first attacker flying into some dark recess in the hold. A vicious backhand slash killed the second.

He hardly paused in his forward progress as he made for the mass of Berbers clustered on the starboard side catwalk. As he neared them, one man, in his excitement, hopped into the hold and charged at the knight with his scimitar flashing. Sir Roger met this challenge with his shield and shoved the man to the rear, where it was his bad luck to meet Declan O'Duinne. In a blur of steel, he died.

Ten feet from the starboard side the Norman halted. Even without armour, there was no way he could mount the catwalk swarming with boarders. With calm deliberation, he passed his shield and battle-axe to the boy behind him and slowly drew his two-handed broadsword.

"Come on ye beggars!" he shouted and glared at his foes.

These proud warriors from the desolate mountains of the Rif could not ignore this show of defiance. Two more leapt into the hold and charged at the man. Sir Roger twisted to his right, swinging his long blade far to the rear—just missing his squire. As Declan O'Duinne jumped backwards to avoid the broadsword's arc, the knight uncoiled forward with such speed and power that both men went down in a heap.

Roland watched, transfixed, as his master blunted the Berber attack with controlled mayhem. He had only seen Sir Roger in combat once before, deep in the forest of Clocaenog, but on that occasion he had been badly wounded and the fight was something of a blur to him. Seen in the full glare of the Mediterranean sun, his master's lethal skill made it clear how the Normans had conquered half of France and all of England.

His eye caught another motion far below and he was shocked to see Friar Tuck leap from the *Sprite* onto the deck of the Berber galley. He had completely lost sight of the monk in the heat of battle. Somehow the man had managed to slip over the side unseen while their enemies were distracted by Sir Roger. The Berber helmsman fled from this unexpected assault, but the slave master was too slow and went down quickly under Tuck's sword. He was fumbling with the keys on the man's belt when the remaining warriors near the bow noticed him.

Perhaps a half dozen of the boarding party had not yet made it up the side of the *Sprite*, and now they turned toward this unexpected threat to their own craft. Rushing astern in a mass, they hoped to quickly overwhelm this intruder and return to the business of seizing the English ship. Tuck tossed the keys to one of the galley slaves in the hold and braced himself for the charge.

At the same time, Roland saw that the remaining archers in the bow of the galley were turning their attention aft and were trying to get a shot at the monk. The boy threw himself to the deck of the sterncastle and reached blindly through the railing to where he had hung his spare bundle of arrows. He prayed that the Berbers would be preoccupied with the deadly knight in the hold and not slice off his exposed arm with one of their lethal looking scimitars. His luck held and his hand found the strap.

Without pausing, he sheathed his sword and took up the longbow. Below, Tuck was being pressed back by the sheer weight of the six attackers. At this range, the boy could not miss. He began with the rearmost swordsman and worked his way forward. After dropping two, the archers in the bow saw him and sent a hail of arrows his way. Flinging himself to the deck he just avoided the barrage—but Master Sparks was not so lucky. Roland heard a cry and saw that the ship's master had taken an arrow in his shoulder. Somehow he managed to keep his grip on the rudder and with his free hand ripped the shaft free, his tunic showing dark blood at the wound.

There was no time to aid Sparks as the battle reached its full fury. No more Berbers dared to take up Sir Roger's challenge; instead they pressed hard on the crew both forward and aft. Some pikes had been splintered and now many of the men were fighting back with sabres. Handy they were with the blades, but against trained swordsmen and still outnumbered, they were again losing ground.

Seeing the shift in tactics, Sir Roger made his way back to the port side and with a boost from Declan regained the catwalk. Forcing aside his own countrymen, he strode into the fray below the sterncastle and began to force back the Berbers.

Above him, Roland worked to blunt the enemy's frantic efforts to regain control of their galley. He focused on the Berber archers in the bow of the galley. In close combat, Tuck had few equals, but the bowmen could kill at a distance and were a greater threat, so he set about reducing their numbers. His deadly accuracy quickly forced the remaining archers to crawl into the hold to escape. There, they found no refuge, for the keys Tuck had flung below had been put to good use. Many of the slaves were now free and they turned on their recent masters with a vengeance. The Berber bowmen had no chance.

"Cut the lines!" Tuck shouted and gestured to the nearest slaves. Roland watched as three ragged men climbed from the hold, took up the scimitars of the Berbers who had fallen, and began hacking at the ropes that held the galley to the *Sprite*.

The change in the balance aboard the galley did not go unnoticed by the three men who had cornered the monk in the stern. One began to scream at his fellows still aboard the *Sprite* until he was abruptly struck down by one of the men cutting the lines. Even from his distant vantage point, the boy saw the shock on the man's face—that a slave should have raised a weapon to him.

Now more slaves were swarming out of the hold and the two remaining swordsmen threw down their weapons and prostrated themselves before Tuck, seeking his mercy, which the slaves were not likely to provide. Tuck motioned for his newly freed crew to chain the Berbers to the oars. The did so without gentleness.

When the last line was cut, the galley, with Tuck's hand on the steering oar, swerved away from the *Sprite*. On the sterncastle, Master Sparks still fought to maintain control of his ship and felt it surge forward once freed from the drag of the enemy vessel.

On the deck of the *Sprite*, the Berbers battle fury waned as they saw their craft moving rapidly away from them. Now the sea was at their back and the onslaught of Sir Roger de Laval was to their front. Still, they were hard men, and far from beaten. They still outnumbered the crew and redoubled their own attack in a desperate effort to gain control of the cog.

"Declan! Roland! To me!" Sir Roger's voice rose above the clash of steel and shouts of men fighting for their lives. Roland dropped his longbow, retrieved his sword and dropped to the deck below the sterncastle, just to the rear of his Master.

"I'm here, my lord!" he shouted.

"And I!" echoed Declan.

"Then for Shipbrook and de Laval—*have at em!*"

There was barely enough room for the knight and his squires to fight alongside one another, but somehow they managed. Where Sir Roger bludgeoned his way forward with mighty slashing strokes of his long blade, Declan O'Duinne advanced behind a quicker, darting blade, his moves too fast to anticipate. Again and again, he forced his opponent to react to a feint, leaving him out of position for the telling blow.

Roland had neither the brute strength of his master nor the deadly elegance of his friend, but he had learned much from his teacher, Sir Alwyn Madawc. As he pressed forward, he gave the man he faced no time to launch an attack of his own. Sir Alwyn said you needed more than skill in a contest of blades—you needed an inner fury to drive you forward. During the long and desperate struggle for control of the *Sprite*, that fury had been building somewhere deep inside. Now it was unleashed and the Berbers fell back before the swords of Shipbrook.

There comes a point in a close fight when foes come to realize who shall prevail. Some choose to fight on for pride, though they know they will lose and likely die. Others lose all heart. As the knight and his two squires pressed forward an almost visible ripple went through the boarders. They were losing and they knew it.

First one, then groups of two and three threw down their weapons and clambered down into the hold. One who got too close to the paddock of Bucephalus was sent sprawling into a water barrel by a savage kick from the warhorse. Now the only man left with fight in him was the leader—the man who had taken Roland's arrow in his shield. He spit at his men and shouted to them in the Berber tongue. There was little doubt he was calling them cowards for surrendering.

"Save yer speeches, ye heathen," Sir Roger shouted at the man, who clearly did not understand English. But the Berber leader could understand a challenge in any language. The man had no quit in him and was as quick as a snake with his scimitar. Several slashing attacks glanced off Sir Roger's mail shirt. Had the angle been a bit different his sword could have penetrated even this protection.

Despite his skill, he could not stand before the Norman knight. A last desperate lunge missed its mark and Sir Roger brought the heavy hilt of the broadsword down on the man's head. The turban he wore could not protect him and he fell senseless to the deck. Sir Roger hardly paused before he began shouting orders to the crew and his squires.

"Boda—secure these prisoners in the hold. Declan check Buc."

"My lord," Roland interrupted. "Master Sparks was struck. He will need aid."

"Then get yourself there, lad. I'll follow shortly."

Roland ran across the deck, which was slippery with blood, and up the ladder to the sterncastle. Henry Sparks was still at his post, but looked pale and weak.

"Take the rudder, Master Inness," he gasped as he slowly sank to the deck.

Roland leapt to take the steering arm from Sparks.

"Push her to starboard a bit," he groaned. "I think the breeze is freshening in that quarter."

Roland moved quickly to follow the Master's direction. Far to the south and behind them, he could see a faint disturbance on the water.

"Pray for the wind, boy, or we will not see land alive!"

"Aye, sir," the boy replied—and in truth he was praying, for bearing down on them from the port side was the forgotten Moorish galley, its oars glistened in the bright morning sun. He could hear the dreadful thud of the drum driving the slaves onward. He scanned the deck below him and knew with certainty that no matter how brave the resistance, the men of the *Sprite*, could not repel another boarding. Three of the crew were dead and six were wounded. Both Sir Roger and Declan appeared unscathed from the fight just concluded, but Friar Tuck was no longer with them.

By now, the Moorish galley was only a few hundred yards away and Roland could see a great knot of men clustered on the deck. These men were dressed in much more of a uniform fashion than the Berbers. Each wore robes of creamy white with a red sash at the waist. They wore no turban, but rather a steel helmet with a drapery of mail protecting their neck. These were true soldiers and their galley was bearing down at great speed upon the *Sprite*, which was only now gaining momentum after being cut loose from the Berber vessel.

Roland's observations were cut short by the arrival of Boda who took the helm from him without a word. He knelt at Master Spark's side and ripped a section of cloth from the man's tunic and pressed it to his wound, which did not seem to be bleeding excessively. Sparks gave him a painful smile. Then from above him, Boda spoke urgently.

"Master Inness, stand to your longbow. I seen what ye did t'other galley, now we've a need of ye once more." Roland looked up and Boda gave him a grim look.

As he finished binding Sparks' wound he saw Declan pull himself up the ladder to the sterncastle. The boy was weary, but seemed to glow with the lingering madness of the fight. He smiled broadly at Roland and slapped him on the shoulder.

"Roland, me lad, did ye hit a thing after sticking that heathen in the rump? I was a wee bit busy down below and saw nothing but screaming Berbers tryin' to carve me like a flank of beef!"

Roland didn't answer. He had killed many men in the frantic moments when Tuck was seizing the Berber galley. He had lost count. For a moment he felt a strange stab of guilt that he had sent those men to their deaths and yet could not account for their number. Declan's sword was dripping with blood but he seemed untroubled.

"Didn't keep count, Dec. More coming yonder though." Roland pointed to port and Declan seemed to notice for the first time the new threat.

"Gad! I'd forgotten about those devils."

"Aye, but they've not forgotten us."

Declan studied the oncoming galley and the force gathered on its deck.

"It looks bad," he said.

"It does. Hand me my arrows, if you please."

Declan sheathed his bloody sword and picked up Roland's quiver.

"Not so many left here, Roland," the Irish boy murmured, some of his bravado fading. "Best make 'em count."

Roland nodded and took the quiver. There were more arrows stored in the hold, but no time to fetch them now.

"You'd best get back. Sir Roger will have need of you."

Before Declan had reached the ladder to the deck below Roland nocked the first shaft. He glanced quickly back to port and was encouraged to see the sea begin to rise in a chop. A wind was coming. Boda edged the helm to starboard a bit to catch every possible advantage from the growing breeze. The *Sprite* was picking up speed, but with agonizing slowness, and the Moorish galley continued to gain on them. They were now within range of his bow.

Roland braced himself—this time against the port railing and took careful aim. *Breathe...relax...release.* The arrow flew like a bird of prey and plunged down into the solid mass of men on the other deck. There was but a ripple, but clearly a man had fallen. These were, indeed, trained soldiers, for at a shouted command they all raised shields in unison. Against this unbroken wall, even his longbow could not prevail. Still, not all aboard the galley were thus protected and he began to carefully pick his targets from among the crew.

He could sense the quickening breeze at his back and feel the cog begin to surge forward—but the enemy vessel was at full speed and closing fast. The wind they had prayed for had come—*but too late.* Roland could see men with grappling hooks in their hands. Soon they would snag their prey and swarm aboard. The young bowman sent a steady stream of arrows at the approaching Moors and some struck home as men prepared to board the cog. Then he reached for his quiver and found it empty.

He looked back across the deck of the *Sprite* and saw the exhausted crew stand to their stations, some with broken pikes and others with swords. Sir Roger was organizing them to meet the coming onslaught. Roland laid his longbow on the deck and took up the sword once more. He moved to the ladder that would take him to the deck below. If he fell, he wished to fall beside Declan O'Duinne and Roger de Laval.

Then a sound came to him—faint at first, but rising quickly to an excited roar from the crew below. He saw the men point to starboard and turned just in time to see the Berber galley bearing down on them from the south. His heart sank. Had the Berbers regained control of their craft? Then he saw the man at the helm. It was Tuck. The monk had the tiller and, somewhere below, the former slaves were pulling with gusto. What was the man doing? If they kept to their course they would pass just astern of the *Sprite* and across the path of the approaching Moors. Was the monk addled?

The *Sprite* shielded Tuck's craft from view until it appeared as if from nowhere heading straight for the Moorish vessel. The man at the galley's tiller hesitated, unsure whether this new vessel was friend or foe. The commander of troops had no such hesitation. He could see that no Berber manned the rudder. He started to shout a command, but the Moorish oarsman had now realized in horror that the Berber galley intended to ram them amidships. Without waiting for direction, he pushed the steering oar hard to starboard and the galley swung around. The two craft almost tangled as they passed within yards of each other.

The unexpected interference of the Berber galley had driven the Moors well off their planned intercept of the *Sprite*, but they were a trained crew and swung around smartly to take up the chase once more. But the moment had been lost. The wind continued to build and the square sail of the cog grew taught as the English ship gained speed.

The commander of the Moors had seized many Christian ships in these waters and he well knew that if the wind was up, his advantage was lost. Reluctantly he ordered the galley to come about and seek a prey they could catch—the captured Berber galley that had tried to ram them.

That ship was now heading northeast toward Iberia. Perhaps they hoped to get far enough up the coast to reach Christian lands. No matter, he knew his slaves were better fed than those on any Berber craft.

"Make these dogs stroke hard," he screamed at his slave master. The drum increased its tempo and the galley accelerated. "We'll have them by dark," he said to no one in particular.

A mile away on the sterncastle of the *Sprite*, Roland watched these events unfold. He turned to the man at the rudder.

"Boda, come about—we can catch the galley and bring the friar back aboard."

Boda shook his head vigorously. "I'll not do it. We turn her to port and we lose the wind. That galley would be back upon

Warbow

us. The good friar knows what he's about. He's headed that way of a purpose—to lead the heathens away from us."

"Boda's right, Master Inness." Roland turned to see Henry Sparks struggle up to a sitting position. "We go to port and we'll go practically dead in the water. Now all we can do is pray for the good Father and get ourselves out of harm's way."

Roland turned and watched as the two galleys fell farther astern. He was angry at Boda and Sparks, but could not contest their knowledge of the winds. He watched helplessly as the two galleys fell farther behind, and finally out of sight in the swells. The land too was falling away on both sides as they plunged eastward into the Mediterranean Sea. He finally gave up his vigil and sank down on the deck of the sterncastle, his face in his hands.

Pray he would—a prayer for Friar Tuck.

The Queen's Agent

Lady Catherine and Millicent took the familiar road from Shipbrook to Chester where they joined the entourage of Earl Ranulf and his wife, Lady Constance. The ladies of the region may have received the summons from the Queen, but their husbands were making a point of accompanying them to London. The men were to attend a banquet with their spouses after the reception, which the Queen had made clear, was for ladies only.

Millicent de Laval had to agree with her mother that early autumn in this part of England was the loveliest time of year. The winter damps and fogs were months away and the heat of midsummer had given way to crisp air in the mornings and a pleasing warmth in the afternoons. Every bend of Watling Street, as the road to London was called, showed the country to best advantage. Wild flowers still fought for space along the old Roman road, fruit trees in each village were heavy with their bounty and golden carpets of grain swayed in the breeze as they waited for the harvest.

She would have much preferred to be riding her bay mare on the trip to being cooped up in a carriage that lurched and bumped with every missing flagstone in the roadway, but she had lost that argument with Lady Catherine. Still, the autumn weather was so agreeable, there was simply no room for a pout. And soon they would reach London!

She had been very jealous when her father and his two squires accompanied Earl Ranulf to the King's coronation the previous year, but now she had her own chance to see the

48

greatest city in the kingdom—and she wanted to see it all. Her thoughts were interrupted by her mother.

"Millie, we will be within the city gates in a few more hours. I hope you will remember all I have advised you concerning your conduct."

"Yes, Mother," she replied with a sigh. "Do not wander off. Do not scratch myself if I itch. Curtsy low to the Queen and do not speak unless spoken to."

"Good girl. And what else?"

"Well Mother, I seem to remember something in your instructions about listening and observing—or something to that effect."

Millicent smiled innocently at her mother, who rolled her eyes at the ill-concealed sarcasm of the remark. In fact, Lady Catherine had been drilling this particular advice into her since first they heard they would be meeting the Queen.

No noble family, no matter how remote they might be from the seat of power, could ignore court politics. Finding oneself on the wrong side of a noble, or worse, royal dispute, could result in losing one's head—literally. In such a world, attention must be paid, and Catherine de Laval was determined that her daughter would do so.

"It's good of you to remember that advice, young lady, and to take it seriously. This summons from the Queen is highly irregular and we must be cautious. I can only surmise that Queen Eleanor is seeking information—outside of the normal communications with the barons. Perhaps she thinks their wives will be more forthcoming."

"Does she not trust the barons?" asked Millicent.

"Not a bit," her mother replied. "She must mind the throne for Richard until he returns, and many think he never will..." She stopped abruptly, but too late. She saw the flicker of fear on her daughter's face.

The girl quickly regained her composure. She knew—they all knew—that if the King did not return there would be small hope that her father would, but she did not want to add her fears to the burden her mother already carried. *Be brave for me, Millie*, her father had whispered to her at their parting. *Look after your mother.* She had promised him that, and would do her best to keep that pledge. She quickly brought the conversation back to the Queen.

"So she fears there may be treachery afoot among the barons?"

"Aye, she does and with good reason. First, the barons are treacherous by nature when it serves their interests, and second, because she has another son, who no doubt would seek to position himself as the next king, whether Richard survives or not."

"Prince John."

"Yes, the very same. And this is why I believe the Queen has particularly summoned the noble ladies to this audience. The King has given his brother control of all the counties in the region. Our own Cheshire as well as Derbyshire and Nottinghamshire are all now beholden to Prince John. The wealth of these counties now flows, in part, into his coffers. It gives John more power than he has ever possessed, but King Richard has no sons and has not named his brother as heir. It is little wonder then that the Queen wishes to hear all she can about these counties and what John and the Earls might be up to!"

"Surely Earl Ranulf will take no part in any plotting against the King, Mother?"

"I think not Millie, but he is young and easily swayed. We must pay careful attention to Lady Constance to see which way that wind might be blowing. As for the rest, I know not how things stand in Derbyshire or Nottinghamshire."

"And where stand we, Mother?"

Lady Catherine leaned close to her daughter and fixed her with a firm gaze.

"We stand with your father—and your father stands with Richard. To the end."

From the driver's bench in front of the coach, their man called back to them.

"Aldersgate, my lady."

They entered London.

The city was magnificent—loud, dirty, dangerous and fascinating. It would never replace the rolling green hills and salt marshes of home, but Millicent was transfixed by the spectacle of it all. As their carriage made its way through the busy streets to the inn where they would take lodgings near St. Helen's priory, the girl was presented with one new oddity after another. Apart from the jugglers and other street performers, it was the sheer mass of humanity that stunned her. She did not think there were this many people in all of England.

Finally they arrived at the inn, and with the usual fussing by their servants and the innkeeper, they were settled in their room. In but a few hours, they would be joining Lady Constance and many other noblewomen at the Queen's reception, followed by a banquet that the men would attend. Lady Catherine supervised her daughter's preparations.

The girl had never dressed for an event of this importance and was a bit baffled by the elegant gown and undergarments her mother had procured for her, but Lady Catherine patiently showed her how to don each item. When done, Catherine stepped back and held her daughter at arm's length. The transformation in the girl was startling. The formal gown, the hair swept up with a band of silk—this was no longer the gangly little girl that could out-ride anyone in Cheshire and loved to muck out the stalls. This was a young woman—and a striking one at that. *How has she grown to be taller than me?*

"Well daughter, you are a sight! We shall have all female company for our reception with the Queen, but there will be young men aplenty at the banquet, and you will surely catch their eye. So be forewarned!"

Millicent looked at her mother doubtfully.

"I don't wish that Mother. I have no interest in young men."

Lady Catherine raised an eyebrow. Then hugged her daughter and stepped back.

"For the moment, young lady, that pleases me, but that will change in due time—mark my words!"

The girl smiled back. *Young men.* She had never cared much for the attentions of boys. In fact she had taken great delight in flummoxing those of her acquaintance, with her wicked japes or besting them at horse. She found boys to be full of pride and rather silly.

But there was the *one* boy—the one who had saved her life. It seemed an age ago when she had walked with him on the walls of Shipbrook and given him a silver amulet as a token of remembrance.

Would she ever see Roland Inness again?

***

William de Ferrers waited impatiently for the summons. He paced about the antechamber while Father Malachy stood by. They waited to be called into the presence of the Prince. This was a meeting de Ferrers had requested at Malachy's insistence and now he vaguely wished he were back in Derbyshire—for what he was about to embark on would be seen as treason in the eyes of any who supported the King. He did not want his own head to end up mounted on a pike outside the gates of the Tower!

Finally, the great oak door swung open and a priest peered out, beckoning him to enter. The room was large and lushly furnished with rich tapestries and soft couches. On one of these, the younger brother of King Richard sat, half reclining.

"De Ferrers! Welcome my friend." The Prince waved him to come closer. "Can I send for drink? Please come sit with me!"

The young nobleman, determined to not show his anxiety, smiled at the Prince and took a seat across from him. The royal brother was only a few years his senior, but seemed much older.

"Your grace, this is my spiritual counsellor, Father Malachy. Shall I bid him leave?"

John barked a laugh. "Nay, my lord. If you trust him, why should I not? I find priests add an air of Christian fellowship to any gathering—even if they do clean out our larders with their appetite! But I see Father Malachy is spare enough, so I think our foodstuffs will not suffer over much. Please sit, Father. And now William, what news of your sire?"

"Your grace, we last heard that Lord Robert was delayed for some time in Lisbon, but did good service there against the Moors. His message said he was travelling overland to avoid

52

the straits at the Pillars of Hercules and would find sea passage for the Holy Land on the eastern coast of Iberia."

"A redoubtable warrior still," replied the Prince with a half-smile. "We will pray for his safe return—along with that of my dear brother. And what of things in Derbyshire, William? With Lord Robert off crusading, I feel a...father's concern... for the welfare of your county."

"Lord Robert left the affairs of Derbyshire in my hands, your grace, and I assure you, my hands have a firm grip. But in this, and in all things, I defer to your wisdom and guidance. We seek only to better serve you."

Prince John beamed. "I think we shall have that drink now, William. We have much to discuss."

The Prince had heard that the son of Robert de Ferrers was ambitious and ruthless, and kept an iron grip on the key county that had come under his sway. What he did not know, until this very moment, was where the young nobleman's loyalties lay. Now he knew. The man had no loyalty.

He was perfect.

***

The reception began near sunset at Westminster Hall, a cavernous building erected by William the Conqueror's son. Neither Lady Catherine nor Millicent had ever been inside such a magnificent structure. It could have held ten times the numbers that now filed forward for their presentation to the Queen. The two women of Shipbrook were in a slowly advancing line behind Lady Constance. She had hardly spoken to them throughout the journey down to London and not at all as they waited in the hall to be presented.

An hour passed as the Queen engaged in animated conversation with each of the noble ladies ahead of them in the line. Millicent used the time to study the women around her. They were all dressed in their best finery. Silks shimmered on flowing gowns and jewellery gleamed from half a hundred pale necks. At last, Lady Constance was called forward. They would be next.

Millicent watched as the Earl's wife exchanged a few words with the woman who sat on a slightly raised throne—

Queen Eleanor—a woman out of legend. Eleanor of Aquitaine was wife to two kings and mother to a third; the royal prisoner of King Henry and now, virtual ruler of the realm with King Richard on crusade. Millicent knew the Queen's history. Lady Catherine had made certain of that! But none of that seemed important as she watched the woman.

She was old. Well past sixty years, but still fair in the eyes of the girl. No, more than fair, she was a beauty. Time may have softened her features but Millicent could see why two kings had fallen in love with her. Though it was not her beauty that most impressed. The woman had enormous presence. She could have been homely and dressed in rags, but the way she held herself left no doubt—here was a Queen.

"Lady Catherine de Laval and Mistress Millicent de Laval of Shipbrook!"

Millicent was so absorbed in watching the Queen that the announcement startled her. But she had the presence of mind to glide forward gracefully beside her mother. Six feet in front of the Queen they stopped and curtsied low.

"De Laval—I know this name."

Lady Catherine and Millicent arose and stood, fixed by the penetrating gaze of the woman before them.

"Come closer ladies. Neither my eyes nor my ears work as they once did. Now, why do I know this name?"

Lady Catherine spoke. "Your grace, you may know of my husband, Sir Roger de Laval, who faithfully served both King Henry and now King Richard."

"Ah yes, that's it! That's it! Richard spoke of him before leaving for Burgundy. Your place, it is out on the frontier with Wales?"

"Yes your grace, we have the honour of protecting the borders of Cheshire from the Welsh."

The Queen pondered that for a moment, then glanced over at Millicent.

"This is a tall one!" she said and smiled at the girl. "So, what do you *do*, Mistress Millicent?"

For a moment the girl was confused by the question, but then realized she was being asked what talents she might have.

"Your grace, I ride—better than most."

The Queen surprised them with a loud hoot.

"Excellent. Too many girls these days just do embroidery or write bad poetry! When I was your age I was a fair rider myself. Rode all the way to Jerusalem with King Louie on the last Crusade! God's breath, I wish I could straddle a horse yet, but I am as old as the hills."

She paused, then beckoned Lady Catherine forward. She leaned in close and spoke in a whisper.

"Come to my chambers in the residence before the banquet begins. I wish to speak more with you—and bring the girl," she said, nodding at Millicent.

Lady Catherine nodded and stepped back. Together, the women of Shipbrook curtsied and retreated as the Lord Chamberlain announced the next to meet the Queen. They moved to join Lady Constance, where they were expected to take up station.

"Whatever was she whispering to you about, Lady Catherine?" asked the Earl's wife when they reached her.

Catherine de Laval smiled.

"My lady, she asked me how many more were in line behind us. She said her eyes were not so good anymore and her rump was starting to hurt."

Lady Constance looked shocked, but they had all heard that Eleanor of Aquitaine could be blunt.

"Really?"

"Word for word, my lady."

***

For the next hour the Queen met her subjects and stopped to speak at length with some, dismissing others with a quick word. Then the Lord Chamberlain ended the affair by announcing "*All rise,*" as the Queen stood and retired through the passageway that led to the private residence of Westminster. It would be several hours before the banquet was to begin and the Lord Chamberlain's men began to politely shoo the noble ladies from the hall. Already a host of servants were hauling in tables at the far end for the evening meal.

Lady Constance and most of the other high ranking ladies retired to their near-by residences on the Strand. Those of lesser rank were left to make their way back to more modest dwellings in the city or to shift for themselves about the grounds of Westminster until time for the evening festivities.

Catherine and Millicent made their goodbyes with Lady Constance and went for a stroll. As they walked, Catherine finally felt free to pass along the Queen's whispered message to her daughter.

"Whatever can she want with us, Mother?"

"I cannot guess, Millie, but I don't like it. Neither your father nor I hold truck with politics."

"This will be politics?"

"Everything a Queen does is politics, girl, so be on your guard. She is not to be trifled with."

When the crowd had dispersed, they slipped back inside and made their way as inconspicuously as possible past the army of servants who were noisily arranging the banquet space. When they reached the arched portal through which the Queen had passed, they were met by two armed soldiers.

"We have been invited to attend the Queen," Lady Catherine announced with more assurance than she felt.

"Your name, my lady?"

"Lady Catherine de Laval and Mistress Millicent de Laval."

The man nodded and swung a heavy oaken door open.

"Straight down the hall until you meet the Lord Chamberlain, my lady. He will escort you."

They entered what proved to be a rather short hallway and were quickly greeted by the Earl of Oxford, who served as Lord Chamberlain. He led them into a small parlour where the Queen sat before a crackling fire in the hearth.

"Lady Catherine and Mistress Millicent, your grace," he announced and quickly withdrew.

"Good, good! Come sit with me, ladies," the Queen smiled and gestured toward a padded bench drawn up across from her chair. "I like a fire, even in the summer. It's hard to keep these old bones warm!" She paused while the ladies of Shipbrook settled themselves, then spoke.

"Do you love your husband, Lady Catherine? Please be honest with me."

For one of the rare times in her life, Millicent saw her mother flustered.

"Why, yes...of...of course, your grace," she stammered.

"There is no 'of course' about it, Lady Catherine. Most wives of my acquaintance loathe their husbands—and with good cause! My own husband locked me up for twelve years and I did, on occasion, plot against him. So, give me an honest answer. I do not judge. Do you love him?"

There was now no hesitation in the reply.

"Yes, your grace, I do. Roger de Laval is my man and there are none better in England or elsewhere, I'd wager."

The Queen sighed for a moment, and spoke wistfully. "I thought of my Henry that way for many a year, but kings make poor husbands." She turned back to the two women.

"This much I know—the King trusts your husband, and Richard has a good sense of who is loyal and who is not—as do I. I have learned the hard way that loyalty is greatly valued because it is so very rare. If you are loyal to your husband, then I can assume you will be loyal to the King. I needed to be sure of that." She paused and turned toward Millicent.

"Now, young lady," she said, "tell me what colour stockings the Lord Chamberlain was wearing when he showed you in."

Millicent glanced at her mother, but turned quickly back to the Queen. "Blue, your grace, light blue."

"And what tapestry was hung on the wall behind me at the reception today?"

The girl hesitated but for a second.

"It was lions, your grace, yellow lions on a field of red."

"Quite right, my dear. It seems you have a reasonable talent for observation—to go with your talent for riding. I think you will do nicely!"

"Do, your grace?"

The Queen turned toward Catherine. "Lady de Laval, Cheshire is a most powerful county and we must be vigilant to secure it for the King. Trouble may come from any direction, even from my own family, and securing Cheshire and the Midlands is the key to keeping trouble at bay. I must know if there is any mischief afoot there. I need someone I can trust to watch carefully what goes on at Chester. I would like you to place your daughter as lady-in-waiting to Lady Constance. She will be my eyes and ears in the Earl's household."

The Queen paused for a moment, letting her words sink in.

"Lord Ranulf seems harmless enough, but I am less certain about his wife. She was once married to my late son Geoffrey and has a son of her own by him—Arthur. My grandson is but three years old and is being raised in Brittany, but I know my former daughter-in-law. Constance is ambitious—for herself, and for her son. She would have the crown on his head if it were up to her. And—she hates your Earl." As she spoke the Queen leaned forward and grasped Catherine's arm with a surprisingly strong grip.

"I believe I can trust you. You or your daughter may refuse this request and I will take no offense, but I need your help. Your King needs your help." Now she leaned back and looked from one of the women to the other.

Millicent turned to Lady Catherine.

"Mother...?"

"Millie...you are no longer a child," her mother managed. "You must choose."

Millicent turned to the Queen.

"You want me to spy on Earl Ranulf."

"On the Earl, and any who pass through his halls. Can you do that, girl?" Millicent glanced once more at her mother. Lady Catherine's face betrayed nothing. She turned and met the gaze of the Queen.

"Your grace, I am no spy."

The Queen frowned.

"But I can be your scout."

Eleanor of Aquitaine smiled.

***

The banquet that evening was a blur for Millicent. Her mind kept returning to their interview with the Queen and to the words she and her mother had exchanged afterwards. The two women had been escorted from the Queen's chambers and

58

strolled arm-in-arm along the Strand while they waited for the evening gathering to begin.

"Mother, am I foolish to do this?"

Her mother sighed.

"Yes, you are. There is peril in this, Millie. If you are discovered, I doubt the Queen will acknowledge or aid you. It is the way of queens. You mean nothing to her. Yet—we both know you really have no choice." She continued, with a bitter edge in her voice. "Just as your father had no choice but to grant the *request* of the King to go off to some god-forsaken desert, we have no choice but to aid the queen, no matter her assurances to the contrary. We are all pawns when thrones are at stake, my love, but chin up, sometimes a pawn makes all the difference."

That night they found their way to their assigned seats near Earl Ranulf and Lady Constance. Queen Eleanor made her entrance accompanied by her son, Prince John, and took up station at a slightly higher table than the rest. During the afternoon, most of the high born ladies had retreated to their great London town houses to refresh and don even more magnificent dresses for the occasion. Now they were kept company by their men, the lords of the Midlands, in their own finery. Men from all the noble families of the region were present, save those few who had accompanied Richard on Crusade.

The meal was sumptuous—fish and fowl of every description and wines better than any they had back in Shipbrook. There were many dishes unfamiliar to the young woman and some unknown to the mother as well. Once the scurrying servants cleared away the remnants, a small group of court musicians began to play and the guests, led by the Queen, drifted away from the tables and mingled at one end of the great hall. Some of the younger members of the group were encouraged to dance by the Queen and soon a circle of laughing young men and women joined hands and began a carole in time to the music.

The spectacle served to divert Millicent from the thoughts that were crowding in on her throughout the evening. She had been taught to dance by her mother and they held small gatherings with music and dancing in their keep, but that was nothing like the swirl of silk and lace before her now. Her mother nudged her.

"Millie, I think we should put aside for the moment our worries and enjoy this evening. There will be worries enough in the days to come. I have not failed to notice that you caught the eye of a number of the young men during the banquet. There is one standing by Earl Ranulf who, even now, is staring at you."

Millicent had the presence of mind not to whirl around and stare back.

"Surely you are mistaken, Mother."

"I think not, child, for here he comes now."

Millicent turned to see a young man approaching. He was tall with jet black hair framing a face that was handsome though a bit severe—giving him a hawkish appearance. His garments fairly shimmered in the reflected candlelight and were of the richest fabrics. As he neared them, he smoothly performed a sweeping bow and smiled.

"My ladies, pardon my lack of introduction, but I understand you are from Cheshire."

Lady Catherine spoke.

"Indeed, you have the advantage of us, my lord. I am Lady Catherine de Laval and this is my daughter, Lady Millicent, and as you have already learned, we do reside in Cheshire. And who might you be?"

The man gave a sheepish smile.

"My apologies, Lady Catherine. It was rude of me. I am Sir William de Ferrers of Derbyshire. My father is Earl Robert— away on crusade I'm afraid, so I rule there in his stead. I was wondering if I might ask the Lady Millicent to join me in the dance?"

Millicent was frozen to the spot. *William de Ferrers. The son of the Earl of Derby.* Roland Inness had spoken of him that day so long ago as they walked together along the walls of Shipbrook. This was the man who had murdered Roland's father. The man who made her friend a fugitive. She had an overwhelming urge to strike him. Instead she smiled and extended her hand.

"With pleasure, my lord."

It was not too soon to be about the Queen's business.

De Ferrers bowed to Lady Catherine and took Millicent's hand, leading her to where the other dancers had gathered waiting for the next tune.

"I must say, Lady Millicent, that I had little hope of finding a dance partner in this company," he said smiling, then lowered his voice. "The Midlands are not famous for producing great beauties, but at least I see Cheshire is an exception. Your mother is quite striking. You look like her."

Millicent recognized flattery when she heard it, even though the young nobleman spoke with practiced sincerity.

"Why, thank you, my lord," she said and smiled sweetly. "My father would agree with you regarding my mother."

"Your father, Sir Roger de Laval I believe?"

"Yes, my lord, he is away to the Crusade, as is your own sire."

"Yes, we have that in common, do we not? I believe I briefly made your father's acquaintance at the coronation—he had a clumsy squire who almost knocked me over!" The man chuckled. "I assume you know the boy—tall, gangly, and tangle-footed?"

Millicent laughed along with the man, but she could feel her cheeks burning and did not like the direction this conversation was taking.

"Why yes, my lord. That would be Roland. He is a good squire, but I must apologize for any injury he did you."

"Oh, no harm done. Your father took him firmly in hand and, no doubt, put him straight. I must say, however, that the boy was a decent shot with a bow. I lost a few pounds betting against him in the Royal Archery tournament."

This produced the first genuine smile from the girl.

"Oh, my lord, had I known I could have warned you."

"Warned me?

"Aye, my lord—warned you to never bet against Roland Inness with a bow in his hand."

Millicent saw a flicker of something behind the man's eyes. Was it anger? Or was it fear?

Good.

Just then the musicians took up a new tune and de Ferrers, recovering, led her to the dance floor. He did not speak again while he led her through the steps of the carole. This was a dance she had practiced before and she moved effortlessly with the music while fighting to maintain a smile on her face. At last the number was over and de Ferrers escorted her back to Lady Catherine.

"Your daughter is an excellent dancer, my lady," he said. "You have taught her well." He then turned to Millicent. "Thank you, Lady Millicent. I hope we meet again soon." With that, he turned and walked briskly away, the crowd parting as he went.

***

Later that night, William de Ferrers sat beside a flickering fire in his father's sumptuous town home on the Strand. Beside him sat Father Malachy.

"My lord, we accomplished much this day. The Prince seemed well pleased with you."

De Ferrers nodded, but did not reply.

"I found his grace's thoughts on Cheshire interesting in the extreme, my lord."

De Ferrers remained silent, staring at the fire.

"The Prince considers Earl Ranulf to be a dunce, but loyal to Richard," the priest continued. "It is the wife that worries him. He fears she will seek to have her son declared the heir over him. It is a situation ripe with..." De Ferrers cut him off with an irritated wave of his hand.

"Do not think me a dunce as well, priest—I do not need you to tell me the Prince's mind."

The churchman shrank back, but spoke again.

"My lord, I recount this to help sort my own thoughts, not your own. You know the affairs of the Midlands better than any living man. I am but a poor priest and know little of politics."

There followed a long silence as the fire crackled. Then the young nobleman spoke with authority in his voice.

"As you say, the Prince is already suspicious of his former sister-in-law. We can use that. Malachy, you will get yourself to Chester by the Feast of Saint Matthew. Appear at Earl Ranulf's keep as you did at our doorstep—poor and humble. He is as easy a touch as my own father I expect. Gain entrance to his household. Observe everything, particularly the disposition of his men-at-arms and the state of the city's defences. Find where they are vulnerable, then report back to me."

Malachy knew a dismissal when he heard it.

"I will not fail you, my lord!"

"See that you don't, Malachy."

The priest hurried from the room. When he returned to his quarters in the small windowless room usually reserved for servants, he lit a candle and took out a quill and a small parchment. He carefully scratched out the events of the day and the progress he was making in fomenting trouble in the English heartland.

He would dispatch this message by trusted courier before he left London. In less than a week, if the weather in the Channel did not prevent a crossing, his report would be in Paris. By now, King Philip may have taken ship for the Holy Land, but his network of spies was extensive and efficient. The message would get through and the King would be pleased with him. Malachy allowed himself a smile. He had certainly heard of St. Matthew. Was he not one of the Apostles? But he had no idea when the man's feast day was. *He would have to inquire.*

Above him, in the room he had just left, William de Ferrers was deep in thought. The Prince had given him much to mull over this day. John's discomfort with Cheshire was clear and there was no attempt to hide his desire to have that county behind him when events came to a head. Cheshire was a rich prize in its own right—richer than any county in the Midlands. If he were bold enough, it could be his! And with John on the throne, he would become the most powerful baron in the kingdom.

When that day came, he would settle certain scores with the de Lavals, both old and new. The girl Millicent was beautiful, but an arrogant little wench. He would take great pleasure in teaching her how to submit to her betters. More importantly, the de Lavals harboured the Inness boy.

His proof was flimsy at best, but he was certain this was the same boy who had almost taken his life with a longbow the previous spring back on Kinder Scout. Ivo Brun had sworn that he killed the owner of that bow, but there was cause to question the assassin's account. To begin with, Brun had gone missing in London during the coronation when Inness and his protectors were in the city. The man had never resurfaced. Coincidence? He thought not. The dagger he had seen on the boy's belt was a twin for one that once belonged to Brun.

And then there was the appearance of the Inness boy at the royal archery match with a longbow! His uncanny skill with that cursed weapon had been on full display that day. He had seen accuracy like that only once before and it had almost cost him his life.

The boy's possession of a longbow and his skill with it, the dagger in his belt—it all pointed to this squire as the one. If Roland Inness ever returned alive from the east, he would find William de Ferrers—waiting for him in Cheshire.

A Nest of Vipers

The blood had been washed from the decks of the *Sprite* and the slain cast into the sea—the two English dead with prayer and solemn ceremony and the dozen or more Berbers with dispatch. Crowded into the hold below were almost a score of captured men, sitting sullenly on piles of provisions. Boda suggested that they be put to the sword forthwith and follow their comrades into the deep, but Master Sparks and Sir Roger de Laval would not countenance such a plan.

"If ye've no stomach fer pitchin' em over the side, sir, then ye must put 'em ashore—and soon. Ye know we've precious little food and water. 'Course all the shore hereabouts is infested with heathens..." Boda trailed off.

"Aye, Boda, t'would be convenient t' slit their throats," Sparks replied. "But it hardly seems the *Christian* thing t'do—what with us being on *Crusade* and all."

"The monk would a' done it, I'd wager," the old sailor grumbled.

The mention of Friar Tuck filled Roland with new despair. For hours he had watched off the stern of the *Sprite*, trying to catch a glimpse of the galley that bore away his friend and benefactor, but the Vendavales continued to blow steadily and they had long since outdistanced friend and foe alike. Now, even land was out of sight. Nothing could be seen but an endless expanse of sea to the horizon as the sun began to set behind them.

"Roland, he's gone, lad." It was the voice of Sir Roger. "He may yet live—none saw him fall—and the Moors had not overtaken him when we lost sight. He is an unusual man. If any could survive, it would be Tuck."

"Aye, my lord. I know he may live, but it seems as likely he's been slain—and we left him to die." There was guilt and anger in the young man's voice.

"Aye, we did," the big knight sighed, "and I'm not much accustomed to leaving my comrades behind on a battlefield—but this battling at sea is strange to me. I think our Master Sparks knows his job and he's no coward. If we could have saved him, we would have."

"Aye, my lord," he replied, with no conviction.

Sir Roger shook his head wearily, then spoke again with a snap in his voice.

"This is the way of soldiering, Master Inness—fer good or ill. Men kill and men die and they are bound together in the face of the dying. It's not fer all, but if yer to be my squire, you must come to live with it. Can ye do that, boy? Can ye?"

The man's words stung. Roland wanted to shout back that he was a farmer and a hunter—not a soldier, but he knew that was no longer true. He had lost count of the men he had killed this very day. Those men had come to kill him and his master—or worse—make them slaves in the galley. He felt no remorse for having killed them. He thought of his father, who had led peasants armed with staves and longbows against armoured knights. He thought of his Viking forbearer who had come to England on a longship and whose name he carried. He looked at the man in front of him, the Norman knight he now served. All of them—*all warriors*. For the first time, he knew there was no going back. He was one of them.

"I can live with it, my lord—and I will," he answered.

Sir Roger nodded and left him alone to stare out across the sea.

***

The night sky was bright with a gibbous moon as the *Sprite* slipped in near the Iberian shore. Boda still grumbled, but dutifully tossed the weighted line off the bow to check the depth and warn them of any hidden shoals. He fairly whispered his soundings back to the ship's master. But Sparks chose his approach wisely, and in time a deserted cove was found. No lights shone from the shore and a line of beach, white in the moonlight, could be seen as they drew nearer.

Quietly he had five empty water barrels lowered over the side, then gestured to the prisoners that they were to follow. Like many sailing men, some could not swim, but they could cling to the barrels and get ashore, if their mates would help them.

"It's the best I can do," Sparks muttered.

For their part the Berbers seemed delighted to find that they were not going to be murdered or made slaves. The last one over the side bowed twice to Sparks.

With a wide grin he whispered, "Ma' al-salāmah!" and was gone.

Free of their captives, the *Sprite* turned back to the open sea and set a course eastward. For ten days they sailed toward the rising sun, until they hove to for fresh water in a deserted cove on the wild island of Sardinia. One crewman finally died of the wounds he received repelling the Berber attack and was committed to the deep, but to the relief of all, Master Sparks and the other wounded among the crew made gradual but steady recoveries. Still, the loss of crew members was an added burden on those remaining, and Roland and Declan pitched in where they could under the watchful eye of Boda.

"Seems ye young gentlemen might be good for somethin' other than ballast and eating up our provisions," he growled as he watched them put their backs into the work.

The squires smiled at each other. By now they had come to know Boda well and understood that he was a hard man but fair—though still suspicious by nature. He knew his place in the world and among this crew and had no patience for any man who did not also know his own.

Young squires who idled about, or worse, puked on his deck were objects of disdain. On the other hand, young men who fought side-by-side with him to save his ship—well that was a different matter. They noticed that the gnarled old sailor had stopped giving them evil looks ever since they had cleared Gibraltar.

Sparks looked down at the boys and smiled. He turned to Roger de Laval who had joined him on the sterncastle.

"Likely lads those two!" he said.

"None better in my experience," replied the knight.

"The young Irishman handles a blade like few I've ever seen."

Sir Roger nodded. "He's deadlier, by far, than he looks."

"And how did you come to have a squire with that kind of skill with the longbow? I have never seen anything like what young Inness did back there in the Straits."

"Well, like most good things, I just stumbled upon him. There were some nasty folk on his trail, so I was a 'port in a storm' as you seamen like to say. For my part, I needed someone to amuse Master O'Duinne, who was threatening to talk me to death. So I took him. Didn't know he had the bow. Didn't know till later that he was perhaps the best shot in England with it. He won the King's archery tournament at coronation, ye know."

"I did not know, but it hardly surprises me. He hit a man from a pitching deck at over a hundred yards—and it was not luck."

"I saw him take down a Welshman at over two hundred yards who richly deserved it, and that with an arrow wound in his leg."

"Extraordinary young man."

"Aye, and what's best is, he does not know just how extraordinary."

"In time," said Sparks. "He will."

"Aye, if we survive this journey, I think he will come into his own. It will be interesting to watch."

Sparks grinned and nodded. "Within another week we should reach Sicily. We will have to stop there to take on supplies and try to recruit a few new hands for the crew."

Warbow

"Aye," sighed Sir Roger, "Sicily."

"A snake pit, my friend."

"So I've heard."

***

With changeable winds it took another five days to reach Sicily. Dun-coloured hills with rocky crags began to emerge over the eastern horizon as the *Sprite* made landfall on the far western coast of the island. Master Sparks steered a little north and then turned east past a headland to skirt the northern shore.

The ship fought headwinds as it made its way east along the coast. When the squires were not assigned crew duties, they studied the land slipping past. The brown hills rather quickly turned to a jagged mountain range that, at times, plunged directly into the sea. These were higher and more barren than the mountains Roland once called home in the Midlands of England, but they still evoked a kind of pull that natives of the high country know well.

On the second morning when the young men took up their vantage point on the starboard side of the forecastle, they were greeted with a sight that made these jagged peaks seem puny. Rising like a huge beast to the southeast was a massive hump of a mountain. And from its summit a huge plume of white smoke rose to the heavens. The two squires were transfixed.

"That'd be Aetna," Boda offered up. "Tis a volcano. Big fire down in the guts of the thing. Hot enough to melt the rocks. Some say it leads to the underworld. Don't know about that, but if ye be up there when she belches up liquid fire, you'll likely get there quick enough."

There was nothing like this in England. All that day and the next they continued along the coast, with Aetna slowly taking up more and more of the view to the south until finally it began to fall slightly astern. Now the land sloped more gently down to the sea and they began to pass fishing villages along the shore. At night, a few flickering lights could now be seen to starboard as they passed, and far ahead there was a faint glow against the night sky.

The boys no longer hesitated to seek Boda's wisdom on the strange sights they encountered almost daily.

"That'd be a beacon at the point for such as us. Bad rocky headland there and around the bend, is the strait, where Charybdis lurks."

"Charybdis?" both squires said in unison.

"Aye, legend is that, where the strait is most narrow, there is a monster hidden deep under the sea, waiting to pull down a ship and eat its crew!"

Declan laughed, a trifle nervously.

"A monster, Boda? Surely not."

"Well, as I say, lads, it's a legend, so take it for what it's worth. What I do know is there are no more treacherous currents anywhere in the sea and in certain seasons, these come together to form a great whirlpool, and then, monster or no, you are down to the bottom!"

Roland could not resist asking.

"In what season does this whirlpool appear, Boda?"

Boda grinned.

"Why, this one, lads. This one."

***

At dawn, the *Sprite* rounded the cape and entered the strait. From here, they could see the mountains of Italy to the east, with Aetna still looming off to the southwest. A strong wind seemed to shift, first from the south, then off the flanks of Aetna. The squires stood to their stations near the mainsail of the craft and watched with a mixture of excitement and nerves. Sir Roger sat calmly below the forecastle and stroked the head of Bucephalus. Master Sparks had a large arm wrapped around the steering oar and his feet planted wide on the deck of the sterncastle, his hair a swirling mass in the wind and his face creased by a broad smile.

"Current running hard south, wind blowing hard north till it changes its mind. Now this is sailing, my boys!" The man was in his element. For the next several hours the crew worked hard under Boda's commands to manoeuvre the sails as Sparks skilfully brought the *Sprite* through the cross sea that ran between the two headlands with their nasty slashes of rock barely two miles apart. No whirlpools or monsters were sighted.

Well before noon, the winds began to die and to the unspoken relief of most of the crew, the port of Messina came into view. Messina's harbour was enclosed by a narrow crescent of land that served as breakwater with a small fortified tower guarding the entrance. Ships of every shape and size were tied up at the docks or were traversing the harbour mouth going about their business. Sparks expertly edged the *Sprite* into an open berth and the crew made her fast to the dock.

"I shall need perhaps two days to find, procure and load provisions," Sparks said to Sir Roger. "I understand you have a task to perform of your own?"

"Aye, Master Sparks, the King commanded me to deliver this letter to his sister, Joanna. Her husband, William, is King of this island." Sir Roger drew out a small leather folder that was bound with straps and had King Richard's royal seal attached. "The King expects to make Messina one of his stops on his voyage to the Holy Land. Don't know what the message says—perhaps, 'Save me a spot for dinner!'" Sparks chuckled, but only for a moment.

"Take care, my friend. This place is worse than Lisbon for intrigue. I say get in and get out and do not dawdle!"

"Aye, Tuck gave me the same warning. Would that he were with me now."

"As do we all, sir, as do we all. Just get yerself back to the *Sprite* and we will be off to war, where I think ye will be more at home."

"That's a fact, Master Sparks," he said, then turned and called to his squires. "Declan! You will come with me to the palace. Roland, get Buc off this boat and let him wander a bit. He'll be as glad as we to be on dry land at last."

Sir Roger and Declan stepped off the *Sprite* and onto the dock and began a wobbling walk up toward the quay. Weeks at sea made moving on land strangely alien. Roland enlisted the help of several crewmen to manhandle a heavy set of planking between the pier and a gap in the ship's railing. A second set of planks was lashed together and lowered from the deck into the hold of the ship where the great warhorse stood waiting patiently.

Roland held the horse's reins lightly in his hand and spoke gently as he urged the stallion up the ramp formed by the planks. For his part, Bucephalus looked a bit bored. He had followed Sir Roger across the sea before, first to France and then to Ireland, and was used to this drill. In a few moments, he was stamping his iron-shod hoofs on the pier—eager to move about freely for the first time in over a month. The horse was clearly pleased to be free from his confinement and flared his nostrils in excitement. No proper warhorse would prance, but Buc was verging on it.

"Settle down there, big fella," Roland whispered loudly to the horse as he rubbed the animal's jaw. He had learned much about the ways of these animals since he joined the household of Sir Roger. There had been no horses among the poor Danish peasants that were his people, and he had never ridden until taught the rudiments by Millie de Laval during a summer that seemed a lifetime ago.

The lessons had been good ones. He did not yet have the easy touch with the animals that Millie had, but he could manage well enough. At the moment, however, he wished he was seated on the horse, for his legs felt strangely unsteady. Roland now knew what Master Sparks meant when he talked of "sea legs." Clearly the dock was solid and unmoving, but the boy felt a distinct sway beneath his feet, as though still on the deck of the *Sprite*.

He walked Bucephalus to the crowded quay and led the animal from one end to the other for near to an hour, reluctant to stop since the horse was so thoroughly enjoying his freedom. In truth, he was loathe to go back aboard the *Sprite* himself.

Messina was a more exotic place than he expected. All about the bustling harbour, strange looking men were tending to the business of the port. Goods of every sort were being loaded and unloaded from every imaginable kind of craft. For a Christian city, there were a surprising number of men with headdresses and flowing robes that seemed to mark them as Muslims. Tuck had told him that this was also the case in Lisbon, where trade continued between the two worlds even as they fought over Spain and the Holy Land.

By the time he returned Bucephalus to his stall and brushed and fed him, it was time for the evening meal. On deck, he saw Boda chewing vigorously on a fresh crust of bread and staring over the side at the city. He grabbed a bowl of stew from the cook and joined the man.

"What are ye watching for, Boda?"

"Yer Master, lad. I should think he would be back 'fore this. Messina is a dangerous city."

No sooner had the man spoken than Master Sparks appeared out of the crowd on the quay moving with more than his normal haste down the dock toward the *Sprite*. The shipmaster hopped nimbly over the railing to the deck. He took a moment to catch his breath, scanning everything on the deck of his vessel, then shaking his head.

"I hoped to find Sir Roger back safely by now. We have a problem I fear. There is talk everywhere in the town. King William died not two weeks ago and some usurper named Tancred has seized the throne. He has imprisoned Queen Joanna and has her closely guarded." He turned and addressed Roland directly. "Would that we had this news before your master and your friend set off to deliver the King's message to his sister. I fear they have walked into a very dangerous situation."

Roland swallowed hard.

"Perhaps they have just been delayed, Master Sparks," he said with more hope than he felt.

"Perhaps, but an English knight trying to deliver a message to an imprisoned queen would hardly be ignored by this Tancred fellow or his henchmen. We need to know what has become of them—and quickly, for I doubt their situation will improve over time if they have been taken."

"I will go to the palace..." Roland began, but Sparks cut him off.

"Then we would have three problems instead of only two. We need to know, discreetly, what has happened, then decide what we must do."

"We must get them out!" Roland now spoke with urgency. "Whatever it takes. I've given my word to Lady de Laval. I cannot fail her."

"Indeed, lad, but we need a plan and first we need sure knowledge of where they might be held—if held they be."

"Agreed," said Roland. "I will go into the city and learn what has befallen them."

"Not alone, Master Inness." Boda spoke for the first time. "I have pissed away my pay in every port city around this sea, including this one. I know where we might find what we need, but you must let me take the lead, young sir, or we'll both have our throats slit. Besides, I like the knight, though the squire talks too much."

Roland nodded at the gnarled sailor. His words rang true. He would have to let the man take the lead. Sparks drew a money pouch from his belt and handed it to Boda. "I don't know this port like Boda nor could I enter places he can without suspicion, but I like the knight too. Some coins can help loosen lips."

Boda took the pouch and stuffed it down his ragged shirt. Roland retrieved his dagger from his kit and likewise concealed it beneath his own shirt. He felt naked going into harm's way without his bow, but it would be of no use in the back alleys of Messina. When all was secure, the two men stepped on the dock, walked to the quay and were lost to view in the crowd.

"Good hunting," Master Sparks murmured.

***

True to his word, Boda knew Messina well. They followed a path through winding streets and alleyways that soon had Roland unable to tell where they were or where they had been. The lanes were so narrow he could barely see a small patch of sky between the encroaching buildings that closed in overhead.

Boda seemed to know what he was searching for and soon enough found it. It was a rancid looking ale house that had seen better days, but Roland quickly recognized the virtue of the choice. Not a hundred yards ahead was the arched entrance to the fortified palace that loomed over the port city. This was not a place where sailors gathered, being too far from the docks.

Here, local folk would come to have their ale and wine. Among them might be those who had seen a large knight and his squire pass by or had heard news of them.

Roland followed the sailor through the entrance into a dimly lit space with low ceilings and a few tables scattered about. The locals in attendance stared at the newcomers for a moment then returned to their drinks. Boda found a seat at one of the rough-hewn tables near the door and motioned to the inn-keeper, holding up two fingers. The man nodded and, in due course, a flagon of wine was delivered along with two dingy cups. Boda took out his money pouch and made a bit of a fuss about extracting coins for payment. The local patrons made a show of not looking in their direction, but there was no mistaking the sense of greedy anticipation that suddenly hovered in the room.

"Drink up, but slowly, lad." Boda whispered to the squire. "We've baited the hook. Now we wait."

The wait was not long. Before they finished half a cup, a very large man rose noisily from his seat and walked up to Boda. He did not look friendly.

"Don't get many of your sort in here," he said with a voice gone gravelly from too much drink for too many years.

Boda gave the man a toothless smile. "And what sort would that be?"

"Why a stinking sailor, of course."

Boda looked embarrassed and turned his head to sniff diligently at each armpit. He got a dreamy look on his face, then leapt to his feet, raising one arm over his head and advancing toward the man. "Smell this—it's like lilacs, it is."

This was not expected. The big man took a half step back to avoid the armpit approaching his nose and did not even see the roundhouse right that landed just above his ear. Stunned, he stumbled and nearly fell over the table he had just left. Boda was on him in an instant, landing blows with speed and precision. The man was going down, but now the inn keeper came around the rude counter with a stave in his hand.

So intent was he on this gnarled sailor who was pummelling one of his regulars that he forgot for a moment the young man still at the table. As he passed, Roland stood and calmly slammed the wine pitcher against his temple. He went down like a felled ox. Boda took a step back and his opponent pitched forward, joining the inn-keeper face down on the floor. The sailor turned, saw the unconscious inn-keeper, and winked at Roland. Together they blocked the door of the inn, a half dozen patrons still inside.

These were hard looking men, but having seen the largest of them reduced to a bloody heap on the floor, none seemed eager to be next. Boda addressed the crowd.

"All right, you lot. Listen careful. You can walk out of here with a few coins in yer pocket or with your teeth in your hands—if you can walk at all. Yer choice."

After a moment of silence, a voice came from the back.

"What ye wantin' for the coin?"

"Information, just information. We seek an English knight. May have come up this way with his squire. Hasn't come back."

"I might a seen 'em!" A wispy-thin man near the front spoke up—and waited. Boda grinned and flipped him a single coin, which instantly got him talking. "It was 'fore noon. Came right up to the gate of the palace, they did. Tried to enter, but words was exchanged with the guards and there was some unpleasantness."

"Unpleasantness?" Roland asked roughly.

"Aye, the guards tried to lay hands on them and the big man banged some heads together. 'Fore we knew it, the place was swarming with soldiers—Tancred's men. Nasty lot, them. They drug the two off through the gate." Boda flipped another coin to the man who had spoken. He caught it in midair and cackled happily.

"Tancred," Boda said it like it left a foul taste in his mouth and spit on the floor. "What sort of man would be stupid enough to imprison the sister of Richard the Lionheart, who at this moment is approaching these shores with a mighty fleet and a mightier host?" Boda's news about the approach of the English king caused a low murmur to run through the crowd.

"Stupid he may be, sir, but bold," a man spoke up, "and he has gained the upper hand, with King William dead and all.

William was a good enough king, as kings go, and we all loved Queen Joanna. We are no friends of the usurper, but he holds the whip hand here in Messina." There was a murmur of assent from the remaining men in the room. Roland spoke up.

"Aye, he does for now, but when King Richard comes calling, the whip will be in his hand. No doubt Queen Joanna will not be harmed. Even Tancred would not be so stupid, but the fate of our friends might be different. We must secure their release quickly, and we are willing to pay for your help." The boy reached into his tunic, withdrew a leather pouch and dropped it on the table.

This was money given to him by Friar Tuck a year ago at the King's coronation. It was a substantial sum, given in return for the golden arrow prize he had won at the Royal Archery tournament. The pouch landed on the table with a satisfying jingle. "This I will give if—*if*—any men among you can help us release these prisoners."

These men may not have cared for the usurper Tancred, but words, not even threats had budged them. Money?—that was a different matter. The money pouch had gained their full attention. A new voice came from behind the crowd. It was female. A girl forced her way through the small group of patrons to the front. She looked down at the unconscious inn keeper and smiling, kicked him in the head. Turning to the two men blocking the door, she stood with hands on hips, head held high.

"This filthy establishment supplies the palace, or at least the palace servants, with their required spirits. I take two wine skins each afternoon to the dungeon guards. I can take you to where they are likely held." The girl was young, perhaps a year older than Roland. She was dark. Her hair raven black, her eyes a deep brown and her skin, of which a good deal was revealed, was the colour of fresh baked bread. She smiled at the men before her and winked. "I am Isabella. The guards like me."

Boda looked at her sceptically, but turned and whispered to Roland. "She's just what we need." Roland nodded. They could not storm the fortress. This girl might be their only hope.

The squire reached into his pouch and laid five coins on the table. Boda spoke, all business now.

"This much now, and the rest of the bag when you get us there. And if you play us false, I'll have back the coins and your heart, for I am, indeed, a wicked man and very familiar with the uses of a knife." He drew out his dagger and smiled a truly frightening smile.

"No," she stated flatly. "I cannot take you. The guards would think it queer if two men came with me. And you," she sneered at Boda, "you *look* like the cutthroat you claim to be. You cannot come. I will take the boy," she said and nodded toward Roland. "He looks harmless enough."

Roland felt his face flush. He turned to Boda.

"She's right. Forgive me, Boda, but you look like death coming to call. It has to be me." Then he lightly touched the dagger in his own belt and turned back to the girl.

"Miss," he said fixing the girl with his gaze, "do not mistake me. I'd wager this bag of coins that I have killed more men than anyone in this room, except for Master Boda here. And I will kill you if you betray us. Do you understand?"

The girl seemed to truly see him for the first time. She shrugged and picked up the five coins from the table.

"Perhaps you are not as harmless as you look."

Breakout

The girl moved with a pronounced sway in her hips as she approached the two guards stationed at the palace gatehouse. It reminded Roland of the Danish women he had known back in the hills of Derbyshire, but here it was done with considerably more calculation. He followed behind her carrying the swollen leather wineskins destined for the dungeon guards. Isabella had sprinkled some sort of powder into each of the skins before pouring in the wine.

"Something the women in my village use when they do not wish to be bothered at night by their husbands," was the only explanation she offered. Somewhere in the shadows of the alley behind them, Boda waited and watched. His role in the plan would come near the end.

"Isabella! Give me a smile!" the older of the two guards shouted before she even drew near.

"Give *him* the smile—and *me* a kiss!" the second guard chimed in and laughed.

Roland watched as she smiled at both and gave them a wink.

"What kind of a girl do you take me for, you ruffians," she said and continued to move forward, smiling.

"The kind I would like to see next to me in a haystack," the older man cackled.

"And what would your wife say to that, Nicolo?" she replied sweetly.

His fellow guard gave out a hoot and punched him in the shoulder.

"And you, Piero—I thought you were courting Margherita, from down the block. Shall we ask her opinion of your request?

The man laughed again, showing a toothless grin and shook his head.

"No, no…but perhaps another time—when Margherita is visiting her mother?"

Roland could tell that this banter was part of a daily routine—then suddenly it wasn't. The older guard put out a hand as Roland tried to pass and stopped him in his tracks.

"Who is this fellow you bring with you, Isabella? I don't like the look of him."

Isabella gave the guard a weary sigh. "I don't like his look either, Nicolo. He is just arrived from the country and knows nothing. I am using him like a mule. He is from my uncle's village."

Nicolo gave the boy a sharp slap to the back of his head.

"Move along mule," he roared, "and don't get any ideas about Isabella. She is mine!"

Roland gritted his teeth and kept moving, following the girl into the darkness of the arched gateway.

"Well done, mule," she murmured.

Ahead of them was another arch leading into a cobbled courtyard, but the girl took a quick left through a smaller passageway. It took them within the walls of the palace and was so narrow Roland could barely pass with the two large wineskins. After a few yards, they came to stone steps leading down. A torch cast a flickering light on the stairway and, far below, a scream broke the silence. The boy froze. Isabella turned quickly and whispered over her shoulder.

"There is always screaming here. I pay it no attention, for it is not my affair and there is nothing to be done."

They began to descend the steps and Roland cringed to think of his master and friend confined in this dark, dank place. *They will be free or he would die trying.*

At length, they reached the bottom of the stairs and entered a much larger arched chamber. More torches lighted this space and two guards sat on low stools near the centre. All around the outer walls of the chamber were small doorways of heavy oak with barred windows—the dungeons of Messina.

"Isabella! You are late my sweet." The guard who spoke was huge, but most of the bulk was fat. The other guard was thin and weasely-looking.

"Toma, my handsome knight!" the girl sang out. "I hurried as quickly as I could! See, I brought my own pack mule to speed me along. Those wineskins were getting too much for a frail thing like me." She deftly caught one of the sacks as Roland slid it from his back and carried it to the fat guard. "This is good stuff, Toma. Just in from Calabria across the straits!"

"Bah, everyone likes the wines from Calabria, but I say Sicily has the best!" He was grinning as he spoke and showed no hesitation in taking the first wineskin, popping out the stopcock and gulping greedily at the contents, some of which rolled down his chin and onto his thin beard. The girl quickly grabbed the second bag and handed it to the weasely guard.

"Lucca, you look thirsty. Please…"

The second guard looked surprised that she had spoken to him. Until now, he had never dared to address the beautiful tavern girl.

"Grazie…Isabella," he managed shyly.

Now both guards were happily swigging on the rich wine and becoming more animated. This was their only relief during the long hours in this hell hole. The darkness, the damp and the screams could fade out for a time—when Isabella delivered the wine.

While they drank, the girl kept up her banter as she collected the empty wineskins from her delivery the day before. Roland fought the urge to try to peek into the nearby cells and attempted to look as dumb and docile as the mule he was meant to be. If the guards noticed that the girl seemed to be lingering longer than usual, they made no sign. Slowly their speech began to slow and they both began to weave slightly on their stools.

"Ho, Isa…Isa…bella, this Calab…labrian wine is too…strong," the fat guard managed, then toppled face first onto the floor, a dark spray of blood erupting from his newly broken nose.

Lucca, his fellow guard, stared blankly at the sight, and began to laugh.

"Look...at...Toma..," he said between high pitched giggles. "He's...," before he could utter another word he toppled backwards from his stool and lay still.

Roland stared in wonder at how quickly Isabella's powder had dispatched the two men, then he sprang into motion. The fat guard had fallen such that the key ring at his belt was now beneath him. He grasped the man's shoulders and began to push.

"Lend a hand here," he whispered urgently to the girl who had frozen in place when the second guard went down. Roland's sharp request snapped her attention back to their task and she helped roll Toma over on his side and tore the key ring from his belt. There were a dozen doors in this warren. Where to start?

"Sir Roger! Declan!" The boy called in a voice between a shout and a whisper. For a moment there was no reply, then from one of the farthest doors he thought he heard a faint call.

He grabbed the keys from Isabella and ran to the door, peering in through the barred window. The darkness of the cell was almost complete.

"The torch!" he called to the girl. She grabbed the smouldering light from its niche on the wall and held it so that a little of its glow penetrated the darkness. Roland could see two figures against the far wall. He fumbled with the ring and was relieved that there were only three keys attached. On the second try, the bolt sprang back and he burst through the door into the foul smelling cell.

It took but a moment to see that both Sir Roger and Declan had been roughly treated by their captors. The Irishman's face was swollen and hardly recognizable. Sir Roger appeared to have burn marks on his exposed arms. Declan tried to speak but his lips were so swollen his words came out as a croak.

"Chains!" Sir Roger held up his arm. It was chained to the wall. Roland again sorted the keys and found the one that unlocked the iron manacles that bound the prisoners.

"Good to see ye, lad," the knight managed as he rose to his feet. Roland could see that even that movement required all of the big man's strength. Declan was also rising and Roland was startled when his friend stumbled forward and embraced him.

"Knew ye'd come," he managed.

"We must go, and quickly!" Isabella hissed. Roland nodded. Thus far their plan was working to perfection, but getting past the two guards at the gate house was going to be a more difficult challenge. Both of the freed prisoners could walk, but moved slowly and painfully. Even if they had been nimble, there was no chance Isabella could talk all four of them past Nicolo and Piero. No, the two men at the palace gate had to be taken out.

They led the freed men back into the main chamber. Before leaving, Roland unlocked several of the doors and threw the key ring in to one of the tattered prisoners. The scarecrow of a man gave him a gapped tooth grin and began removing the fetters from his cell mate.

Roland draped Sir Roger's arm around his shoulders and led him, a step at a time, up the stone stairway and down the narrow passage within the fortress wall. Isabella followed with Declan. When they reached the door leading to the main archway, he leaned Sir Roger against the wall.

"Wait here, my lord," he said and gave a quick nod to Isabella. The girl straightened her skirt, ran a hand through her raven hair, and stepped out of the doorway. Roland followed, carrying the empty wineskins they had collected from the dungeon. As they moved toward the two guards at the outer gate, he noticed the girl's hips began to swing once more. Some part of his brain whispered—*lovely.*

As quickly as that thought intruded, he pushed it aside. The guards had heard them and turned to watch the girl and her "mule" approach.

"Ah, my Isabella," the older guard greeted her. "You lingered much longer today. You have not given your heart to that fat pig Toma I trust!"

Isabella smiled prettily, shook her head and laughed.

"It is not my heart that Toma wants, I think!"

The man leered at her and never saw the blow coming. Isabella had stopped just in front of the two guards, but Roland continued forward and drove a fist directly into the guard's face. The shock staggered him as much as the blow and he reeled back into the alley outside the gate. From out of the shadows, a wiry figure slid forward and applied a stave of firewood to the staggering guard's temple. He went down in a clattering heap on the cobbles, his long spear ringing sharply on the stones.

The second guard seemed rooted to the spot for a moment and that was long enough. Roland turned and hit him in the face with an empty wine bladder. Boda finished him. But this one also made a fearful clatter on the stones when he fell. It did not go unnoticed.

"You there—halt!" the command came from above them on the palace wall. Two guards could be seen peering over the battlements and pointing at them. Roland turned and sprinted back into the gatehouse to the passageway where Sir Roger and Declan were waiting. The big knight seemed stronger now and had draped his squire's arm around his broad shoulders. Roland relieved him of that burden and Boda stood by to aid Sir Roger, if needed.

"We'll have to run for the docks," Boda said. "They will be on us soon."

With agonizing slowness, the group made its way into the maze of back alleys that led to the harbour. Isabella, who knew every shortcut and dead-end, led the way. As they lurched onward, Roland looked at his friend's face. Both lips were split and swollen and a dark bruise covered his right eye and half of his cheek. He could feel the heat rising in his own face as he saw what they had done to Declan and he cursed under his breath. They had no choice but to flee, but he longed to kill the men who had done this.

Despite the alarm having been sounded, the pursuit was slow in forming. But soon enough, the sound of clattering hooves on the main thoroughfare could be heard. The search was on, but Roland felt certain Isabella was leading them down paths the guards would not follow. Sooner than expected, they turned a corner and spilled out onto the crowded quay. At the opposite end, a group of mounted soldiers were forcing their way through the crowds, gazing over the heads of the throng looking for their escaped captives.

Moving slowly now to avoid attracting attention, they made their way onto the long pier where the *Sprite* was secured. Master Sparks, who had been watching the quay for hours, saw them approach and quietly ordered his men to cast off all but a single line and unfurl the sails.

"There!" the cry went up from behind them. They had been seen. Riders turned off the quay and spurred their mounts down the pier toward them.

"Isabella!" Roland shouted. The girl turned toward him and he motioned for her to take Declan's arm and help him the rest of the way. Roland looked at Sparks.

"Master Sparks, my bow!"

The master of the *Sprite* had anticipated the boy's intentions and, plucking the bow and quiver from the deck, heaved them at Roland. By now, the riders were but fifty yards from their quarry and were spurring their mounts eagerly. The quiver landed at Roland's feet and the arrows scattered on the pier. The bow he caught in midair. With a practiced motion, he strung it, picked up and fitted the nearest shaft, and drew.

The leading rider saw this and immediately reined in his charging mount, but his horse's hooves could gain no purchase on the slippery pier. It went down with the rider trapped beneath. The other rider tried to bring his mount to a halt as well, but with his companion blocking the way his horse had no place to go but into the harbour. It plunged in with a tremendous splash and began to swim for shore, but the rider was seen no more.

Roland scooped up his scattered arrows from the pier and ran for the *Sprite*. Standing by the gangway was Isabella. He fished in his tunic and brought forth his coin purse, tossing it to the girl. She caught it with one hand, but did not take her dark eyes off of him. She stepped in front of the gangway, blocking his path.

"You must take me," she said calmly.

"No!" the boy blurted. This was not part of the bargain.

"They will kill me," she continued.

"She has a point," Boda observed from the deck of the *Sprite*.

The girl looked at Roland with a pleading look in her eyes. "Take me with you."

He had never seen a girl look at him this way. His face flushed.

"Girl!" it was the voice of Sir Roger. "Come aboard." The words were hardly out of the man's mouth when the girl vaulted nimbly over the rail and onto the deck. He turned to Roland.

"Master Inness, we are making way. Are you coming?"

Roland could but shake his head and follow her as the *Sprite* was, indeed, beginning to edge away from the pier. He landed lightly beside her as the crew drew the gangway back aboard. She threw her arms around his neck and hugged him fiercely. Over her shoulder Roland could see Declan O'Duinne attempting to smile through his swollen lips. Boda made a kissing shape with his mouth and Master Sparks just grinned. Roland tried to extract himself, but the girl was surprisingly strong.

Sir Roger cleared his throat loudly and the girl finally released her grip.

"Miss, we are in your debt. We will take you to safety, then you may go your own way."

The girl stood with her arms crossed and nodded toward Roland.

"I will go where he goes."

Now it was Roland's turn to speak.

"We are going to war. It is no place for a girl."

"I am no girl. I am a woman and we have followed our men to battle since days of old," she replied. "I will wash your clothes and cook for you."

Roland looked helplessly at Sir Roger but found no relief there. He turned back to the girl.

"I am not your man! You will *not* come with me," he stated firmly, then turned his back and walked away across the deck.

"We'll see," she replied sweetly.

***

The *Sprite* ran southward before the wind down the Straits of Messina, with Sicily to starboard and Calabria to port. The sea foamed around the ship, the sails were full and the sky was a magnificent blue in the late afternoon sun. A swift-looking craft with a lateen sail had sallied out from the harbour and given chase for a short distance until Roland sent a few well-aimed arrows amidships. That was enough to cause it to tack away and turn back for home. He unstrung his bow, wrapped it carefully and put it away. At last he could turn his attention to the two men they had rescued from Tancred's dungeons.

Both Sir Roger and Declan were reclining beneath the forecastle. They looked a sight. Declan's lips were swollen and cracked and his right eye was completely closed. Sir Roger had ugly burns on both forearms and several visible knots on his balding scalp. Angry bruises were forming under both eyes. The wrists of both were raw where the shackles had bound them. Isabella was gently cleaning their wounds and had cut strips of clean cloth to bandage their wrists. Declan tried to smile as Roland approached and revealed a missing tooth.

"What took ye so long?" he managed, and winked with his one good eye. "Did this lass distract ye?"

It was a relief that his friend could still make jests at such a time, but Roland was angry. Declan was more than friend, he was clan, and he had been very roughly treated. So had Sir Roger, the man he had sworn an oath to defend. Was his whole life going to be fleeing from men like Tancred who harm those dear to him? He had run from William de Ferrers, and he was still running. When would it stop?

Sir Roger de Laval had been studying his squire and could see he was near his boiling point. He beckoned him near.

"Master Inness, you must let this go. We are hardly the worse for wear. And we have you to thank for that."

Roland shook his head.

"Tancred should pay for this."

Sir Roger shook his head and snorted.

"Why, because he threw two Englishmen into the gaol? Lord, the man has imprisoned the sister of the King of the English. If he is to pay, I will let our King set the price—and so must you. Can you see that?"

Roland gave his master a half-hearted nod.

Of course I can see it—but I do not have to like it!

But if Declan can make jests and Sir Roger can claim to be none the worse for the experience, then there it must lie. He dropped cross-legged to the deck.

"Tell me what happened."

And the story was told—a bit by Sir Roger and a bit by Declan. They had walked completely unawares into a political tinderbox and had unknowingly struck a spark. They'd been seized and treated like spies.

"Had we known Tancred had usurped the throne only a fortnight ago, we'd have never knocked on the front door—so to speak."

"Tuck would have seen trouble brewing here, I expect," added Declan and they all nodded. The monk had a keen sense for the complexities of politics in this region and for that, and much more, he was sorely missed.

"I can see why a usurper would be suspicious of two Englishmen come to pay call on the former Queen," Sir Roger continued. "He questioned us himself, but was honestly not very practiced at breaking prisoners—just a few applications of the hot iron and a few lumps and bruises. But he could have racked us to no avail, for we possessed no useful information for the man. Frankly, he knew more than we did since he had read the message from the King to Queen Joanna, and I had no idea of its contents."

"What was he disposed to do with you?" asked Roland. Sir Roger shrugged.

"I do believe he would have had us executed in a day or two if you and this lovely lady had not appeared. So tell us—how did you come up with this plan?"

So Roland, with some interjections from Boda and a few from Isabella, told the tale of the inn, the fight, the girl and the plan. When he had finished, Sir Roger rose slowly to his feet, stepped forward and gave Roland a bear hug, lifting him completely off his feet.

"Risky plan, my lad, but executed with panache! There is a lesson there."

He put his squire down. Roland didn't understand the French word *panache*, but he understood the sentiment.

Sir Roger turned to Boda.

"Master Boda, I saw what stuff you were made of at the Pillars of Hercules. Tancred could not prevail against such as you! I am much in your debt."

"We were not leaving without you, your lordship."

Sir Roger nodded and beckoned Isabella to him. Her he hugged gently.

"And thanks to you, miss. You are as brave as any man I've known. I have a daughter—about your age. You remind me of her."

The girl blushed shyly when he released her and, for the first time, she seemed very young.

"As for Tancred, whatever our King decides to do with him, he'll not last long. He is too stupid and even the guards are not happy that Queen Joanna has been put away. So let us put Sicily astern of us—for it is a nest of vipers indeed!"

For the rest of the afternoon they continued their southern course as the land fell off on both sides and the strait opened back into the Mediterranean Sea. As the sun began to dip low, Sir Roger motioned for Roland to join him at the bow of the *Sprite*.

"Son, you must speak to the girl. You are right, she has no place where we are going, but she is a headstrong one. You must convince her to go, but have a care. She has her heart set on you, it would seem."

Roland gave a heavy sigh. She did have to go, and he knew it was up to him to send her away, though they were much in her debt. He sat for a long time below the forecastle, stroking the nose of Bucephalus as he pondered what to do. But nothing would come to him. He must just tell her she would be put ashore and be done with it. He could think of no gentle way to do that.

As the moon rose full over the mast, he found her back at the sterncastle talking with Master Sparks.

"Isabella, may I speak with you?"

The girl smiled and nodded. They walked to the rail.

"Isabella, we are much in your debt, but I have kept my end of the bargain. I've given you all the money I have in the world. It's all I have to give. Tomorrow you must tell Master Sparks where you wish to go."

The girl crossed her arms.

"I will tell him I wish to go with you."

"But why? There will be little but dust and death where I am going."

The girl gave a shrug.

"For people like me, there is dust and death everywhere in this world. You must take me."

"But why me?" he demanded.

She smiled at him. It was a smile with no innocence to it.

"Because you are brave. You did not desert your friends in the prison. Because you kept your bargain, and didn't cheat me. And… I think you might be… kind. Few men are." She stopped for a moment, searching for words.

"Because…"

With no warning, she threw her arms around his neck and kissed him fiercely on the lips, then pulled away. Roland recoiled in surprise. The girl laughed. It was a sweet sound.

"Can you not find some use for me where you are going, Roland Inness?"

Now he was flustered. This was unfamiliar territory. His lips burned where her's had been. His face felt hot, but it was a *pleasant* heat. The confounded girl was making this harder than it should be!

How shall I get out of this?

Then it came to him. He must lie.

"Isabella, you are beautiful and I would gladly take you with me, but I have already given my heart to another." He gestured forward to where Sir Roger was resting, "The big knight said you reminded him of his daughter. It was she who gave me this when we left England." He withdrew the silver amulet with the yew tree design that Millie de Laval had given him an age ago and held it out for Isabella to see. "I could not be false with you—or betray her loyalty."

The girl slumped.

"Ah I see. You hope to someday inherit the father's land by marrying this girl?"

"Uh…yes…of course. It is good land."

90

Isabella sighed and shook her head.

"Then I cannot blame you. My father is dead, but when alive, he was a pauper. I have nothing to offer so rich."

Roland looked at the girl and thought otherwise.

"Not every man is looking for land or riches, Isabella. I think you shall find a man who deserves you. It is just not me."

"Apparently not," she said pointing to the amulet and giving him a wry smile, "but you won't forget me, I'll wager!" Once again she surprised him with a kiss that lingered for just a bit. He did not recoil. No, he would not forget this girl.

Then she drew away and walked over to where Master Sparks was manning the steering oar and trying to look uninterested. As she walked away she swung her hips as she had done for the guards at Messina. Again the thought came to Roland—*lovely*. He heard her speak to Sparks.

"Shipmaster, by morning we will be near the mouth of the River Melito. There is a port a bit upriver from the sea. You can set me ashore there. My village is a day's walk further north."

***

The next morning the *Sprite* made its way a mile up the River Melito to a small village with a dock that reached out to the deep channel. The crew of the vessel lined the rail to watch Isabella take her leave. She turned and waved to them after jumping lightly onto the pier.

"Thank you all! Pirates stole me from this place two years ago and sold me in Messina. You have brought me home. You are honourable men. There is a great shortage of these in the world. May God keep his eyes upon you and keep you safe!"

Roland was surprised to see the tender looks on the faces of the hard crew of the *Sprite*. There were even a few tears, quickly wiped away.

"And you, Roland Inness," she looked at him boldly with her hands on her hips. "If that little *sgualdrinetta* won't marry you, come back to Calabria and see me!"

The crew snickered and Declan punched Roland in the shoulder. The girl blew the crew a kiss, then turned toward home. They watched her until she was out of sight amongst the small houses of the village. *Lovely.*

"Back to work, ye sluggards," barked Boda and they cast off the lines, turning the *Sprite* back into the current and toward the sea. Declan, his face a bit less swollen this morning and his spirits much revived, threw his arm around Roland.

"So, am I invited to the wedding?"

Roland could only give a sheepish grin.

"No wedding, Dec. I lied. I lied like I was born to it. It was my only way out."

The Irish boy grinned back. It would take a while before Roland would grow accustomed to his friend's missing tooth.

"Well my friend, if it had been me, I'm not sure I would have looked for a way out. Lovely girl, that."

Yes she was, he thought.

***

The *Sprite* drifted downstream to the open sea. As they reached the deep water, the wind was against them, but Master Sparks skilfully tacked to starboard and back to port, gaining what speed he could. The weather was fair and for the first time in days, Roland felt at ease. He negotiated the catwalk forward to where Sir Roger reclined under a blanket rigged as a shade.

The big knight was eating an unfamiliar fruit. It was a strange colour. As his squire approached he reached into his sack and extracted another, tossing it to him. Roland saw that Sir Roger had cut his into quarters so he unsheathed his dagger and did the same. Mimicking the older man he bit down on the pale fruit within and winced. Sour, but very juicy! It was unlike anything he had ever tasted.

"Master Sparks managed to acquire a sack of these in Messina 'fore our hasty departure. I had one once in France and always wanted to try another. Locals call them *limones*. Sparks says it helps with the mouth sores his crew gets on the longer voyages. Don't know about that, but I fancy the taste. It grows on you."

Roland sucked the juice from another quarter and felt his mouth pucker. For a moment he flashed back to the feel of Isabella's lips on his—*not sour.*

"My lord, how do you fare?"

Sir Roger smiled. "Passing well, Master Inness, if I do say so. I've been treated more roughly by Catherine on occasion than by these amateurs." He took a thick finger, squeezed a bit of juice from his limone and dabbed it on one of his burns.

"Stings!" he said with a smile. Roland smiled with him. It was a great relief to see the big man recovering so quickly from his captivity. To have lost him and Declan was something he could barely contemplate. They were his family now. He still had a brother and sister, hiding somewhere back in England—children that he vowed he would one day see again—but fate and many trials had placed him with this Norman knight and Irish squire. He thanked God, Odin, and whatever other deities that meddled in the affairs of men, for leading him here.

"So what did ye tell the lass to get her to go?"

Sir Roger's question brought him back to the moment.

"My lord, I confess that I lied to her. I told her I was pledged to another back home. It's all I could think of at the time."

"Ahh. Well let me advise you that you are not the first man to lie to a woman about affairs of the heart, but usually it's the other way around."

"My lord?"

"Aye, usually ye lie to get them into your bed, not out of it!" He gave a loud hoot, pleased with his jest, and clapped Roland hard on the shoulder. Then he spoke with no jest in his voice.

"She was a comely thing, but yer lie was for the best, lad. In truth, where we go is no place for her. Ye did right by the girl."

Roland appreciated his master's understanding, but he wondered what Millie de Laval would have thought of his lie. He absently fingered the amulet at his neck.

I wonder what she is doing right now.

Lady-in-Waiting

It had been quite simple for Lady Catherine to secure a position for Millicent as lady-in-waiting to Lady Constance. Earl Ranulf's wife did, indeed, loathe her husband and everything associated with him, including Chester Castle, the city of Chester and, it seemed, the people of Cheshire in general.

"Dolts," she called them, and pouted and grumbled her way through most days.

So it was no great surprise that the noble ladies of the county were not eager to serve the dour wife of the Earl. With few other eager candidates, Lady Constance instantly agreed to add Lady Millicent to her retinue.

Millie spent a week in Shipbrook preparing for her departure. In that week she was reminded of how closely-knit this remote outpost on the frontier with Wales had become. From birth, cooks, house servants, stable hands and men-at-arms had doted on her as though she were their own and she had fully returned that love. One by one, she said her farewells to each person down to the last swineherd.

Her own preparations were minimal. She had few belongings to pack beyond her somewhat humble wardrobe. On the last day before departure, she took a final ride out to the low hills overlooking the estuary of the River Dee to watch the sun set into the Irish Sea. Shipbrook never seemed as lovely. The harvest was in its final days and workmen were moving from field to field bringing in the crops. The air was crisp, but the sun was warm when the chill winds off the water abated.

The last wild flowers lifted their dusty heads along the trails and birds flushed from thickets and brambles as she passed.

Watching the sun dip toward the horizon, she wondered if her father and his squires were watching the same setting sun in some foreign sea. She sighed and patted her horse's neck. "Everything is changing."

On the day of her departure for Chester, Lady Catherine reminded her of their agreement.

"I will come to Chester once a month on market day. If you have any information for the Queen, you may pass it to me then. If there is something afoot that demands her immediate attention, you will tell Lady Constance that you have received word that I am ill and have asked for you. With luck, your sudden departure will not arouse suspicion. Remember Millie, you do the Queen's bidding, but do not forget your father's oath to Lord Ranulf. I pray that whatever may occur, we will not have to choose between the two loyalties."

"I understand, Mother. I will keep my head about me."

Lady Catherine nodded and pulled the girl to her.

"Stay keen, daughter," she whispered, "or you might lose that pretty head of yours. They execute spies, Millie."

Millicent stepped back and gave her mother what she hoped was a confident smile.

"Not spy, Mother—scout!"

***

Millicent's arrival at Chester Castle was inauspicious. She was met at the stone gate to the inner bailey by Lady Agnes de Kevelioc, Earl Ranulf's sister and primary lady-in-waiting to her brother's wife. Lady Agnes interrogated the girl as she was being shown to her quarters.

"Do you sew?"

"Yes, my lady."

"Dance?"

"A little, my lady."

The older woman suddenly stopped.

"Can you read, girl? Lady Constance hates her priest and will have no more truck with the man. She says he smells and I can vouch for the truth of that! But the Lady insists on having the bible read to her each evening."

"I can read well enough, my lady. I would be happy to perform that service for Lady Constance."

Lady Agnes nodded. "Very good. None of the other ladies can read a word. That will be your evening duty. There will be other chores to attend to during the day."

And there were. Each morning at dawn the small group of ladies attending the Earl's wife arose and accompanied her to the chapel in the inner keep for morning prayers. In some ways, this was the most pleasant part of the day for Millicent. She prayed earnestly for the safe return of her father from the Crusade and never failed to include an entreaty on behalf of Declan O'Duinne and Roland Inness. It made her feel that she was doing her part to help bring them back to England.

She had various tasks assigned by Lady Agnes to fill her mornings and was left to her own devices most afternoons when both Lady Constance and Lady Agnes took long naps. She took these opportunities to be about the business that the Queen had assigned to her.

As it had growing up at Shipbrook, her easy manner won her many friends among the Earl's staff of servants and these were the best of all sources of gossip and news. But as the autumn drifted into winter, it became clear to her that there was really no news that would be of interest to the Queen.

She had learned about the late night carryings-on of some of the other ladies of the court, the bitter spats and long silences between the Earl and his Lady, and the speculation as to whether Lady Agnes would ever find a man, but no intrigue to upset any save the participants thereof. She didn't know whether to be relieved or frustrated. She was certainly bored.

Her evenings reading scripture to Lady Constance added little to her understanding of how things stood with her or with the Earl. Her mistress barely acknowledged Millicent's presence as she read, and at times produced a faint snore as she dozed off during the recitations. It at least gave the girl a chance to practice her Latin.

What seemed an exciting secret mission was turning into nothing but drudgery. As the days passed she found herself longing to be back at Shipbrook and not cooped up in Chester Castle. After her evening readings, her chores for the day were done and she took the opportunity to get more familiar with the castle and the town.

Chester she knew very well from many trips there on market days, and the castle she came to know by innocently wandering down any passage not locked or guarded. She found no treachery afoot against the King, but she had little access to the Earl himself, and shared no intimacies with Lady Constance. If there was a plot in the works, how would she know?

What she did see was troubling in a different way. Earl Ranulf was one of the Marcher Lords that ruled over the borderlands between England and Wales. The King had given these nobles extraordinary rights to rule their domains as they saw fit. They were the buffer between England and the fierce Welsh princes and were expected to be hard men.

By contrast, the young Earl seemed more kindly than commanding. He was a man who seemed forever *hesitant*. She watched him during audiences with his subjects and he seemed to agonize over rather obvious decisions—often seeking advice from his counsellors on trivial matters. Here was a man born to a noble inheritance, but who seemed to have little of the iron will to rule that was expected of his rank.

She recalled her father speaking about what a likable boy the Earl had been, but also worrying about his ability to rule over a vast region that was key to controlling both the border with Wales and the Midlands itself. Millicent concluded that Earl Ranulf was no threat to the King, but wondered what would befall him if the King should not return. The Queen said Cheshire was the key to the heartland of England. If other nobles saw weakness here, *they* would not be hesitant!

And how would that affect my father—and Shipbrook?

As Christ's Mass approached she found herself ranging further from the castle, there being little useful information to be gleaned there. Wrapped in a warm cloak, she wandered at sunset along the great wall of the city. She noted with concern that the place was barely garrisoned and that in several places the battlements had crumbled into the overgrown moat below.

Chester may have been the capital of a frontier province, but it was places like Shipbrook that kept the warlike Welsh at bay. At Shipbrook there were patrols out daily and men maintaining an alert watch from the walls on all of the approaches. If any had shirked, her father, or more likely Sir Alwyn, would have had their hides. Chester was different. Chester was soft and so was her ruler.

She paused along the west wall and gazed toward where the sun was dropping to the horizon. Shipbrook lay that way. She missed it. For her, Chester was a lonely place. As she turned to leave, a movement farther down the wall caught her eye. A figure in a black robe was walking along the south wall heading in her direction. It was a priest she had not seen before.

She saw him stop at one of the damaged sections of the wall and peer over. For a long moment she watched him. What was he looking at? After a bit, he rose and slipped a piece of parchment from his robe and began to mark upon it. *Odd.* What was this priest up to?

Millicent was almost to the tower that marked the northwest corner of the city walls. It would be a good vantage point to observe this stranger who was showing so much interest in the town's defences. She hurried to the tower and climbed the circular stair to the top. It did not surprise her to find the place deserted. The few guards she saw on her strolls tended to be at Northgate and Bridgegate and not on these watchtowers.

Looking down she saw the priest had turned north along the west wall of the town and was coming toward the tower. He had stuffed the parchment back inside his robes and appeared to be casually strolling along the parapet. He passed through the arched entrance and Millicent listened as his footsteps echoed up the stairs. The man kept walking and exited onto the north wall of the city.

The girl watched him as he stopped several more times, usually where the wall was in poor repair, and made more annotations on his parchment. He was clearly taking a careful inventory of the state of the structure—but to what purpose? After the priest passed out of sight beyond a smaller tower in the north wall, Millicent clambered down the stairs and followed. Perhaps the local bishop was concerned about the security of his city and his flock and had sent one of his own to inspect the walls. Perhaps it was nothing. *Or perhaps not.*

When she passed through the small tower the priest was no longer in sight. The girl sighed. The man's interest in the walls was odd but probably innocent. It had, at least, broken up the monotony of her day. The monotony was further broken that evening when she arrived for her readings. Lady Agnes greeted her as she entered Lady Constance's chambers.

"Lady Millicent, Lady Constance thanks you for your services reading the scriptures, but you are now relieved of that duty."

Millicent bowed her head.

"My lady, did my reading displease Lady Constance?"

The older woman softened just a bit.

"Why no, child, it is just that the Lady has at last found a priest to her liking and he will now have the honour of reading her the scriptures." She paused and Millicent saw a rare smile flicker across her face. "It seems this one doesn't smell!"

Millicent gave a small smile in return and started to retire when the door to the chamber opened behind her. Through the door came a tall man in a black robe. His hair was almost golden in colour and he was the handsomest priest the girl had ever seen. He stopped upon seeing the two ladies and gave them a sunny smile. It was the priest from the wall.

"Why here he is now," said Lady Agnes.

"Lady Millicent de Laval, may I present Father Malachy."

Millicent fought to hide her surprise as she curtsied to the priest. The man smiled at her.

"A pleasure, my lady. De Laval? That name is familiar to me I think. Have we met?"

"No, Father. I am but lately come to Chester from Shipbrook."

"That would be out near the border, would it not?"

"Yes, Father. Sir Roger de Laval is my sire and he guards the fords over the Dee, down near the sea."

"Ah, that's right. He is off on Crusade, is he not? I've heard it said that he was a favourite of the Earl's late father."

"Yes, he fought in many campaigns with Earl Hugh and, as you say, he is on Crusade. We have not had word yet from him, but God will preserve him I'm sure."

"Your faith is strong, my child," the churchman said. "I will add your father's name to my evening prayers as well. Now I must take up your old duty of reading the scriptures to Lady Constance." He gave the girl a warm smile. "I humbly hope I can maintain the high standards I'm sure you have set."

Millicent smiled back at Father Malachy, curtsied again and took her leave. As she walked through the now familiar passages toward her quarters, her mind raced. This priest worried her. Why had he been so interested in the walls of Chester and how did he know so much about her and her family? She was sure she had never seen the man before this afternoon. Behind his warm smile she sensed a steely purpose. What was it? As she hurried on, one thought consumed her.

Smile all you like Malachy—I'll be watching you!

***

Later that night in his small, cell-like room in the servants quarters, Father Malachy had his own thoughts to keep him company. *This is easier than I hoped, but that could change. I must not get careless.*

The de Laval girl. She had recognized him! He was certain of it—but how? He knew she had been in London for the Queen's reception. De Ferrers had described his encounter with her with evident bile. He knew the nobleman suspected the de Laval's of harbouring a young man that he wanted dead, but Malachy neither knew nor cared why de Ferrers hated this boy. Petty hatreds were of no interest to him, though he could perhaps use them to his advantage. The girl's presence here at Chester might add some small additional incentive to help him prod Sir William to action.

While in London he had avoided all public occasions, so he was certain the girl had not seen him there. But there was definitely a flash of recognition in Millicent de Laval's eyes when he entered that room.

I shall have to keep my eye on that girl!

The Shores of Zion

A fortnight of sailing brought the *Sprite* to the south shore of Crete where Master Sparks put in at a small fishing village to replenish supplies. While taking on stores in the protected cove, their favourable weather turned foul. For most of a week, they rocked at anchor while late autumn rain squalls whipped the open sea into a maelstrom. Finally, the weather broke and seven days of fair sailing found them off the coast of Cyprus. Sparks noted that an unhinged Byzantine who thought of himself as an emperor ruled that island and they would steer clear. He heeled the *Sprite* over to starboard and sailed south.

At last, they were approaching the end of their long journey. On the third morning, a man on the forecastle shouted "Land!" And there it was, a distant shore—the land of the Bible, where prophets and saviours, demons and angels, had contended for the souls of men since the dawn of time.

Roland and Declan clambered up to the bow and watched intently as they drew nearer. There was a crowd of boats between them and a good anchorage, and, as though summoned, a small galley sallied out to meet them. Not knowing the local situation, Sir Roger ordered all to arms and they stood by as they were hailed. Roland did not understand the language, but it did not sound unfriendly. Sparks quickly cleared up any confusion.

"They are Genoese—from Italy. They are blockading the city from the sea. They will lead us to an anchorage."

They followed the galley in toward shore. Boda did not trust the Genoese to find them a proper place to drop anchor and insisted on casting the line at the bow to measure the depth. Two hundred yards off shore he called "Shelving!" Sparks ordered the sails reefed and let the *Sprite* drift a little closer in before commanding: "Drop anchor."

The men Master Sparks had been commissioned to deliver to this place lined the rails and looked out upon the field of battle. A little to the south stood the great fortress of Acre, the banners of Saladin rippling from its ramparts. The walls were blackened and gouged in several places by the ongoing bombardment from the Crusader siege engines. They could see little movement on top of those walls.

Perhaps a mile northward up the coast, two lines of earthen fortifications separated by barely half a mile could be seen stretching from the beach up toward the unbroken line of high hills a league inland.

"The besiegers are besieged," observed Sir Roger. "Those are Christian banners on the inner earthworks, which means the Muslims have cut off the supply routes overland from Tyre in the north and are attacking from the rear to harass our forces. It's hard enough to storm a fortress without having to worry about your rear."

"But supplies can come to the Christian forces by sea, can they not?" Declan said, pointing to the small fleet of friendly ships patrolling the area around the Crusader beachhead.

"Aye, Master O'Duinne, and that is the only reason this siege might succeed. Otherwise, this lot would not last long." The big knight shook his head and looked grave.

To their front was the Crusader camp. Perhaps at the beginning it had been picturesque with the multitude of banners and coloured tents, but the relentless sun of this barren shore had faded all to a uniform dull cast. Smoke rose from numerous camp fires. It looked like a pauper's camp and the smell on the offshore breeze stank of sweat and dung and rot.

"Take a deep breath if the wind changes, boys," Sir Roger said. "It may be the last one you get that doesn't offend the nostrils."

A boat was rowing out from the surf line toward the cog as it bobbed at anchor. Two men were at the oars and a third was manning a tiller.

"How many for shore?" cried the tillerman from a distance.

"Three, and a good horse," Sir Roger shouted in reply.

"Horse will have to come later. We have a barge for animals. Gather yer kit and I'll come alongside."

Sir Roger waved his acknowledgement, then all three hurried to the sterncastle to bid goodbye to Sparks and Boda. Henry Sparks had made it known to them that his orders from the King were to deliver the Crusaders and then take up station as part of the blockade of Acre's port.

"You have brought us safely to shore, Master Sparks. You are indeed a master sailor and a good man in a fight," Sir Roger said and gave the man a bear hug. "I shall be comforted knowing you are bobbing around off shore here."

Sparks seemed touched by this show of affection.

"It has been our honour to have you and yer young men as our guests these many days at sea. I'd sign ye on as crew anytime," he replied, making no effort to hide the tears that had started to trickle down his round face.

"If it's crew they'd be, I'd have me hands full whippin' 'em into shape," added Boda with a rare smile. "But they'd be welcome."

Roland and Declan gravely shook hands with the master and the mate of the *Sprite* and made their farewells. It was time to go. They gathered their belongings and lowered them over the side to the waiting boat. Each in turn slid down a line from the deck of the cog to the boat below, and the tillerman shoved the craft away from the *Sprite*. Roland watched as they began to draw away. The ship had been his home for four months. It seemed much longer. He turned away and faced the shore.

In short order, the Genoese boatman delivered them there. They reached the gently breaking surf line and all leapt out onto a pebbled beach. Boats were hauled up and left in chaotic confusion up and down the water's edge. Boatmen lounged about or tended to minor repairs.

No one came to meet the contingent from Shipbrook or paid them any mind, so Sir Roger led the way into the camp. Here there was more of an attempt at order than they had seen among the Genoese boatmen at the beach. A broad central path led between tents and huts of every size and description. This thoroughfare ran far off into the distance. Here and there a tall pole flew a proud banner announcing the headquarters of one Crusader contingent or another. As they walked, Sir Roger pointed out the flags he recognized.

"White cross on red—Pisans. White cross on black—Hospitalers. Gold fleur-de-lis on blue—Franks. Red cross on white."

"Templars!" Roland and Declan answered together.

"Aye, Templars, lads. At least what's left of 'em after Hattin."

Roland recalled the story Tuck had told of a hundred and fifty Templar knights beheaded on Saladin's orders after that battle. He wondered how far they were from that horrible killing ground. As they continued along the main road through the Crusader encampment, they were swarmed by flies and, as Sir Roger had predicted, the smells got worse. The Norman knight hailed a passing Knight of the Hospital.

"Whereabouts are the English?"

The man pointed further on.

"Not many here, but what there is, ye'll find about a mile that way."

The continued on their way and Declan nudged Roland in the ribs.

"Look—rats. Big ones!"

Roland had already seen the vermin that were scurrying between the tents.

At length they came to a large tent with a banner that caused Sir Roger to pause and consider.

"I believe I know this standard. Master Inness, is it familiar to you?"

With a shock of recognition he looked at the flag with its white shield emblazoned with black horseshoes and topped with a plumed helmet. This symbol he had seen his whole life. It was the coat of arms of de Ferrers, the Earl of Derby. He looked at Sir Roger just as a knight emerged from the tent. He was old, but not stooped. Anyone could see that there was still power in the man's bearing. It was Lord Robert de Ferrers himself. He saw the three men standing before him and spread his arms wide. Sir Roger gave Roland a warning touch on his arm.

"I believe I heard English spoken! Praise God, for there is too much gibberish spoken in this camp. Welcome gentlemen. I am Robert, Earl of Derby, and I am much in need of more stout Englishmen here in this hell hole!" He stuck out his hand and Sir Roger took it.

"Sir Roger de Laval of Shipbrook, my lord, and my squires Masters O'Duinne and Inness. We have just arrived."

"Well, you are most welcome here. Shipbrook? I haven't heard of it."

"It is a small fort on the border with Wales. I am the sworn man of Earl Ranulf."

"Ah, Ranulf. Good man. Now, tell me…what news from England? I was halfway to here when the news came of Henry's death and Richard's coronation. I expect my son William attended the crowning in my stead. Does the new King hasten to our aid?"

"Aye, my lord. He is coming. I cannot say when he will arrive, but he was to depart England but a month after we took ship."

The Earl nodded and clapped Sir Roger on the shoulder.

"You look like an experienced fighting man. Let me have one of my retainers help find you a spot to settle in and we will get better acquainted in due time." The Earl barked a command and a man emerged from the tent.

"See that Sir Roger and his men have shelter—over next to the Frisians. I believe there is some space there."

The man lead the Shipbrook contingent to a dusty, trampled spot with a woebegone tent drooping in the middle.

"This belonged to Sir Reginald," the retainer said. "He's dead. You may have it." When the man left, Sir Roger gave Roland a hard look.

"There is no place here for settling debts, lad. Earl Robert is the senior English lord here and we will naturally fall under his command. I must be certain I can trust you on this. Do you forswear your grudge?"

Roland looked up at the sky for a long moment, then back at Sir Roger.

"My lord, the Earl has crimes enough to answer for, but it is his son who must pay for what he did to my father. One day I will kill William de Ferrers, but the Earl is safe enough—from me."

Sir Roger nodded.

"Good...and Inness—when the day comes to settle your debt—you will have my blessing."

War in the Land of God

The first week in the Crusader camp left Roland wondering which was worse, the heat, the sand, the rats or the fleas. All conspired to make life miserable. For the first few days they were left alone to arrange their living quarters. The squires fetched Bucephalus from the beach and got him settled. As Roland and Declan went about their labours, Sir Roger wandered far, inspecting the entire length of the siege lines that surrounded Acre. His observations were not promising.

"King Guy of Jerusalem commands this rag tag host and from what I can see, he is no soldier. It was he who led his Christian army into the massacre at the Horns of Hattin. He has lost Jerusalem and most of his kingdom. The rats and fleas could take Acre before he could. I swear Saladin released him from captivity to vex us." The big knight sighed and shook his head.

"Look up there," he said, pointing to a high hill covered in brush and stunted carob trees. "Do you see that tent? It is Saladin's tent. He sits up there and sees everything below. We have not the strength to dislodge him and he has not the strength to break the siege—yet." He paused and swung his arm in an arc before him.

"Along our siege line, each of the European contingents has a section and there is little coordination among them. The French have been hurling stones for months where the north wall meets the east. They call that high structure where the two walls meet the Accursed Tower. It's claimed that this is where Judas' thirty pieces of silver were minted, but legends hereabouts come cheap. It is an exposed salient and vulnerable, but the Franks have neither the men nor the siege engines to reduce it." The Norman knight spread his hands as though seeking to make sense of what he had seen.

"Further along, the Germans pound at the defences in front of them with no concern for what the Franks are doing. What little damage they do is quickly repaired. There are not enough siege engines and not nearly enough men to storm the city if there were a breach. No one seems to really know what conditions are like inside, but unless they are near starvation, this siege is hopeless!"

The squires looked at each other. Had they come half way around the world to risk all in a fruitless campaign?

"Help is coming though?" asked Declan. "The French...King Richard."

"Aye, help is coming, but who knows when. Armies never move quickly, and kings? They are easily distracted. The question is, can Saladin gather enough strength to throw this dog's breakfast of an army into the sea before help arrives? I would not bet against him."

"So what are we to do?" asked Roland.

"We endure. We keep our eyes open. It is what we are here for. We fight when we must."

At least someone here knows what they are about, thought Roland. That night, he lay in his bedroll and thought about the man in the tent on the hill and wondered if he were watching.

The next morning, Sir Roger was called to the tent of Earl Robert for a council of war. The Earl addressed the dozen knights crowded around him.

"We English are few—and we have only a few horses left alive. We have no siege engines of our own. Until we get succour, we cannot move against the city. The Franks and the Germans and the knights King Guy has left from his own forces will continue to pursue the siege of the city. We and the Pisans have been given the task of protecting the rear of our lines north of the city when the enemy tries to attack us there. Saladin has not been able to break the siege, but he can keep us off balance. It is up to us to keep him at bay."

The men around the small table in the Earl's tent were all hard-bitten warriors. Each had come for his own reasons. Some, like the Earl, came to pay off a spiritual debt. Others hoped to gain glory or perhaps plunder. In the months they had toiled before Acre, there had been little of glory and no plunder. The mission the Earl outlined for them was clear enough. Patrol the outer breastworks. Counter any spoiling attacks Saladin may launch. Sally out to hit the enemy if the opportunity presents itself.

For the next hour, the talk centred on practicalities. What section of the breastworks would they hold? How would the structure of command be handled? In the end, as the most recent arrival and lowest in rank, Sir Roger was assigned to command the English forces along the breastworks during the hours of darkness. He accepted his assignment without complaint.

***

Thus began the siege of Acre for the men of Shipbrook. Each night, Sir Roger stationed his two squires a mile apart along the breastworks with instructions to light signal fires should any enemy activity appear to their front. He stationed Pisan foot soldiers and crossbowmen at lookouts along the line and a small cadre of armoured knights was held in reserve, ready to ride to any section of the line that was threatened.

Nothing happened that first night—nor the next or the next. Anxious men stared into the darkness and watched for an enemy that would not show himself. Each day, after the sun sank into the sea, the land quickly gave up its relentless heat. Men wrapped themselves in cloaks or huddled near fires to ward off the cold. Winter was approaching fast and Roland had to wonder just how cold the nights would get in this sunbaked land.

The days were filled with fitful rest as the desert heat prevailed, even this late in the year, and the vermin of the camp made sleep a trial. Five times a day, from the tall, thin tower behind the city walls, a high wailing call rose and fell—the Muslim call to prayer. At first men in the camp had banged together swords and whatever metal was at hand to drown out the sound, but in time gave up the effort. Roland found the call strangely hypnotic and often fell asleep at dawn to the sound of it.

Days turned into weeks with no change in this routine. By day, they tossed under the feeble shelter of their tents to the sound of stones slamming into the sturdy walls of the fortress. They ate meagre rations of greasy mutton and chick peas, when they could get them, and drank rancid water. By night, they looked out into the darkness trying to catch any sign of the enemy. But Saladin's patrols were cautious. Weeks into their nighttime vigil, Roland and Declan saw a few distant riders silhouetted against the night sky, but little else to show that the enemy was even there.

Then a rumour swept through the camp that the French were losing patience with trying to breach the wall. They were planning an attack on the outer siege lines of the Muslims to clear a way through to Tyre, the only other Christian stronghold to the north.

The rumour was confirmed when King Guy declared his support for the plan and ordered the Germans and the English to join the Templars and Hospitallers to form the heavy cavalry force for the attack. The foot would lead the advance against the Muslim defences and penetrate their lines. Then the heavy cavalry would sweep through to complete the breakout. The attack was set for dawn.

Sir Roger gathered his squires and laid his own plans.

"The French are behaving like children who do not get their way. They've been pounding that wall for months and the best they have done is to turn the top to rubble. They are tired of waiting. They can't take the city, so it seems they must do *something*! This plan might work, but to what end? They open the road to Tyre tomorrow and it will be closed the next day. And this will most definitely stir the man on the hill to action." He paused and pointed to Saladin's tent on the Hill of Carob Trees. "That man knows what he is about. The French do not!" He looked at his two squires.

"We have no choice in this, but I will be damned if I get you two killed for King Guy and this folly. Roland, you will advance with the Pisan crossbowmen who will be behind the foot soldiers. Make the best use you can of yer longbow, but if things go badly let the Pisans be your guide—and run like hell. Declan, someone must be left behind to guard against the garrison of the city making a sally into our lines. You will be with the few English foot in the trenches opposite the north gate." Declan started to protest, but Sir Roger cut him off.

"Don't fret lad, you are as likely to be killed there as anywhere, and I assure you there will be no glory in this attack." The Irish squire had no reply to that and nodded his acceptance of the assignment.

"And you, my lord? What of you?" asked Roland.

"I will be with the heavy cavalry. Our mounted knights are a match for any three of their light cavalry, but our numbers are small. If we stay close together, we can cut our way through— and back again if necessary, but there's the rub. Will knights from every realm in Europe fight as a unit? Will they have discipline? If we let ourselves be carried away pursuing the Saracens, we will be scattered. I have heard tales of how that happened at Hattin—and it was a slaughter." He paused once more.

"It is in God's hands, but I have a bad feeling. I would rather it was in the hands of a capable general, but none reside here at the moment. We must look to ourselves, lads. Understood?"

"Aye, my lord."

"And lads—don't do anything stupid!"

***

The attack was launched at dawn. Catapults were repositioned in the night and began to lob stones at the Muslim earthworks that stood less than three hundred yards from the Christian lines. A gap had been cut in the Crusaders' own earthen wall and the moat filled in during the night to allow close-packed ranks of foot soldiers to swarm forward.

To his credit, King Guy rode in the vanguard of this force along with the ranking Frankish nobles. The end of the infantry column was still exiting the Crusader lines as the attack began against the outer ring of defences that hemmed in the Christian forces. As soon as the infantry had cleared the gap in their own lines, the Pisans moved forward to pour volleys of crossbow bolts into the enemy lines.

For once, it appeared Saladin had been taken by surprise. There was resistance at the Muslim defensive line, but it was light. Foot soldiers fell from enemy arrows, but maintained their ranks and stormed into the moat and over the enemy earthworks. The defenders began to break and many fled in what looked like the beginnings of a rout. Once the way had been cleared by the first assault troops, following units paused to cut a gap in the line and fill in the moat for the heavy cavalry that followed.

With a path cleared for mounted knights, King Guy and his retinue surged forward and saw nothing but open ground and fleeing enemies before them. Excitement rippled through the small group of Frankish nobles. This was what cavalry was made for—riding down a broken enemy! Without waiting for the heavy cavalry and with no command given, they began to spur their chargers forward and fan out in pursuit of the Muslim foot soldiers.

Cheers went up all along the Crusader column, and King Guy spurred his horse into a gallop. The Frankish nobles did the same as they began to ride down fleeing men. At the rear of the column of foot, the heavy cavalry had just reached the break in the Muslim earthworks, when a breathless rider spurred up.

"The King orders the heavy cavalry forward—at once! The enemy has broken and you are to pursue them."

Sir Roger stood up in the stirrups of his saddle and looked quickly around the site of the breach in the enemy lines.

Not enough dead here.

This victory had been far too easy. Instinctively, he looked up to the Hill of Carob Trees. Three riders sat motionless on their mounts in front of Saladin's tent watching the plain below. And then he knew. Knew it in his bones—it was a trap.

In front of him, the leading riders among the armoured knights began to urge their massive warhorses forward and others behind were following. Sir Roger hesitated but a moment before digging his spurs into Bucephalus' flanks. The great destrier snorted and lunged forward.

He could not countermand the King's order, but if he could reach him with a warning he might avoid a disaster. As his horse gained speed he saw Roland Inness trudging forward with the Pisan crossbowmen and reined to a stop.

"Take a dozen of these Pisans and get yourself behind that berm." He pointed to the break in the earthworks they had just passed through. "We'll be back this way shortly and I expect we'll be in a hurry. Do what you can to slow the pursuit!"

With no further explanation he spurred off toward the front of the column.

Roland stepped out of ranks and called to a Pisan he had come to know. He asked for a squad to join him at the berm. The man was only too happy to oblige. Resting behind a berm was better than following in the dust cloud stirred up by a thousand trudging foot soldiers. Roland positioned a half dozen of the crossbowmen on either side of the cut and waited.

At the front of the column, the heavy cavalry was plunging ahead of the foot soldiers as they joined the pursuit of Saladin's fleeing troops. King Guy had come to a halt as his mounted forces thundered by. He looked exhausted from the morning's exertions, but there was a gleam of triumph in his eyes. Sir Roger reined to a halt by the monarch. The King seemed intoxicated at the sight of his hated foe in panicked flight.

"We have them on the run, man! Have at, or you'll miss the fun."

"Your grace!" Sir Roger interjected. "I pray to God I am wrong, but this smells of a trap. They made no fight to hold us at the berm, and now our heavy cavalry is scattered. We've seen no sign of Saladin's cavalry. They must be somewhere."

The King looked at him for a long moment—seeming to not comprehend what he was being told.

"Trap? Trap, you say?"

"Aye, your grace. I think they are waiting until our cavalry is too scattered to defend themselves or the infantry." As he spoke he stood again in his stirrups and looked intently at the low brown hills off to the right. And there it was—a cloud of dust rising up from a defile between two of the hills. It could only mean the approach of enemy cavalry. He turned back to the King and pointed in that direction.

"There, sire. They are coming to drive a wedge between your knights and your foot. It's what they did at Hattin. Sound a recall!"

The King blinked.

"Hattin?" His stunned look was now replaced by a look Sir Roger had seen on many a battlefield—fear.

"Aye, damn it man. Sound the recall or those knights and those foot will be butchered 'fore noon." He turned in his saddle and saw the King's herald and a bugler a little distance off and motioned them forward.

"Give the order, sire."

The King, all triumph now gone, raised a weary arm to the bugler.

"Sound recall."

The man instantly obeyed and the bugle sounded. How many heard the call that day would never be known, but some did. Some heard and ignored it, caught up in the fight, their bloodlust up. Some had already ridden out of earshot. Those that did not heed the call were not seen again.

As the dust cloud grew higher and nearer, some of the knights who had been in pursuit rode up, their horses covered in dust and some spattered with blood. They were angry. Some of the Frankish knights began to curse the King, but Sir Roger bulled forward on Bucephalus and pointed to the east where the unmistakable cloud of dust was fast approaching.

It silenced any protest and, before the King could order a withdrawal, some of the knights kicked their horses into an exhausted run back toward the berm and the safety of the Crusader lines. Sir Roger spit on the ground in disgust. Then he spoke to the King, as though to a lost child.

"We must go, your grace."

The King nodded and turned his horse back toward the rear. Dejectedly, he followed his fleeing knights. No order had to be given to the foot soldiers. They knew to retreat as soon as the first knights flew past them in a headlong gallop to the rear. At first, they moved with some order, but as more knights passed them their retreat fell into panic. They fled in a vast mob, many clogging the gap cut through the enemy berm, and others climbing over it and through the moat.

The fleeing knights struck about them with the flats of their swords to clear their own path to safety. As the mob surged by them, the Pisan who had joined Roland called to his fellows and more crossbowmen joined those already guarding the berm. From where he stood, Roland could not see beyond the dust cloud created by the panicked foot soldiers. He looked in vain for Sir Roger and the King.

Off to his right front, he saw the spreading cloud of dust descend from the hills and knew this was what Sir Roger had warned of. Slowly, the infantry cleared the area in front of the berm. Except for a few stragglers, the foot soldiers now had a fighting chance to escape the trap that Saladin had laid.

As the dust cloud settled, he could see a knot of mounted knights galloping toward him. Close on their heels was a swarm of Saladin's light cavalry. Roland climbed to the top of the mound and shouted at the Pisans.

"Make ready!" He raised his arm. Crossbows came up in unison.

"Now!" He lowered his arm and two dozen men loosed their bolts in an arc over the heads of their own knights. Ragged gaps appeared in the pursuers' ranks, but they came on. Roland needed no further commands, for the Pisans knew their business. He swung his longbow off his shoulder, fitted an arrow and searched for a target. He cared not for the King or the other knights, but had sworn to Lady Catherine he would guard her husband's back. He was going to fulfil that oath this day.

He now had no trouble finding his master in the chaos of the retreat, though he was in the very rear of the fleeing knights. The big knight mounted on the massive horse towered over the men to his front. He was holding a position at the rear of the group to guard the King. Roland kept his eyes on him as they sped toward the gap and safety.

The Muslim cavalry, not weighed down by heavy armour and riding horses bred for speed, had no problem closing on the King and his escort. Many were falling from the bolts landing among them from the Pisan crossbows, but now their battle fury was aroused. The honour of killing or capturing the Christian King of Jerusalem would bring great reward to the one bold enough to do it. This King had been paroled by Saladin and had given his oath not to take up arms against them. Now was their chance to make this oath-breaker pay.

Rider after rider spurred forward to challenge the big knight on the grey charger at the rear of the group. Sir Roger had his great battle axe out and turned in the saddle to challenge his pursuers. As they surged forward he saw one fall and then another. Two riders came at him at once. He unhorsed the first with a mighty swing of his axe and saw the second pitch backwards out of his saddle, a steel-tipped arrow in his chest.

Good shooting lad!

At last the King galloped through the gap in the berm, but there were still hundreds of the enemy in close pursuit. Sir Roger wheeled Bucephalus around and halted, blocking the gap. Roland could see that Saracen infantry were gathering behind the cavalry.

He and the Pisans, even with Sir Roger to anchor them, could not hold back this horde for long and once they broke for their own earthworks the bowmen would be slaughtered before reaching safety three hundred yards away. He turned to watch King Guy and the remainder of the Crusader heavy cavalry disappear into the safety of their siege lines.

No help there.

Then he saw a sight that gave him hope. Men were coming toward them through the ranks of their own panicked forces—men running on foot, men shouting battle cries. At their head was Earl Robert de Ferrers, a great broadsword in his hand, helmetless, his grey hair streaming wildly behind him. Beside the Earl was Declan O'Duinne shouting something unknowable in Gaelic. They were not many, but they might be enough!

Saladin's infantry were a hundred yards out. Roland had turned back toward the attack and was methodically delivering death into their ranks, but they came on. The Pisans, who had held their ground so staunchly, were beginning to waver. Their leader ordered a final volley and twenty bolts cut bloody gaps in

116

the charging ranks. The crossbowmen then began to sprint for their own lines.

Seeing their withdrawal, Sir Roger turned Bucephalus and rode down the side of the berm to where Roland still stood shooting into the oncoming tide. He stopped and reached down with his free hand, swinging his squire up on the back of the warhorse. Together they rode toward the oncoming rescue force.

The Saracens now fell victim to the same loss of discipline that had ruined the Crusader attack. When they saw the berm abandoned they sprinted forward hoping to overtake the retreating Crusaders, only to be met by the fierce counter charge led by Sir Robert. He waded into their ranks and many fell at his hands. Declan O'Duinne fought beside him and once more showed his mastery with the blade. Around enemy campfires that night there would be tales of the infidel with the strange red hair who had cut down so many of their comrades.

The enemy charge was checked and the Earl now began a slow retreat of his own, maintaining a rear guard to protect the fleeing Pisans. Sir Roger and Roland joined him and, as they neared the safety of their lines, the Pisans regrouped behind their breastworks and began pouring death into the enemy ranks. To the north, horns began to sound and the attackers melted back toward their siege lines. It was over.

Exhausted, the men who managed to escape the well-laid trap collapsed in heaps inside the breastworks they had left at dawn. King Guy was nowhere to be seen. On the Hill of Carob Trees, the riders were gone. It was not yet noon.

Philip Augustus

Despair hung over the Crusader camp like a pall in the wake of the disastrous attack on the Muslim lines. Grumbling could be heard around the campfires and in the trenches, with the Franks in particular blaming King Guy for the failure. Morale was further damaged when news arrived that the two kings who were sailing to their aid had been distracted by trouble in Sicily and would be much delayed there. A week after the repulse of the Crusader attack, King Guy called the leaders of the national contingents to a counsel.

"My lords, despite all of our efforts, Acre will not fall. I have prayed on the matter and believe that it is God's will that I leave you and seek to hasten the arrival of the aid we so sorely need. My lords, I pledge to return with a great host at my back! Until then, I leave my kingdom in your capable hands." The King of Jerusalem read this from a piece of parchment that rested on the camp table in front of him. He had no more to say and there were no questions from the assembled Earls and Barons. As the word spread through the camp, there were quiet celebrations.

With the departure of the King of Jerusalem, life in the camp settled into a monotonous routine of patrolling and waiting. The garrison of Acre could not break out, the Crusaders could not break in, and Saladin still lacked the strength to throw them into the sea. And so it stood through the winter and into spring. Easter came and priests said mass with as much ceremony and fanfare as they could muster. It did little to raise morale.

Less than a week after the Easter celebration, Roland and Declan were awakened near noon by a terrific din that suddenly erupted in the camp. Groggy with sleep, they crawled from the shade of their tent to see a great crowd of Crusaders from every contingent thronging the main road leading down to the beach. A euphoric air hung over this parade of grizzly, dirty warriors as they rushed past. From a distance, drums could be heard and bugles blared. A priest walked by with his hands upturned toward the heavens, praising God.

They looked at each other.

"What can it be?" Declan asked.

Before Roland could venture a guess, an English knight shouted at them as he rushed past.

"It's the French King! Philip and his army have come at last!"

For the squires, the arrival of a king of any stripe was worth a view, so they joined the parade heading down to the sea. Sleep could wait for another day. When they arrived, they found a dense mass of knights and nobles clustered near the shore, many shouting with excitement while others turned aside and knelt to thank God that help had come to them. For the ragged force that held onto the siege lines around Acre, it seemed a miracle had finally arrived.

Offshore, they could see that about a half dozen new ships bobbed at anchor and the Genoese boatmen were already about the business of landing the French forces. One of the larger barges was now approaching the beach and above it rippled the blue and gold banner of Prince Philip, King of France.

Some of the Frankish knights cleared a passage for the King through the crowd as the barge surged onto the rocky beach with a final pull of the oars. A host of men-at-arms in royal livery leapt over the sides and a wooden step ladder was lowered from the rail. Roland noted that it was not the most regal entrance he had ever seen as the French monarch manoeuvred over the railing and descended the ladder backwards. But the man had certainly dressed the part.

As he alighted, he turned and, for a moment, seemed to strike a pose as a great cheer went up from the gathered knights.

He was wearing a steel helmet with a circlet of gold at the top and the most beautiful armour Roland had ever seen. It had been shined to such a gloss that the glare of the reflected sun was near blinding. Over his shoulders was draped a short cape of royal blue silk lined with ermine. His hair was dark and he sported a thin beard at his chin line.

One of the Frankish knights approached leading a horse by the reins and the King mounted. A retainer leaned over the railing of the barge and the King extended his arm to receive a magnificent snow white hunting falcon. He lifted his helmet from his head and addressed the assembled multitude.

"Warriors of Christ! For too long you have carried the burden alone of cleansing this land of Saracens. No longer! France has come to Palestine!"

A roar went up from the crowd. Philip basked in the adulation and continued his prepared remarks.

"I bring you the blessing of the Pope. He assures us that all who labour here in the service of the Lord will have their sins washed clean and a place prepared for them in heaven."

More cheering erupted. Then he pointed to the walls of Acre with a dramatic flourish.

"I have brought men and siege engines. We shall have that place in our hands within a fortnight. That is my pledge and my promise."

As a new round of cheering arose, the white falcon on the King's arm suddenly took flight. At first the men thought that Philip had launched it to punctuate the end of his speech, and cheered the magnificent bird as it circled once overhead. But one look at the royal face betrayed the King's surprise.

The bird rose high over the Crusader camp, did another lazy circle, and flew south. Had it kept going, little would have been said, but it alighted on the highest rampart of the Accursed Tower and sat looking down on the Christian lines. Philip did his best to look unconcerned, and the desperate men on the beach continued to cheer, but some in the crowd took it as an evil omen and crossed themselves.

Having roused the crowd, Philip was led away toward the French contingent by one of the Frankish knights. Still astride his horse, he reached down to bestow his benediction on the outstretched hands of the ragged and weary men who lined the way. To them, he looked like salvation at last.

"Quite a spectacle."

Roland and Declan turned to see Sir Roger had come up behind them.

"Does this mean we will finally take the city?" asked Declan.

Sir Roger let his gaze follow the French King as he moved away.

"Perhaps, but I would not put a wager upon it. The fresh troops and siege engines will help, but getting a city to yield takes more than numbers. We must break the will of the defenders. I do not think Philip is a man to break another man's will or to bring a determined foe to his knees. For that we need a man who is relentless and clever and bloody-minded. For that, we will need Richard."

Sir Roger drifted back to his tent and the squires stayed at the beach through the afternoon to see the new troops come ashore. These men were neither thin nor filthy as most of the local crop of Crusaders had become during the siege. Among them were French barons and other nobles who seemed to compete with each other in the richness of their dress and the magnificence of their armour and weaponry. For all that, they looked like hard men and ready for battle. Roland turned to Declan.

"If King Philip can't take the city with these men, then he is truly no warrior."

Declan nodded and then yawned. The night guard was not many hours away. They returned to their tent and turned in.

***

The French king held a scented piece of silk to his nose as he surveyed the small tent he was to occupy until his large pavilion was ready. The smell of the place was ghastly and he feared he would be sick to his stomach. But men had started to file in and he was determined they would not see him retch. He had been prepared for the heat and the sand, but the filth of this two-year-old camp was appalling.

The men who gathered around him were the flower of the French nobility and it was easy to tell the new arrivals from those who been here from the beginning. Looking at the veterans, Philip saw men burnt as brown as any Saracen, men grown gaunt from poor food and little rest, men whose best garments would have shamed a beggar on the streets of Paris. He solemnly vowed to himself that he would stay no longer in this hellish place than honour required. He spoke to the assembled men.

"I will inspect the siege lines on the morrow and will make a plan for the taking of the city. This stalemate must end, and I intend for it to end in triumph for France. Mind you, the English king has been distracted once more and is attempting to seize Cyprus, but he is coming in strength and may be only weeks behind us. I want to welcome Richard to *Christian* Acre. Am I understood?"

"Aye, lord" some answered. Others nodded grimly. They had too often been overshadowed by the haughty English—first by Henry and lately by Richard. It was time for all to see the growing strength of France.

***

For weeks, the Crusader camp was alive with new activity. Huge siege engines that had been built in France and disassembled for transporting were unloaded and reassembled. Great towers on wheels designed to get men to the top of Acre's walls were built. Mangonels and other bombardment devices were constructed. Plans were made, cancelled and remade.

Finally the French king ordered a concentrated bombardment of the walls near the Accursed Tower. What had been a feeble pecking at the great ramparts of the city by the few catapults at King Guy's command became a storm of stone on stone. At the same time, sappers were ordered to mine under the same section of the walls in the hopes of creating a collapse and a breach. After much delay, a general assault on the wall was ordered for an hour before dawn on the following day. This was to be a Frankish assault and the other contingents would join in only after the French stormed their way over the walls and into the city.

That night, the sappers entered the tunnel they had excavated under the foundations of the wall. They would light the timbers they had used to shore up those foundations and when they collapsed, so too would the wall. Instead they were met by Muslim defenders who had dug a countermine that intersected the French tunnel. The lightly armed French sappers were slaughtered. The failure of the mine was reported to Philip, but he seemed unconcerned. His siege engines had managed to turn the top of the wall into rubble, though no breach had been made. The attack would go on as planned. The English knights gathered at a vantage point to watch the proceedings.

In preparation for the assault, the French rolled a siege tower to within fifty paces of the wall. Its highest platform overtopped the battlements and a wide ramp was positioned there to drop onto the top of the wall. The moat at the base of the wall had been filled and the engineers who had built the great tower now put their shoulders to the base of the thing and pushed it the last few yards. Over a hundred French knights had marched forward behind the tower and once it was in place they clambered up the interior ladders to make ready for the assault.

All of this the defenders of Acre had watched. They waited until the tower was jammed with the Franks to unleash their own plan. Before the ramp could be lowered, brightly glowing orbs flew over the ramparts and struck the top of the tower. It was Greek fire and within a minute the tower was ablaze. Many of the men jammed on the top platform or crowded onto the ladders could only burn or jump and some did both. The fire illuminated the entire sector of the line.

Despite the destruction of his siege tower, Philip ordered the attack forward at the appointed hour. Men rushed to the wall through a hail of missiles with scaling ladders. The bravest started up the ladders. None made it to the top of the wall.

From his headquarters, the King watched his careful plan come undone one piece at a time. Finally, unable to stomach the carnage, he ordered the attack halted. Once more, the Crusaders drew back inside their lines leaving many of the newly arrived French host dead at the unyielding walls of Acre.

The day after the failure of the French assault, a lone man entered the King's tent. He wore the robes of the church. He was the Bishop of Beauvais and the king's cousin. He was also Philip's spymaster. The two men looked at each other.

"I see no profit in this place, sire," said the Bishop.

"Nor I, cousin. Richard cannot be long in coming and he will strut and bluster—and may even take the city. Let him, for while he may find glory here, he may lose a kingdom in the bargain. The reports you received from your agents in England were most interesting. I commend you for picking men with a talent for fomenting mischief."

"Thank you, sire."

"I know Richard well. He will be consumed with this war. We will go home at the first opportunity, but he will stay to the end. By then, half of his kingdom will be in my hands and the other half in chaos. "

The Bishop nodded.

"With the right nudge, there will be civil war in England."

The King smiled.

"Add that to your prayers tonight, cousin. I shall."

The Earl's Backdoor

Millicent de Laval was frustrated. In Chester, weeks had turned into months as winter fixed its hold over the land. She had been unable to gather information that was of use to anyone. Father Malachy had not, to her knowledge, returned to inspect the city walls—but why would he? The walls were still crumbling in places and the blackberry brambles still filled the dry moat. That much he had already seen. Any endeavour to repair and strengthen the city's defences would have been visible to anyone in Chester who was not blind, and no such effort was underway.

What she noticed was the priest's growing closeness to Lady Constance. It had started as an hour of scripture reading in the evenings, but now extended to long walks through the castle grounds after morning prayers. She had watched them from afar when she could, and Malachy seemed to grow more animated in his conversations each time she saw them together.

From a distance, he appeared to be entreating her, but for what she could not know. That the lady had fallen under the influence of the priest would have caused her no concern if he were what he presumed to be. But she remained convinced that he was not. This was no simple travelling priest who had chanced upon their doorstep. What his game was she did not know, but she was determined to find out.

Lady Catherine arrived for market day a few weeks past Christ's Mass and listened to her daughter's account of her stay at Chester and her suspicions of the priest.

"I do not think this rises to the level that calls for a report to the Queen, but I agree that the priest bears watching. Trust your instincts, daughter, and keep your eye on him—but do not think even a churchman incapable of violence. I beg you to be careful, Millie."

"I'll take precautions, Mother, I promise."

But precautions would not help her find out what Malachy was up to, and her task was made more difficult by the man himself. The girl had the distinct feeling that while she was watching him, he was doing the same with her. It was nothing she could prove, but there were several instances when she saw him gazing in her direction across a hall. Had she given something away? Did the man know she was spying on him?

As winter began to give way to spring with no progress made on her suspicions, Millicent reluctantly reached the conclusion that poking about and passively observing the situation would simply not do. She needed help to get to the bottom of the priest's intentions, and that help appeared in the form of a scullery maid who loved to gossip.

When not attending to her duties, Millicent spent as much time as possible cultivating the trust and friendship of the castle servants. And it was here that the solution to her problem was found. One afternoon, Prudence, known as Prudy to all in the kitchen, mentioned the young priest who was paying such devoted attention to their mistress.

"'Andsomest friar I ever seen, that one," said Prudy. "'E could read my scriptures any night, 'e could!" The kitchen staff laughed at that, which only encouraged the girl.

"I'll bet after 'e leaves her chambers, 'e sneaks back in the night."

"Through the Earl's Backdoor!" another of the scullery girls added with a cackle.

Millicent waited until the hubbub died down and spoke up.

"What is the Earl's Backdoor?" This prompted another loud round of laughter throughout the kitchen, with much nudging and winking among the servants. The head cook quieted the crowd and turned to the young noblewoman.

"Why, miss, it's the special passage old Earl Hugh Kevlioch built so that he could slip unseen into his wife's chambers at night."

"But why would he need to sneak into his wife's chambers?" Millie asked, puzzled. This produced a round of snickers until the old cook hissed for silence.

"Well, old Hugh was a hound with the ladies, he was. He built the passage so that his mistress would not know he was still getting connubial with his missus!"

Millicent shook her head in wonder. The dalliances of the higher nobility were beyond her ken and just a bit shocking, but she instantly recognized the opportunity this new information afforded her.

"Would someone show me this secret passage?" she asked eagerly.

A flood of volunteers immediately offered to be her guide.

"No danger in it," one said. "Earl Ranulf's off at 'is hunting lodge and besides, he uses neither the front or back doors to his lady's chambers." This set off another round of snickers, until the cook sternly shushed the crowd. Then Prudy spoke up.

"I'll show you, my lady, but we must do it all secret like. The Earl may not use it, but 'e would not appreciate us poking about in such a place."

"Of course, Prudy. When shall we have our look?"

"Why, miss, now would be best I think. The Earl is off on the hunt and her Ladyship never budges from her quarters at this hour."

So with the encouragement of the kitchen staff, Prudy grabbed a candle, cupped her hand around it to guard against drafts, and started up the stairs.

"This way, miss."

Millicent followed her up back stairways that she had come to know over the past months to the second floor where the Earl and Lady Constance had their quarters. The place seemed deserted. Prudence led the way down a hall toward the Earl's bedroom.

Millicent had never ventured in this direction down the hallway, always turning left toward Lady Constance's chambers when she had business there. The hall was long and very dimly lit. They passed through two stone arches and could see the entrance to Earl Ranulf's quarters just ahead. With the Earl absent, it was unguarded.

As they approached the door, Prudence signalled a halt and held her fingers to her lips. She passed the candle to Millicent. Inside the arched stone entryway to the Earl's room were wooden panels on either side. Prudence pointed to a small lever set into the edge of one of the panels and pulled it down. This unlocked the panel, which she slid noiselessly to the side and stepped through. Reaching back, she took the candle from Millicent and beckoned her to follow.

The passageway was narrow, but had a high ceiling, and the girls did not have to crouch as they started forward. Dust clung to the walls and the occasional cobweb attested to the fact that this secret passage had not been used in years. The hidden path ran parallel to the hallway for most of its length, but near the end took a sharp turn to the right.

Here there was another panel, like the one they had entered near the Earl's room. It was set in the wall of Lady Constance's bedroom next to the large fireplace. Both girls put their ears to the panel and listened intently. The only sound that emerged was a faint wheezing noise that Millicent instantly recognized as her Ladyship's delicate snore.

From here I can hear everything!

Millicent motioned to Prudence to move quietly and the two girls retraced their steps. After listening carefully for any sound outside the entrance panel, they emerged unseen, though a bit dusty. Millicent turned to the scullery maid.

"Prudy, this must be our own little secret. Can I trust you?"

"Oh, aye, miss. I won't tell and none of the scullery or kitchen staff either. They like you, miss—all of 'em."

Millicent blushed. Gaining the trust of the castle servants was part of her strategy for gaining information, but being kind and respectful had not been feigned. This was how she had treated the staff at Shipbrook since she could barely walk—with the occasional exception of certain squires. Her mother and father would not have tolerated anything less. She liked these people—more, in fact, than the nobles she had come to know here. Lady Agnes had more warmth and wit to her than she let on, but the rest were a dull lot—Lady Constance included.

"Thank you, Prudence. I am grateful for your trust and for that of the others. Now, you'd best get back before cook falls out of her good humour."

"Aye, Miss," the girl gave Millie a quick curtsy and was gone.

Now she needed to plan her next steps carefully.

***

William de Ferrers ate his breakfast with gusto. He was well pleased with the progress of his plans. A message arrived in the night from his man Malachy. He had sent the priest to spy out the state of things in Chester—and the news was good. Not for Chester, of course. The city's defences were a jest—the walls falling down, the moat dry, the guards fat and lacking vigilance. He had known that Earl Ranulf was weak, but the weak should be vigilant or the strong would take what was theirs. Chester was ripe for the taking—for someone strong enough to grasp it.

But the niceties must be maintained. He could not simply seize the city and with it the lands of Cheshire—not unless there was an urgent cause for action against the Earl. And his man Malachy would see to it that there was such cause. The priest reported that the Lady Constance was eating out of his hand. Perfect. The silly woman would be the key that would give him Chester.

He would have to wait for all to come to fruition, but he had faith—faith in his very own man of God. Father Malachy would see to it that Lady Constance cast a shadow of treason over her husband. The priest was too clever by half, but could be relied upon to obtain the evidence he needed to support a charge against the Earl. And with that evidence in hand, he could move decisively against Chester.

He would appear to be rooting out treason against the absent King, but the fall from grace of the loyal Ranulf would benefit John, not Richard. With Cheshire and the Midlands completely in friendly hands, the Prince's position would be almost unassailable. And John would have William de Ferrers to thank for that. His reward would be rich. Of that he was certain. On the morrow, he would lead a large group of his men westwards toward the border of Cheshire—hunting. There, he would await a signal from his man in Chester.

"Two counties are better than one," he whispered to himself. "And with Cheshire comes that dung heap they call Shipbrook. Then I will settle with the de Lavals."

Smiling, he finished his breakfast.

***

Millicent's plan was a simple one. She had learned that the Earl was staying another night at his hunting lodge and would not be back till the morrow. This would be her best opportunity to find out what was transpiring between the Earl's lady and the charming Father Malachy. The Earl's Backdoor would provide her with a hidden place where she could overhear what passed between the two at their daily scripture reading. A part of her fervently hoped he would simply read the verses and go, that her suspicions would prove baseless—but her intuition told her otherwise.

Well before the priest's arrival, she made her way into the secret passage and down its length to Lady Constance's chambers. She blew out the candle, afraid that some light might shine through the edges of the panel. The narrow space plunged into complete darkness and she waited. As she sat alone in the dark, she thought of the charge given her by the Queen. Up till now, she had been an observer—a scout in her own mind, but this was no longer scouting. This was spying, plain and simple. The thought made her uncomfortable, but she was committed now, come what may.

After what seemed an eternity, Father Malachy arrived. Lady Constance gave him a warm greeting. It was far warmer than any she had ever extended to Millicent or, for that matter, to her husband, the Earl. Malachy, in turn, showered the woman with airy compliments that made her shush him out of embarrassment. Millicent listened intently. She could hear every word.

When Malachy began to speak, he uttered no passages from the Bible. He addressed Lady Constance in an urgent tone.

"My lady, have you considered the matter we spoke of last evening?"

There was a long pause.

"Father, I know you are right, but I am frightened. How can I be sure that we will succeed? How can I be sure that this will not bring harm to my son? The King is ruthless, as was his father before him. They forced me to leave Arthur behind in Brittany and come to this God-awful place. They forced me to marry this milk sop of a man so that I would be well out of the way. They keep watch on my son and I'm sure Ranulf watches me. What you suggest is dangerous—to all of us."

"My lady, you know that no venture is without risk and no man ever grasped a crown by shying away from danger. But, my lady, you now have before you the opportunity you have long awaited. Richard is sailing away to the Holy Land and most think he will die there. Should he return, you can expect no better treatment from him than you suffered under his father. The time to act is now." The priest paused and Lady Constance broke in.

"But if Richard dies on Crusade, could I not expect more consideration from the Prince? He has always expressed his sympathies to me—in private." Millicent heard the priest give a derisive snort.

"John is ambitious, and has not a sympathetic bone in his body. The Queen keeps watch over him and the nobles think him weak. That will keep him in check while Richard still lives. But if news comes of Richard's death, John will not hesitate to destroy you and your son. Should Richard die, Arthur is the only stumbling block that stands between John and the throne. On this matter, the Prince will not be weak. He will kill your son."

"But he is hardly more than a babe."

"He is the grandson of Henry and Eleanor, with perhaps a stronger claim to the crown than John. The Prince knows that many nobles would rally around your son. No matter his age, John would have him killed."

"What am I to do, Father Malachy? Please tell me."

"My lady, you have but one place to turn and there you will find the strong support your son will need to survive what is to come—and to someday claim what is his birthright. As we spoke last evening, you must write to Prince Philip. You must seek the French king's aid. Only he has the strength to protect your son."

Millicent almost let out a gasp, but caught herself. What she had heard to this point was most troubling, but the priest's suggestion that the wife of Earl Ranulf should seek the aid of the French king was shocking. It was treason!

"But why should King Philip aid me," Lady Constance asked plaintively. "How do you know his mind on this matter?"

"My lady, let me just say that I dwelled in France for many years and I have friends in the King's inner circle. Philip hates Richard with a passion—has for years. He finds our King boastful, high-handed and not to be trusted. Surely you yourself can vouch for that! King Philip wants peace. He wants a brother king on the throne of England who will tend to his own realm and cease meddling in France. He is fond of Arthur and thinks that you have been treated unfairly—first by Henry and now by Richard. I am certain he would do all in his power to protect your son."

"And what sort of help can I expect?"

"Men, money, siege engines—whatever it would take to put Arthur on the throne."

"But Philip has also gone to the Holy Land. What if he should die instead of Richard?"

Malachy actually chuckled at that.

"You can be sure that King Philip will not get himself killed in this war. Unlike Richard, he feels no need to seek glory through his own feats of arms. He is a king, not a warrior. He will come home alive—and sooner than anyone might suspect. He has much to gain by returning while Richard remains in the desert."

Lady Constance sighed and fell silent for a long time. Millicent wondered if they had perhaps moved out of earshot, but then she spoke.

"What shall I say to the King, Father?"

"My lady, I have taken the liberty of drafting a message. In it, you will ask Philip for an army to enter Brittany and protect Arthur from any harm that Richard or John might intend for him. You will ask him to use his forces to threaten Richard's lands on the continent—Anjou and Poitou in particular. The price Richard will pay for preserving those lands in France will be his designation of Arthur as his heir over John. Honestly, I doubt he will object too much to that demand. He hates John, you know."

Millicent could hear parchment being produced.

There was a long silence as Lady Constance read the contents of the message.

Don't sign it! Millicent screamed in her head.

"Have you a quill, Father?"

Oh God. So there it was! Malachy was an agent of the French and Lady Constance was too dense to see it. He has convinced her that the only way to safeguard her son is to commit treason against her King. If the King didn't have her head for this, then Prince John surely would. And who would believe that her husband was not a part of the plot? Earl Ranulf's head would be on the block along with hers. *Where would that leave the de Lavals?*

Was it possible the Earl knew? *Not a chance,* she thought. He cannot stand his wife and would find himself subordinate to her if her son were king. No, Ranulf must be in the dark. The Queen would surely want to know this, but her mother's words came back to her.

"You do the Queen's bidding, but do not forget your father's oath to Earl Ranulf."

The Queen could wait. She had to get to the Earl.

***

Father Malachy tucked the parchment into his robes and tried to suppress the look of triumph on his face as he hurried from the inner keep of the castle. Passing from the outer bailey and into the dark streets of the city, he made straight for an ale house near the East Gate. There he met a man and passed him a message that would be taken to William de Ferrers, who was encamped just over the border between Cheshire and

Derbyshire. From there it was but a hard day's ride to the gates of Chester.

They would strike after sundown on the morrow and he had no doubt the city would be theirs. De Ferrers would strut about like a cock—as though this stroke had been his doing—and Malachy would encourage him in that. With Ranulf seized for treason, Cheshire and the Midlands would be fully in the hands of those loyal to John. *And John is ambitious.*

Trouble was sure to follow. At the least, there would be civil war. At best, Richard will be overthrown and a weakling king would rule Britain. In either event, France would prosper.

King Philip will be very pleased...

Lionheart

The wave of gloom that pervaded the Crusader camps after the failure of the latest French attack lasted hardly a week, for over the horizon came a great fleet and a new army. At its head was the greatest warrior of Europe, Richard of England. The joy that had greeted Philip was nothing compared to the outpouring that met King Richard. Where Philip came with six ships, Richard brought twenty-five.

The men of Shipbrook joined the great throng gathered by the sea to greet the arrival of the King. Richard did not disappoint. A barge carrying his great black war horse had already reached the beach and as the King's launch slid onto the sand, he stepped on the rail and mounted his charger in an easy motion—no ladder for the Lionheart!

He wore his hauberk and a simple white surcoat with a red Crusader cross on the chest. A broadsword hung from his belt and a great battle axe from his saddle. Energy seemed to radiate from the man. Some men cheered and some wept. Here at last was a commander who could give them victory. The King raised his arm to silence the crowd.

"Soldiers of God, I swear by the one True Cross that we shall have this city. Your sacrifices shall not have been in vain. Prepare yourselves!" With that, his speech was done.

Philip was on hand to greet his rival, which he did with a great show of royal delight. Together the two monarchs rode a short distance to a small sandy hill where a tent had been prepared by the King of France for their first meeting since

135

Sicily. Amid much public display of affection, the two long-time enemies disappeared into the tent. Within minutes those who lingered nearby could hear contentious words being exchanged and not long after, the King of England made his exit. By now his household guards had established headquarters near the English contingent further down the siege lines and Richard rode there, acknowledging the cheers from all sides as he passed.

Sir Roger, Roland and Declan stayed on the beach as barges began unloading the English army that had followed the King to these shores. It was a tonic to hear English spoken by such a host after more than a year away from home. All through the morning, the barges ferried more English nobles, knights and troops ashore. Sir Roger reluctantly ordered his squires to head back to their tent to rest before their night patrol when a shout stopped them.

"Sir Roger de Laval I believe?"

They turned to see Sir Robin of Loxley striding down a ramp from the nearest barge, a broad grin on his face.

Sir Roger returned the smile and strode across the sand to grasp the man's hand.

"Sir Robin! You are well met, sir. Welcome to hell!"

Sir Robin looked past the Norman knight at the squalid camp and made a sour face.

"I can see no one freshened up the place for my arrival—but who are these scarecrows trailing behind you?"

Before their master could answer, Roland and Declan descended on the new arrival with whoops of excitement.

"Sir Robin! It's good to see a familiar face," Roland said.

"I see you've brought your longbow," Declan added, pointing to the weapon slung over the man's shoulder.

"Aye, lads, it's good to see you as well. Yer both a bit taller but not so well fed as when last we met—and I'd feel naked without the longbow. I had hoped that I would be the greatest archer in the Holy Land, but I see I will have to defer to my betters on that score," he said, smiling at Roland. "You've not lost your touch, have you, lad?"

"Not a bit, Sir Robin, but you are welcome to a rematch at your convenience."

"Perhaps, but no shooting at melons in the sky!" The knight smiled ruefully, recalling the shot that had cost him the royal archery tournament and won it for the young man before him. Sir Roger interrupted the exchange.

"Sir Robin, there is a newly vacant tent near us if you wish to use it. It is no more pestilent than any of the others. We can show you the way."

"I'd be obliged, Sir Roger, but I have a comrade who I'd have take quarters with me, if it will accommodate two." There was an odd, sly look on his face as he made this request. "I believe he is on the barge just landing now."

One of the large Genoese barges rasped ashore on the beach and a broad plank ramp was lowered to the sand. First over the rail was a broad, muscular man in brown robes with a broadsword at his belt and a beaming smile on his face. All three of the men from Shipbrook stood rooted to the spot. Walking down the ramp was Friar Tuck.

***

"Tuck!" Roland was first to break free from the shock that had frozen them to the spot. He ran down the beach and met the monk as he reached the bottom of the ramp. "You're alive! Thank God."

Tuck took the boy by both shoulders and beamed.

"I am indeed and with no small help from God, I can testify!"

"But how? Where have you been?"

Tuck laughed as the others came forward to greet him, Sir Roger slapping the friar heartily on the back.

"I knew you were a hard man to kill, Father, but 'pon my soul, I thought the Moors had you!"

"Ah, it's a grand story, my friends, but let's get some food and drink in me and I'll tell it from the start."

For the sake of hospitality, they held the questions they were burning to ask as Roland and Declan ran ahead to fetch food and drink for the new arrivals. When they returned, the two men were gathered with Sir Roger by the small cook fire that served the nearby tents. Tuck began his tale.

"The Berbers—now there is a warrior race! Few have survived being boarded by men such as they. But they did not count on the mettle of the men on the *Sprite*!" He looked from man to man in the circle surrounding him.

"Woe unto the Berber who faces a Norman knight in full battle fury!" he nodded toward Sir Roger.

"Or an Irishman with a blade quicker than a serpent's strike," he nodded to Declan.

"Or a Dane, who can use that longbow for more than just straw targets. Hitting a man on a pitching deck from another pitching deck—extraordinary!" he nodded to Roland.

"And Master Inness, I greatly appreciated yer assistance with the crew of the galley. Taking the vessel seemed a good idea at the time, but if you had not thinned their ranks, it would have gone poorly for me, I fear. I owe ye for that."

Sir Roger spoke up.

"Father, if ye had not come at that Moorish galley when ye did, we would all be dead or in shackles pulling on oars. I think all debts have been paid. But how were you able to escape them? It's said the Moors feed their slaves well, better than the Berbers. They should have been stronger and swifter."

Tuck smiled.

"That is true. Those on my galley were some of the gauntest men I've ever seen, but they had something more than full bellies and the lash to spur them on—they had a chance for freedom. Once we captured the vessel, they were no longer slaves, and no galley of slaves can catch a galley of free men." The monk said this last with the conviction of one who knew whereof he spoke.

"They chased us through the night and into the next morning, but finally gave up. Most of the men at the oars were Spanish, so we made for Tarragona. I arranged for the sale of the galley there and the crew went their separate ways, each with enough gold to get him home. I took passage to Marseille where the English fleet was to gather. I arrived on the very day the flotilla was setting sail for Sicily and took ship there."

"Sicily!" Sir Roger turned up his nose. "Not my favourite port-of-call."

Tuck laughed heartily.

"Aye, nor mine, and I offer my apologies for not being there to guide you. For there was still talk among the harbour folk that a large English knight and his squire had come to grief with the usurper Tancred and were rescued by a wench."

Sir Roger grinned sheepishly.

"Loose talk that—but the wench *was* a comely lass—ask Master Inness!"

Roland blushed furiously and Sir Robin threw an arm around him.

"Now that is a tale I would like to hear!" said the young knight.

Before Roland could make reply, the tale-telling was interrupted. A messenger arrived wearing a tunic emblazoned with the King's lions.

"His grace requests the presence of Sir Roger de Laval," he said, scanning the group.

Sir Roger sighed. "That would be me."

"What shall you tell him?" asked Roland as the knight rose to follow the messenger.

"The truth, lad. It's what he sent me here for."

***

King Richard was waiting for Sir Roger in a tent that was large, but otherwise spartan. As the knight bowed, the King stepped forward and embraced him.

"Sir Roger, I beg your forgiveness. I am late and you have endured this pestilent place for much longer than we planned. I had a bit of trouble in Sicily with a usurper named Tancred. The man locked up my sister! I sacked Messina, which brought the upstart to his senses."

"Aye, your grace, we had a bit of trouble with him as well, but no matter. You are here now and thank God for that. There is much here that needs to be set right."

The King nodded.

"Guards, leave us." He motioned for Sir Roger to sit beside him.

"Now tell me, old friend, what is the situation here?"

"Lord, it is the Tower of Babel here. The King of Jerusalem commanded until the French king arrived and the

King of Jerusalem..." Sir Roger spit on the ground. "The King of Jerusalem is an ass, beggin' your grace's pardon. We were lucky that over the winter Saladin could not muster the strength to sweep us all into the sea. Would that he had kept the man a hostage after Hattin."

The King shook his head, but motioned for the knight to continue.

"Then, what was left of Emperor Barbarossa's army finally arrived. They say one hundred thousand marched from Germany, but after the Emperor drowned in some nameless river, the Turks cut them to pieces in the deserts of Anatolia. Most of the survivors stayed on in Tyre, there to fulfil their Crusader oaths by drinking and chasing wenches, I'm told. Only a few thousand, under the Duke of Austria, marched here to Acre, though they were welcome. When Philip arrived a month ago, there was hope. He had fresh men and siege engines, but he dawdled, then came up with a bad plan and executed that poorly. Many a good man died at the walls as a result." Sir Roger's voice rose sharply as he spoke, his anger barely under control.

"Your grace, this place can be taken, but only with a decent plan and hard fighting." Sir Roger concluded his report and fell silent, waiting for his King's reply.

"Sir Roger, this information is troubling, but not surprising. You have been most helpful. I knew I could count on you." He rose and Sir Roger made ready to take his leave, but the King was not finished.

"Things are about to change here at Acre. On the morrow, you and I will walk the siege lines and decide where we shall strike our blow. We will have a simple plan and will execute it with vigour—a notion that escapes my royal friend Philip. We will assemble the siege engines and knock a breach in the wall. Then you will have your hard fighting. Then we will take the city." Sir Roger nodded.

"Aye, your grace. That we will."

***

As the King promised, the following day they inspected the defences of the city. The French were continuing to hurl stones at the Accursed Tower, and there was damage to be seen, but no significant breach. Further along the lines the Germans with their few siege engines pecked away at another section of the great wall. Richard shook his head and turned to Sir Roger.

"I hoped that somehow your report was exaggerated, but I see now that it was all too true. This is madness! I've seen enough."

When they returned to the English sector of the lines, the King summoned Earl Robert de Ferrers and the other senior nobles for a council of war. He pointed to the north gate of the city, which was opposite their position.

"That is where we will strike! I want our siege engines assembled here. There is damage to the left of that gate. I want every machine that can hurl a stone focused on that point. I want the tower I brought from Sicily assembled in two days. I've hired the Pisan crossbowmen away from Philip and they will keep defenders off that section of the wall. Each night, I want sappers and any other men in our camp not bearing arms to fill the moat with stones." He paused and looked at the circle of men who surrounded him.

"We will breach that wall within a fortnight. We will storm the breach and take the city." He paused once more. "We will show this bootless bunch of Franks and Germans what Englishmen can do! Is it understood?"

As one, the nobles shouted their reply.

"Aye, sire!"

Into the Breach

A young man peered into the deep darkness outside the flickering light of the campfire. He looked toward the fortress of Acre and could see nothing in the night, but felt the heart pounding in his chest. *So loud. I wonder if Declan can hear it.* Roland Inness had been frightened many times since landing on these shores, but this was the worst. There would be no sleep this night.

Since King Richard's arrival, feverish preparations had been underway for this day. During the hours of darkness, English sappers slipped forward to fill in the moat at the base of the north wall. Night and day they tunnelled under the wall until a whole section of the foundation was supported only by timbers. Then torches were sent forward to fire the wood. Armed men guarded the sappers against any counter-tunnel being dug from inside the city. There would be no repeat of the underground butchery suffered by the French.

The King's great siege tower, Mategriffon, had been built in Sicily and was reassembled before the walls of Acre. It was manned by Pisans who kept up a galling hail of crossbow bolts on any defenders who showed themselves along the north wall. The tower was faced with iron and tanned hides that were drenched with vinegar, keeping the Greek fire from igniting its timbers.

Richard had assembled almost three hundred catapults that kept up a steady pounding of the wall until a section near the northern gate had crumbled. Late the same day, the burned out timbers under the same section gave way with a sound like thunder and a breach was formed. Through that gaping wound, the King was sending his men at dawn to fight their way into the city.

Roland turned back to the campfire and warmed himself against the chill of the desert night. He shivered and wondered if it was from the cold or his fear of what was to come. At dawn he and Declan would be in the first wave of English troops fighting their way up the rubble of the breach. The defenders of Acre knew they were coming and he knew that death waited at the top of that heap of stone.

The King had called upon Sir Robert de Ferrers to lead the first wave of the assault and assigned Sir Roger de Laval to command the second, passing over many men of higher rank. The second wave was to burst into the city once the wall had been taken by the first men up the slope. Sir Robin, Tuck and the small Templar contingent were assigned to Sir Roger's command.

The first wave was largely manned by volunteers. Most of these were younger knights and squires, many of whom were in search of glory and advancement. Sir Roger had urged his squires not to join them, but could not bring himself to forbid them. He was not surprised when they stepped forward with the others of their rank. His squires could not abide being counted as cowards by their fellows.

Of all the dangers of war, forcing a breach was the most desperate. The enemy knew that if the breach were lost, so too would be their cause, their city and likely their lives. They would defend it with the fury of cornered animals. The English attacking force would have to match that fury, fighting its way up a steep and jumbled slope with arrows and stones raining down on them. They would be funnelled into a narrow space at the top where all of the might of the enemy would be marshalled. Taking the breach seemed impossible, but take it they must if Acre was to fall. The King had ordered it and they must obey.

English foot soldiers manned the earthworks to the north to counter any attempt to disrupt the final assault on the walls.

Starting well before dawn, a great booming beat of drums came from inside the city—the signal to the man on the Hill of Carob Trees that a Crusader assault was imminent. Saladin knew Acre hung in the balance and would surely hurl all of his available forces against the Crusader rear, diverting what strength he could from the English attack. Richard knew this tactic had frustrated previous assaults and was determined that it would not alter the outcome of this dawn.

Near midnight, Sir Roger gathered his squires together.

"You lads are the finest squires I've ever had the honour of employing..." he began, his voice gone husky.

"Better than Harold, who ran off with the milkmaid?" Declan chimed in with a weak attempt at humour. No one laughed.

"Yes, better than Harold. So stay together—and don't be stupid," he said and fell silent. They nodded in response. It was advice the squires had heard many times since arriving in the Holy Land. Their master then walked off into the darkness to gather the troops for his own assault on the wall in the second wave.

After midnight, a messenger arrived to announce that the last stones had been placed and the path across the moat was complete. They now had a clear approach to the rubble slope in front of the breach. The bombardment of the catapults continued to pound away, seeking to crumble the wall further and prevent any repairs being made.

Roland turned to watch as Declan pedalled the action of a large grindstone. Sparks flew from the rapidly spinning wheel as the young Irishman sharpened the edge of his sword. Roland had already done the same. He fingered the longbow by his side. This was his preferred weapon and, while it usually wasn't used in close quarters like this, he was determined to carry it. The bow could kill at close range as well as long. And besides, he felt naked without it.

"Declan, are you afraid?" asked Roland. His friend paused at his labours and gave a slow nod.

"That clattering sound you hear over this way is my knees knocking together. If I had a hole, I'd climb in and pull it in behind me!"

"As would I. Why are we doing this?"

"Because we are insane and hope to be cut into tiny pieces by big Muslim swords," Declan replied ruefully. Then, ceasing his work at the grindstone, he spoke more seriously.

"I could not stand to see the others go and not join them. They would have thought us cowards had we not."

"True enough," said Roland. "But I wonder what they will think of us if we end up dead on that wall?"

"Martyrs to the cause, my friend—and celebrated by all," replied Declan.

"Aye, but I would rather be alive at the end of this day than a martyr to this cause."

The two squires grew quiet for a moment, then Roland spoke again.

"There is something else at work here," he said. "I think it's the King. He makes you want to risk your life for him. I wonder if he knows that?"

"He knows all right," said Declan. "It's a king's job to send men to die and this king is good at his job. Being king is a bloody business. We have about a dozen kings in Ireland—all with bloody hands."

"Do you think Saladin is like the King?"

"Yes—and just as bloody," replied Declan.

As he spoke, the first faint light began to appear in the eastern sky. There was a trumpet blast. It was time to assemble.

Roland hitched up the new mail shirt Sir Roger had presented him and pulled its hood over his head. He buckled his sword belt and slung his quiver with twenty arrows over one shoulder and the bow over the other. With one hand, he gripped the hilt of his sword and ran the other through the straps of his shield.

Declan looked him over as though performing an inspection. The many months since they left England had changed his friend. Despite the meagre rations in camp, he had added muscle to his shoulders and arms and the face was no longer that of a boy.

"You've come a long way since our meeting on the road to York," he declared.

Roland laughed. "How so?"

Declan did not laugh. "Ye look like a killer, my friend, and that's a fact."

Roland waited a moment to see if the Irishman would break out his sunny grin, but it did not come. He looked at Declan and saw little of the carefree Irish boy who had befriended him, what seemed an age ago. His sandy hair was long and tangled and he had the beginnings of a curly red beard that framed his fair face. But it was the eyes that were different. They had seen too much since leaving England. They were not the eyes of a boy. He guessed that Declan saw the same in him.

"Killers we must both be this day, my friend," he said after a bit. "Up there," he gestured with his shield toward the city walls still cloaked in darkness, "up there it will be us or them. And I intend for it to be them. What say you?"

Now the grin returned.

"Them—for certain!"

Together they moved off until they reached a deep ditch that led toward their attack positions. Eighty men had volunteered for this act of valour and they gathered in a series of connected trenches near the moat as the first hint of a red dawn began to show.

Some were there because the King had promised them favours. Some had come to prove their courage. Others were there because they sought the grace of God and the expunging of their sins as the priests had promised. All knew that to be first into a breach was deadly, for few were expected to survive the forcing of the gap. Those who did would be expected to hold the top of the breach for the second wave.

Roland looked at them as they arrived in ones and twos—mostly young and eager to prove themselves—but also frightened. You could see it in their eyes. Some coughed nervously. Others shifted slowly from side to side in the narrow confines of the trench and fidgeted with their weapons and mail. One squire retched, his stomach betraying his nerves. No one spoke. Sir Robert de Ferrers stood above them on the lip of the trench, his back to the walls of Acre.

Then there was movement to the rear. Men were coming across the broken ground. At their head was Richard Lionheart

146

who stood above the men in the trenches below. All grew silent and turned toward their King as he spoke in a quiet, but commanding voice.

"Men, you must take that breach or die like Englishmen in the effort. Now, kneel and pray." Eighty men knelt as one and prayed silently—some for victory, some for glory and all for survival.

"God go with you," said the King. He turned and marched away into the growing pink light of the new day. At that moment, the bombardment of the catapults stopped. An eerie silence fell over the field. Earl Robert de Ferrers rose and addressed his troops.

"This day you will do a thing many a man would fear to do," he said looking at Roland and several others in the group. "Any man among you who reaches that breach this day can never be counted a coward." He paused.

"Are you ready?" he roared. Old he might be, but the heart of a warrior still beat strong in the chest of Robert de Ferrers.

An echoing roar arose from the eighty and a rhythmic beating of swords on shields began. The clang of metal on metal grew louder as more men took up the beat. There was no more need for stealth here. The enemy knew they were coming and where. The first rays of sunlight were just peaking over the hills to the east as they approached the moat, now filled in by the sappers.

"On my signal, lads, we all go up at once. Don't stop for anything. If we don't reach the top and secure the flanks of the breach, we are all dead men." He turned toward the slope above them and raised his broadsword, pointing it directly at the notch of the breach, still hidden by shadows.

"*Now!*"

The first wave hurled themselves from the trenches and ran for the moat. Instantly, arrows from the wall began to land among the attackers. Men were hit and some went down. As they had been drilled so long ago by Sir Alwyn, the two squires raised their shields to ward off the hail of death from above. Roland could hear the arrows splinter on his shield face. In response, the Pisan archers on Mategriffon poured a torrent of return bolts over the wall, and the enemy onslaught lessened.

Roland and Declan ran side-by-side across the uneven stones filling the moat and were surprised to arrive at the rubble pile unhurt. Sir Robert immediately began climbing up the shattered rocks toward the top of the breach. From above, someone began to dislodge stones and tumble them down toward the Crusaders. Only the covering volleys of the crossbowmen kept more defenders from starting an avalanche to bury the climbing Englishmen.

As he scrambled upwards, Roland dodged several bouncing stones and caught sight of a huge man, hidden from the Pisans in the tower, hurling them down the slope. He stopped, quickly swung the bow from his shoulder, nocked an arrow and loosed it at the man. It was a difficult uphill shot, but the arrow took the defender in the arm and he fell back.

For the moment, the cascade of stones slowed to a trickle. He slung the longbow back over his shoulder and clawed his way upwards. Declan had climbed past him as he had switched to his favoured weapon and now Roland hurried to regain his place next to the Irishman.

The Crusaders were halfway up the slope when Declan grabbed Roland's arm and pointed above them to the wall on the left of the breach. They could see men struggling with a black object. It was a cauldron. A knot of English knights were working themselves along the edge of the rubble heap beneath that wall. The squires screamed a warning, but it was too late. A foul, steaming torrent of searing oil poured down, striking two of the English. They died screaming.

More men were lost to arrows, but still they came on. The first wave was only twenty feet from the top now, but the slope was steeper and harder to climb. Roland could hear the defenders just a few yards away on the opposite slope shouting orders and preparing to meet the English at the top. He and Declan were right behind Sir Robert as he crested the summit of the breach. A dozen Muslim swordsmen surged forward to meet them.

The three armoured knights had to struggle to maintain their footing on the uneven stone and were in danger of simply being overborne by their attackers. They chopped and thrust at the oncoming mass as shield met shield...and held. Behind them, other knights and squires were reaching the top and the English line began to lengthen and thicken. They pushed back the defenders.

For a moment, it seemed they had won. Roland found himself beside Sir Robert at the top of the shattered wall and could see down into the city below. The sight made him gasp. Where any two streets crossed, there were piles—piles of bodies. Even from a distance he could tell that some were soldiers, but most were not. There were women...and children in those heaps of the dead. Perhaps they had died from the bombardment or perhaps from starvation or disease. But the number of the dead was shocking to him.

This city is dying.

Now, by ones and twos, more of the Crusaders were reaching the top, until a small force of about half their original number had gathered. Down the slope, the bodies of their brethren were scattered like driftwood on a rocky shore. A few struggled to rise and a few others called out, but most lay still.

Those at the top fought for breath, some falling to their knees in exhaustion. Roland dropped to one knee and used the hem of his doublet to wipe away the sweat that poured into his eyes. He looked down at the rampant white stag of de Laval on the cloth—the symbol that had been so brilliant on the day of Richard's coronation. It was now faded and streaked with dirt and blood. He could hardly believe he was alive.

The English barely had time to gather themselves when a new horde of warriors appeared on the remaining sections of the wall on either side of the breach. A hail of arrows rained down on them from two sides, and as Roland raised his shield, he watched in horror as Sir Robert de Ferrers staggered backwards, a shaft buried in his neck just above his mail shirt. He caught the Earl as he fell.

"My lord!"

The old warrior was bleeding profusely and his eyes were cloudy. He blinked and looked at Roland, then grasped his arm in a still-iron grip.

"Inness! I am a dead man. Hold the breach." He tried to speak again, but blood foamed at his mouth and he was still.

Roland had no time to think on the meaning of this death. Screaming their defiance, the defenders of Acre came pouring down the sides of the notch like a wave, directly at the gasping Crusaders. An odd anger seized him. He stood, stepped to the front of the ragged English line and braced himself against the oncoming tide.

"Shield wall!" he roared.

Declan O'Duinne was the first to reach his side. The two stood shoulder-to-shoulder, their shields overlapping as they waited for the wave to break over them. Others heard the command and saw the two squires braced for the assault. For the sake of survival, they joined them to form a rough curved line of locked shields and waited for the impact as this mass of men bore down on them. The two forces came together with a deafening clash of steel on steel and the shouts of desperate men.

This was battle as Danes had known it for uncounted generations—a shield wall! A strange madness seemed to come over Roland. Somewhere in his blood, the Viking stirred. He heard the voice of Sir Alwyn Madawc in his head calling him to the killing fury and he gave himself to it.

The Saracens broke against the tightly packed English like an avalanche of flesh and steel. The English line bowed inwards, but did not break. Men cursed, men sweated, men flailed across the barrier of shields. A warrior grasped Roland's shield to pull it down so he could bring his wickedly curved scimitar into play, but Declan used his broadsword to take the man's arm off at the elbow. He fell screaming to the rubble and Roland lunged forward into the gap, slashing at the more lightly-armoured enemy that surrounded him. Declan closed up beside him and the English line edged forward a step.

There was little stratagem here. Men dug in their heels and pushed, shield on shield, grunting with the effort. A huge English knight used a long-handled battle axe to hook the shield of an attacker to his front, pulling it forward and down so that men to his left and right could cut down the exposed warrior. Roland and Declan held the centre of the line, pressing forward and looking for openings to kill those who had come to kill them. With their leader down, the English stubbornly held the breach.

Across the shields and straining bodies of the foe, Roland could see the enemy commander shouting at his men, but could hear nothing over the din. The swarms of attackers seemed to be gaining strength from the man's exhortations, and almost imperceptibly, the tide of battle began to slip away from the Crusaders. Without thinking Roland began to shout, his voice hoarse but strong.

"Come on, lads! For Richard and England!"

A ragged cheer went up from his own ranks, but there were just too many men on the other side fighting for their own cause. Slowly the English line grew thinner as concealed archers high atop the Accursed Tower sent waves of arrows into their ranks. They began to give ground until they were pushed back onto the rubble slope.

Now the Crusaders faced a foe that pressed them hard from higher ground. Even the arrival of a few stragglers from further down the slope could not stem this tide. Step by step they were forced back, but the line would not break. To do so would have meant an utter slaughter. Still, sensing victory, a new wave of troops swarmed down from the walls with a great ululating war cry.

Roland fought like a man possessed, hurling defiant insults at the men to his front who were desperately trying to kill him. He took a small wound to his shield arm and another on his thigh, but hardly felt them in the heat of the battle. He glanced to his side and saw that Declan had lost his helmet, but was still in the fray. The squires guarded each other's flank, trading blow for blow with an endless stream of brave men fighting to save their city.

The scimitar was a wicked weapon for slashing and particularly good for fighting from horseback, but it wasn't as effective in the close combat of a shield wall as the straight, short swords the squires wielded. Still, men in the front ranks of the Crusader line were falling with none to replace them. A few more such losses and the line would break. Then the wolves would be on the fold and few of the English would survive.

At that moment, from down the slope, a great blast of bugles sounded. Roland dared not turn to look, as two black clad men were trying to relieve him of his head, but he heard a roar rise up from below him.

"For England, lads!"

Roland knew that voice. Sir Roger de Laval was coming with the second wave up the slope! Sixty English knights followed him into the carnage at the top of the breach. Among them was Sir Robin of Loxley and Friar Tuck, his brown robe replaced with the red cross of the Knights Templar.

As the reinforcements reached the beleaguered men of the first wave, Sir Roger bulled his way to the front. The English line began to thicken and edge forward once more. Warriors who had braved English arrows and swords shrank back from this fearsome knight who swung his battle axe in wicked arcs into their ranks.

The big Norman fought with skill and a grim purpose, pressing the attack relentlessly. To his right, Tuck kept pace as they pushed the enemy back. Beside him, Sir Robin charged the defenders to his front with reckless courage. Slowly, the tide turned and the Crusaders regained the high ground at the top of the breach.

As the second wave swept past, Roland could hardly find the strength to follow back up the slope. He was gasping for breath and sweat blinded his eyes. His sword felt like it weighed a thousand pounds. He stole a glance at Declan who looked his way and gave a weary nod. They once more began to climb, stepping around the dead as they went.

Finally, they rejoined the English line as it came to a halt at the top of the breach. The incredible din of the battle had fallen oddly silent. The two squires forced their way to the front and looked down once more onto the streets of Acre. They saw that this day would not bring them final victory.

The Emir had opened the gates of his citadel in the centre of the city and sent forth his last reserves. A horde of defenders were pouring out into the broad street, heading straight for the breach. Even with the fresh English troops of the second wave, they could not hold the breach against this. Acre hung by a thread, but a thread that would not yet break. Sir Roger turned to the thin line of English standing there.

"We will withdraw! Now!"

A few of the younger knights in the second wave protested and he turned on them glaring.

"If it's a martyr you wish to be, then stay. We have done all soldiers of the King can do this day." He gestured toward the city below, its streets filled with the dead. "Look about you. The breach is lost, but the city is doomed—let's be gone!"

He turned and started back down the rubble slope. None stayed behind. Like a receding wave on the shore, the English made their way back to where the attack had begun at dawn. Roland and Declan stopped to help two of the wounded and all limped and staggered back into the Crusader lines.

***

Mashtub, Grand Emir, servant of Saladin, and commander of the garrison at Acre nodded to the man standing beside him on the tower. The man flung his arms out, releasing a grey pigeon to the sky. The bird circled for a moment then turned toward the east.

In less than an hour, the message from Mashtub was in the hands of his master on the Hill of Carob Trees overlooking the plain of Acre. Saladin read the message twice then laid it on the table before him. His commanders had gathered around and waited to do his bidding.

He knew that he could order another attempt to break the Crusader siege lines, but the attack would surely fail. More ships were arriving from the west and men were pouring into the enemy camp. Somehow the Christians had been able to bring many men across the vastness of the sea, when he had recieved but a trickle from his own lands much nearer at hand. He would not send his men to die for show. The lots were cast. He turned to his generals, and spoke with a sharp sadness in his voice they had not heard before. He hoped they would not see the tears glistening in his eyes.

"Acre is lost."

Acre

Two days after the failed attack on the breach, the mighty fortress of Acre capitulated. The terms of surrender were harsh. The leaders of the garrison, to include the Grand Emir Mashtub, were to be held for ransom. Another fifteen hundred from the city would be exchanged for all Christian prisoners languishing in Saladin's dungeons. The rest could buy their freedom for ten dinars each. Those who could not, would be sold as slaves. Saladin was also required to return the True Cross, upon which Jesus had been crucified. This holiest of relics had been captured from the Christian army at Hattin. He had to fulfil all of these terms within one month.

The Crusader dead from the attack on the breach, including Earl Robert de Ferrers, were given Christian burials in the makeshift graveyard that held so many of their fallen. As the man was laid to rest, Roland struggled to make sense of what it meant to him. As Tuck had told him long ago, not all Danes or Saxons were good men and not all Normans evil. He had seen the truth of that in the man he now called master. He did not know how to judge Earl Robert, but this he did know—the man's son was now Earl of Derby and vengeance for his own father seemed further away than ever.

As Roland had seen from the top of the breach, Acre was a city barely alive. He and Declan watched as the dead were taken out and dumped in the moat east of the city to be buried in a mass grave. A long column of starving and weakened citizens, those who could pay the ransom, were filing out of the south gate. Muslim cavalry still lurked in a wide circle around the city, but Saladin's tent had disappeared in the night and the bulk of his army had retired toward Jerusalem.

King Richard and King Philip entered the city with great pomp. Bugles were blown and heralds announced their coming. Invigorated by victory, Richard rode through the northern gate like the conqueror that he was. He established his headquarters and residence at the royal palace in the centre of the old city, raising his lion banner there. Philip made an equally grand entrance through the eastern gate and set up his court in the former palace of the Templars.

The only thing to mar the triumphal entry of the victors was an altercation between the English troops and the remnants of Barbarossa's army. The Germans had sacrificed much to maintain the siege for two full years and, in their joy at the victory, they raised the white and red striped battle flag of the Holy Roman Emperor over the city's battered ramparts. English troops tore it down and threw it in the gutter. When the Germans protested, they were set upon and driven from the city by the English.

Duke Leopold of Austria, who commanded the remnants of this once great force, confronted Richard in a rage. The King dismissed the man and offered no satisfaction. Whatever their role in maintaining the siege over the years, the Germans had played little part in the final capitulation of the city. It had been the arrival of the English that had won the day—or so went the thinking of the English troops—and Richard was of like mind. The Duke swore to the King's face that this outrage would be avenged and led the tattered remnants of his dead Emperor's great army from Acre.

A day after the fall of the city, a summons came to Sir Roger. He was to present himself and his squires to the King at the royal palace later in the day. He was puzzled.

"The King can see for himself what the situation is here now. He no longer has need of reports from me." He shook his head. "I suppose we'll know what's on his mind when he tells us. Now let's see if we can scrub off some of this dirt and make ourselves presentable!"

The men of Shipbrook trooped down to the sea, stripped naked and scrubbed off the accumulated sweat and grime of weeks in the desert. They had moved into a small room in the city after the surrender and there they pulled on the tunics that Lady Catherine had made for them to wear at King Richard's coronation. That grand day seemed an age ago and the tunics had faded from black to a dark and dingy grey. There were stains on the fabric—stains from more than dust and sweat. But the de Laval coat-of-arms, with its rampant white stag, was still proudly emblazoned on the front. Sir Roger looked his squires over.

"It's the best we can do," he declared. "Now let's go see what's on the King's mind."

The three made their way down the main street of the city, grateful that the smell of death had started to wane. At the royal palace, they were greeted by Sir Robin of Loxley who wore an impish grin on his face.

"Sir Roger! You look well turned out." He gave the squires a quick inspection. "Even these raggedy young men are passable!" Sir Roger waved off this puffery.

"What's this about, Loxley?"

"Ahh...I think it best to let his grace explain. I'm just to escort you into the hall."

Sir Roger snorted. Loxley knew something he wasn't telling and was mightily amused. Sir Roger de Laval did not like surprises, especially when they came from the King. The last such surprise had dragged him away from Shipbrook and landed him here.

"This way, my lord."

Sir Robin led them into the hall. The place was magnificent, even if a bit in need of repair. Their steps echoed on the arched stone high overhead. Oddly, the hall was empty.

Sir Robin crossed to a small wooden door and pushed it open. They filed into what had once been a chapel until Saladin had seized the place. It had been hurriedly restored to its former function, as a large crucifix hung on the wall between two high narrow windows. Standing before the cross was Richard of England, dressed once more in the triumphal garments worn for his entry into the city. He seemed solemn.

"As you ordered, your grace," Sir Robin announced and stepped back into the shadows.

The King stepped forward and clapped Sir Roger on the arm.

"It would have been another month to take this place without your reports and your wisdom, sir. I thank you." He handed Sir Roger a leather bag that, by its heft, contained a small fortune in coins.

"You have more than earned this, de Laval."

Sir Roger stood stock still. He seemed stunned.

"Sire…"

"Just take the money, man. They may have been starving here, but there was no lack of gold. You deserve a share as much as any in my company."

Sir Roger bowed and stepped back.

"And now, for the chief purpose of our meeting. Two days ago, I ordered Earl Robert de Ferrers to lead our attack on the north wall breach. I watched the attack go in from Mategriffon. Against great odds, our first wave reached the top, only to have the Earl fall mortally wounded—I saw him fall, God rest his soul. It was then that I saw a great host of the Saracens fall upon our men and my heart sank. I sent word to Sir Roger to go in with the second wave, but I feared it was too late. The first wave was doomed. Or so it seemed."

For a moment the King paused, emotion overtaking him as he recalled the dire scene.

"Then I saw two of our knights rally the men into a shield wall. By all that is holy, I have not seen a braver act in twenty years of campaigning and it saved the lives of the men at the top of that breach. We did not take the city by storm that day, but no matter. We showed what Christian men can do!"

He paused and looked at Sir Roger.

"I have it on excellent authority that the two men who held the line and rallied the men were your own squires, Masters Inness and O'Duinne. Master Inness I have met before. It seems he is as useful with a sword as with his bow. And Master O'Duinne has surely shown what my Irish subjects are made of.

Would that I had many more like you! Now, the two of you, come forward and kneel."

For a moment, both froze to the spot, but Sir Robin gave them a gentle shove in the back and they stepped forward and knelt before the King. Richard drew his great two-handed broadsword.

"As knights of my realm, do ye swear to speak the truth, be loyal to your lord, honour all ladies, be charitable to the poor and helpless, and come, when summoned, to the defence of the crown?"

"I swear it," they said, almost in unison.

He lowered the great sword to Declan's left shoulder, then right. He turned and did the same to Roland.

"Then rise, Sir Declan of …?"

"Ulster, your grace."

"Sir Declan of Ulster, rise." Declan rose, a little unsteadily to his feet.

"And rise, Sir Roland of…"

Roland hesitated but a moment.

"Kinder Scout, your grace."

"Then rise, Sir Roland of Kinder Scout, and go with my thanks."

***

Sir Roger de Laval was bursting with pride. As they made their way out of the royal palace and into the street he beamed at his two charges.

"Oh, if only Catherine and Millie could see you two now—and, of course Alwyn—ye owe much of this to him!"

Roland walked in a daze. It was almost too much to take in. He wondered what his father, Rolf Inness, would have thought of this. His family had been laid low by the Normans, but he had been saved by one and elevated by another—the mightiest Norman of them all. It was passing strange.

He was now Sir Roland of Kinder Scout, the youngest knight in the army at sixteen, but landless and practically penniless as well. He owned nothing but his longbow, the dagger he had taken from Ivo Brun so long ago and the yew tree amulet around his neck. Everything else—his mail, his sword and the clothes on his back had come from Sir Roger de Laval.

Under the law, he could now own land, but that counted for little if you were a pauper. Like so many things that had come his way since that horrible day in his father's field, knighthood would take some getting used to. At least there was Sir Declan of Ulster to share the experience of being a penniless knight!

"Did I not tell ye?" Declan asked him, as they trudged to their new temporary lodging inside the city. "On the road to York. I told ye then, if fortune smiled on a squire he could become a knight. Sometimes I surprise myself with my wisdom!"

Roland laughed. He realized that it was the first time he had laughed in a very long time. *Thank God for Declan O'Duinne.*

Sir Robin caught up with them.

"My lads, well done! The King has high standards for knighthood. I was in the second wave and thought I would be recovering bodies, but you held! The sight of you two on top of that rubble heap holding back the tide…Well done, indeed!"

Both boys blushed a bit at this praise.

"I did not know what else to do, but call for a shield wall," Roland said sheepishly. "It just came to me."

At this, Sir Robin laughed heartily.

"Spoken like a true Dane!" The young knight then turned serious.

"One word of warning, Sir Knights—the King does not grant favours without expecting something in return. Mark it. He has something in mind for you two."

***

For six weeks the Crusader army rested and refitted after the fall of the city. In that time, Sir Robin's words were half forgotten, but then a summons came for Sir Roland and Sir Declan to attend the King at the palace. Sir Roger was not included in the summons and was not happy.

"He's up to something, lads. I don't like it. But like it or not, he is the King, so get yerselves there and keep yer heads about ye."

Roland and Declan made their way to the royal palace in the heart of the conquered city and were taken to a room that had books and scrolls scattered across a massive table. They waited. An hour later, King Richard arrived, trailed by several high-ranking nobles, all in animated conversation. When he saw the two young knights, the King flung out his arms and embraced each of them warmly.

"Ahh…the heroes of the breach! My lords, mark these two well. I see great things ahead for them. A Dane and an Irishman! What will be next?" The great nobles laughed politely, but seemed little interested in the two young men dressed in worn and ragged garments. One sniffed and held a scarf to his nose. Richard paid them no attention.

"Lads, we are moving south down the coast to Jaffa, and soon. It's the nearest port to Jerusalem and I intend to take it forthwith. From Jaffa, it is but a six day march to Jerusalem. Saladin has withdrawn his army southward, but his patrols infest the high ground inland from the coastal road. He is screening us so that I will not know where he plans to strike. I cannot lead this army south into an ambush. I am sending you two to find out where the man has taken his army."

Both men stood mutely for a moment, not knowing how to respond to this task the King had set before them. Finally, Roland spoke.

"As you wish, your grace, but…we do not know this country well."

The King smiled until he heard tittering from the gathered nobles. With no warning, he turned on them, his face red.

"Which of you shall I send out among the heathens? Who wishes to take the place of one of these lads? Speak!"

None of the highborn men in the room met the King's gaze. They knew these two had been picked because they were of low rank and expendable, but the King, in his fury, could order any of them out. The silence in the room was deep.

"I didn't think so," Richard grunted in disgust and turned back to Roland and Declan.

"Of course you cannot know the way, but I will give you a guide who will get you through the Saracen patrols that hem us in. He knows the land between here and Jerusalem and can advise you on the best path to take. Sir Roland, I've heard that you once tracked a band of Welsh brigands across the border to their lair and entered their fortress unseen. That is the kind of skill this task requires. Once you learn where Saladin has gathered his strength, make your way back to me in haste. I intend to march south within the week."

"Yes, your grace." There was no other answer that could be given.

"You will meet the guide at the south gate at midnight. Godspeed to you both."

And that quickly, the audience with the King was over. A retainer motioned for the knights to follow him and they filed out of the room. Roland noticed that the King was still scowling at the noblemen as they left.

Sir Roger was not happy.

"Is this how he rewards men who held the breach on the walls of Acre? He may be King, but he is a schemer!" The knight spoke the word through clinched teeth. "*Schemer,*" he hissed again, and it was as close to a curse as the man could hurl toward his King. "I cannot have you two out alone among the enemy. I will go with you!"

Roland sighed and looked at Declan.

"My lord, we may now be knights, but we are your men to command, as always."

The big man nodded.

"But you cannot come with us."

Sir Roger started to object, but Roland continued.

"My lord, there are none better than Sir Roger de Laval in a fight, but we are not seeking a fight. We must go unseen behind the lines of the enemy, and you, my lord, are not a man likely to go unnoticed."

The master of Shipbrook started once more to object, but shook his head.

"You are right on that count. But know that if you two do not come back, Catherine will blame me."

"Well, we can't have that, my lord. So expect us back."

The Fall of Chester

Millicent de Laval sat in her quarters clenching and unclenching her hands. She had always been headstrong, but now she agonized over what action she should take. Lady Constance had committed treason. Of that there was no doubt. Malachy, the priest—if priest he was—had the parchment and she assumed it would soon be sent by messenger to Paris. Or the priest would take it himself. God only knew what horrors this would set in motion. Whatever Malachy's assurances, people would die, and those most likely to die were Lady Constance and her young son—not to mention Earl Ranulf. But something in this line of reasoning troubled her.

If Malachy was acting as an agent of the French king to offer his support to Lady Constance and her son, the logical step would be to spirit her away to the continent where she would be under Philip's protection. Leaving the woman in Chester would expose her to the wrath of King Richard, or more near at hand, Prince John—or even the Queen. Then there was the matter of the priest inspecting the defences of Chester. To what purpose was that?

She was missing something, but what?

It had been a day since she overheard Malachy suborn treason in Lady Constance's chambers, but neither he nor the lady had done the logical thing and fled. The Earl had not returned from his hunting lodge, which was almost a day's ride from Chester, and dusk was approaching. She considered finding a horse and flying there as fast as it would take her, but

162

the sudden clatter of many hooves on the cobblestones of the courtyard below cut her short. She ran from her room to a small window nearby that looked down on the inner keep. It was the Earl.

Now what?

The man barely knew she existed and a simple request for a private audience would raise more questions than she wished to answer. She needed an excuse to speak to the Earl alone, for this dreadful news could not be spoken of to any but him. Then it struck her. Earl Ranulf had been close to her father when he was younger and had always maintained a respectful regard for Sir Roger de Laval. She would trade on her father's name and hope it would be enough. It would have to be.

The girl took a moment to compose herself, then hurried from her room to intercept the Earl before he reached his own quarters. Surrounded by a large retinue, Ranulf, Earl of Chester, entered the main keep slapping his sleeves with his hat, the dust from the ride leaving small clouds in his wake. It was not an opportune time to make an entreaty. He would be anxious to change from his hunting clothes and perhaps even take a bath. He would not likely to be patient with interruptions, but she had to act.

As he reached the top of the stairs, she stepped forward and curtsied, blocking his path.

"My lord, forgive me for intruding."

The Earl looked startled by her approach. He recognized the girl, barely, and would have put her off, but something in her manner stopped him. Sir Charles Abernathy, one of his retainers, stepped forward.

"Girl, the Earl is tired. Speak with him later!"

Ranulf raised his hand and silenced the man.

"You are, I believe, the daughter of de Laval, are you not?"

"I am, my lord, and I come to you with an urgent message from my father." She spoke, but kept her eyes respectfully cast down.

"Urgent? How could it be urgent when he is halfway around the world, my dear?" Several of the party that gathered below the Earl on the stairway snickered, but he silenced them once more with his hand.

"My lord, it was urgent enough for him to send it by ship from Sicily a month ago, and I do not think the urgency has diminished in that time." She had no idea if her father had ever been in Sicily, but she couldn't be concerned with that now. She had to get this information to the Earl in private.

"I received it this very day and was instructed by the messenger to deliver it to you only."

"Well give it to me then and I will judge if it is urgent enough to interrupt my bath!" Once more, the Earl's retainers began to laugh.

Lickspittles, the girl thought. She lifted her eyes and met the Earl's gaze.

"My lord, the message was not in writing. It was my father's wish that I should tell it to you in private."

The Earl was clearly annoyed, but again, something in the girl's face—an appeal in her eyes—made him hesitate to dismiss her.

"Well, all right then," he said, the irritation clear in his voice. "Let's get on with it so I can soak before dinner." He turned to the men who had gathered around him.

"Off with you. You are a dusty lot and I'll expect you cleaned up before we sup." He turned and headed toward his quarters.

"Follow me girl."

Millicent trailed behind. As they entered the Earl's chambers, one of his men-at-arms took up station outside the door. The Earl threw his dusty cap on a bench and turned toward her.

"Now what is this urgent message from your father—and be quick about it!"

Millicent took a deep breath.

"My lord, it was a lie. I have no message from my father. Forgive me, but I do have information of the greatest urgency."

"Lie...you lied? You have some nerve, young lady. I shall not have liars in my household." He turned as if to summon his guard.

"My lord, *please*! Hear me out. After, you may do what you will with me. But there is treason afoot and you are in grave danger."

"Treason? What nonsense is this? Speak girl, but tread carefully. There is no treason here at Chester!"

"My lord, there is." And the story came out in a rush.

"The priest…that counsels your wife. I believe him to be an agent of the French king. He has convinced Lady Constance to sign a letter to King Philip begging his aid on behalf of her son. She asks the French to threaten King Richard's domains in France to force him to name Arthur as his heir."

Earl Ranulf seemed stunned by her tale.

"Constance? Constance has sent a letter to the King of France? How do you know this?"

"My lord I overheard Malachy convincing the Lady that her son needed King Philip's protection. Do not ask me how—it is not important. She agreed to sign. That document is now in the hands of the priest. It is proof of your wife's treason and you will be suspect as well. He must be seized and that message retrieved." She finished, breathless.

The Earl sat down on the nearest bench and looked at Millicent. She could tell in an instant that he did not believe her.

"Girl, you have a remarkable imagination. If you heard anything, you have misunderstood it. And I'm troubled that you have been sneaking about here listening in on the conversations of your betters. This is all nonsense and you are lucky that I hold your father in high esteem or the consequences of your childish intrigues would be much worse. You will return to Shipbrook tomorrow. Now get out!"

She knew she was beaten. This had been her best, her only chance of stopping something frightful from happening to this man. And if he should fall, would the house of de Laval stand? She shivered in fear and frustration. The Earl was glaring at her. She gave a quick curtsy and turned to leave. Before she reached the door, a new clatter arose from the courtyard outside the Earl's window. They both stopped to stare. It grew louder and now there were shouts and the sound of steel on steel.

What now? Her banishment forgotten for the moment, they both rushed to the windows and looked down at a scene of violence and chaos. Men were striking at each other with swords and lances. A large group of mounted knights were overwhelming the household guard.

"What in God's name..." the Earl began. The chaos subsided as the intruders finished subduing the few remaining men-at-arms. In the quiet that followed, a tall man in a black robe hurried into the courtyard and could be seen speaking to a knight mounted on a pale white charger. After a short exchange, Father Malachy withdrew a roll of parchment from his robe and handed it to the man, who was clearly the leader of the band. He removed his helmet.

"De Ferrers!" Earl Ranulf croaked out the name, almost strangling with shock and rage. "What is the meaning of *this*?"

Millicent did not know. She had heard nothing of the nobleman from Derbyshire since her return from London. How he was connected to Malachy and why the message for the French king was being placed in his hands was a mystery. She must dwell on these questions later. For now, a party of armed men were dismounting and heading for the entrance to the keep.

"My lord, I think they mean to arrest you and your lady. We must flee."

"Flee?" The young Earl looked confused. "I have done nothing!"

"Aye lord, but those men mean you ill and if you are silenced, who will defend you?" She could tell that her words were starting to get through to the man, but still he hesitated.

"Where shall I flee to?" Millicent at least knew the answer to that question.

"We shall go to Shipbrook, but we must go now!"

"Of course, you are right." He grabbed his dusty hat, jammed it down on his head and started for the door. The guard had already rushed to the first floor to defend the keep and Millicent prayed that what was left of the Earl's men could delay de Ferrers' troops from reaching this floor. She grabbed Earl Ranulf's arm as he started down the hall.

"This way, my lord." She found the hidden latch to the panel and slid it aside. The Earl's Backdoor would be their escape route. She lifted a small torch from its holder in the hall and led the Earl into the passage, closing the panel after them.

"I haven't been in this place since I was a boy," the Earl whispered as they made their way toward Lady Constance's chambers. Millicent turned and put her finger to her lips and the Earl nodded. They continued in silence. Beyond the wall to their left they could hear the sound of men rushing up the stairs and on toward the Earl's chambers. Soon muffled shouts could be heard as the room was found to be empty.

By then they had reached the panel at the far end of the passage. Millicent flipped the hidden latch and slid the panel aside. She heard a gasp as she entered the room followed by the Earl. Lady Constance stood there looking at them as though two ghosts had materialized out of the air.

"My lord...What is the meaning...?" Earl Ranulf silenced her with a look of fury Millicent had never seen on his face.

"Constance, you stupid cow! What have you done? You have ruined us!"

For a moment, the Earl's wife looked dumbfounded.

"What do you mean...ruined?"

"You've signed a document that is proof of treason, woman! It is even now in the hands of our enemies."

Slowly comprehension began to dawn on the woman's face.

"But, my lord...my son..."

"Your son is but three years of age and is a pawn between Richard and Philip. You have no idea what you are doing. You have played a dangerous game and now we are the losers. Those men outside are coming for us now."

As the Earl spoke, the sounds of the search were drawing nearer. Millicent spoke up.

"My lord, there is no time for sorting this out. De Ferres has his men searching for you. We must flee." Millicent gave Constance a hard look. It was time to lie.

"We must get to London, my lord, to seek help from the Queen." The Earl seemed to grasp what the girl was doing.

"Yes, to London, but how?"

"Follow me, my lord." As they started for the door, Lady Constance began to wail.

"Ranulf...what of me? You can't leave me..."

"I can and I will. You have made your bed. And Constance...you have been a poor wife to me. Good luck with de Ferrers!"

He turned and followed Millicent out the door after she had carefully checked that the hallway was clear for the moment. Her many forays through the back ways of the castle paid handsomely now as she took little-used stairs down to the kitchen and out the scullery. There was a narrow passage from the keep that led to the top of the city walls and she led the Earl there. As they hurried along the wall, crouching to avoid being seen from below, Millicent outlined her plan.

"My lord, unless I miss my guess de Ferrers will have all gates guarded. We will have to go another way."

"What other way is there?"

"The Dee, my lord. We must get to the river."

***

William de Ferrers was furious. He had the town. He had the castle. He had a wailing Lady Constance. But no Earl Ranulf! He couldn't imagine how the man had slipped through his cordon at the castle. But then Lady Constance, gibbering in fright, had said that he had been led away by one of her ladies-in-waiting.

"Lady-in-waiting?" Sir William snarled. "What lady-in-waiting?"

"It...was...was...the new one...Lady Millicent," the woman managed.

The de Laval girl! The insults to his person by the de Laval family seemed to have no end! He would have them all dead!

"Malachy! You know this pest hole, find the Earl before he leaves the city—and the girl. I want them before dark!"

"They are going...to London, my lord," offered a sobbing Lady Constance. "I heard the girl say... to see the Queen..."

"Post sentries on the road to London—and the road west," de Ferrers ordered. "That damned girl may try to reach her keep on the frontier."

168

Lady Constance, still weeping, turned to the priest. "Father, why have you done this? I trusted you!"

The priest smiled sweetly at her.

"You placed your trust unwisely, my lady." The distraught woman flinched, as though struck. She turned to William de Ferrers.

"Sir William, what will become of me?" De Ferrers gave her a sunny smile.

"Why I expect they will cut off your head, my lady. It is what we do with traitors."

In the Midst of the Foe

It was midnight when Roland and Declan found their way to the south gate of the fortress of Acre. Each carried a few days' rations in a bag and a water skin. Both of the newly-made knights had a short sword and Roland slung his longbow and a quiver over his shoulder. They must avoid a fight, but would not go unarmed. They had heard tales that there were other things besides Saladin's men in those dark brown hills to the east that could kill. Each left their personal possessions in the care of Sir Roger.

A man dressed in long robes met them at the gate. He looked every inch a Saracen and held the bridles of three horses. In the flickering light of a torch, Roland could see a square jaw framed by a coal-black beard, but little else of the man's countenance.

"My lords, I am Ibrahim. I am an Arab by birth and a Christian by conversion. I have been ordered to get you through the screen of patrols in the hills to the east and set you on the right path. Put these on." He handed each of the knights a robe much like his own. They pulled the garments over their heads and each took a bridle of one of the horses.

"Ibrahim, I am Roland Inness and this is Declan O'Duinne. What is your plan?"

"Sirs, I know who you are. I was in the second wave at the breach. It is my honour to do you this service. But you must listen carefully to what I propose, for if we are caught, our heads will be forfeit!"

"I am all ears," offered Declan.

The man doused the only torch that illuminated the gate house at the south wall.

"We will lead the horses out on foot. There is a ravine just outside of our old earthworks that leads back into the hills. A week ago, we could not have gone a thousand paces before we were discovered, but I have been watching. The army of Saladin is gone. He has left only a few patrols to keep watch and they cannot be everywhere. I believe we can slip into the hills and once there, we mount and ride openly for a time, as though we ourselves are a patrol. When we are well past the screen around the city, I will go no further. It is your task to find their army."

Roland listened carefully to Ibrahim's plan. It was simple. Simple was always best.

"Lead the way, Ibrahim, and we will follow…and may God go with us."

"Amen," he heard the man mutter.

Penetrating the thin screen of cavalry that kept watch on the Christian army proved easier than Roland had feared. They reached the ravine without being challenged and saw no sign of patrols until they mounted and rode out onto a high ridge. Off to the south and farther to the north, campfires could be seen. Their enemies clearly did not expect any major movement of the Crusader forces in darkness and were taking that time to rest themselves and their horses.

For an hour, they rode east, higher into the hills. Even in the dark, Roland could see that the land was continuing to rise as they passed through broad valleys with hills growing higher on each side. When all chance of discovery by the patrols was past, Ibrahim signalled a halt and reined in his mount.

"This is as far as I will go, sirs. I encourage you to ride only at night and conceal yourself during the day. Even with your robes, you will arouse curiosity if any see you. Better to travel in the dark when all are seeking their beds."

Roland looked at Declan and could see him nod agreement. This plan made sense.

"Ibrahim, the King believes Saladin is withdrawing toward Jerusalem. What roads lead in that direction?"

"Sirs, many roads lead south to Jerusalem. If you were an Arab, you could reach the Holy City in four days following the most direct roads, but to approach the city from the north or west you will be riding through the places that Saladin will likely be marshalling his forces. Wearing dirty robes will not be enough to let you pass through there unchallenged."

"If you had this task, Ibrahim, how would you do it?" Declan asked.

"Sir, I would come from an unexpected direction—from the east where they will not be watching. Sir, you should ride directly east to the Sea of Galilee. When you can see it from a distance, you have gone far enough. You must then turn back southwest to come upon the enemy from behind. It will be roundabout and still dangerous, but better than being caught between the patrols and the army."

Roland turned to Declan.

"Dec, this plan seems sound to me, but we will be hard pressed to find Saladin's army and get back to Acre before the King marches. What do you think?"

Declan rubbed his chin for a moment.

"I think his plan may be the only one that makes sense. We would be stopped on the main roads leading to Jerusalem and, while I can talk my way out of most things, I cannot do it in their heathen tongue. Uh…beggin' yer pardon, Ibrahim."

In the dark, he could not see the face of their guide, who remained silent.

"I see no profit in goin' straight in. Ibrahim's way is round about, but it's the best chance of keeping our heads attached to our shoulders. Besides—I fancy seeing the Sea of Galilee."

Ibrahim gave a small grunt.

"There are Christians that still dwell near the Sea. Perhaps you could be baptized in the Jordon which flows south from there. I was—as were many other heathens."

Declan smiled. "Well said, Ibrahim. I deserved that. But I was baptized in the River Finn back in Ireland, and that was good enough for me!"

"Ibrahim, we are in your debt," Roland said. "I ask you to find Sir Roger de Laval and let him know what our plan is and that you saw us safely through the enemy lines. And, Ibrahim, tell him we will stay together and not do anything stupid. Tell him that."

"It shall be done, sirs, and may God watch over you."

"And you."

Then he was gone—back toward Acre and out of sight in the darkness.

Declan pulled his mount up close to Roland.

"So which way is east?"

Roland grinned. His Irish friend was not used to navigating in the dark. He looked over his left shoulder and found the North Star where his father had taught him to look. It seemed odd that it would still point the way for him so far from home, but there it was. If north was left, then east was straight ahead. He leaned over and spoke to his friend.

"Remind me to teach you about the stars, Sir Declan, but follow me for now. We have much ground to cover before dawn."

***

For the rest of that night and the next, they rode hard to the east. Through broad valleys and narrow passes they rode unseen, hiding in a remote thicket in the hills during the day and circling around the few villages they encountered at night. On the second night, with dawn still hours away, they came to a broad plain rising toward the east. Ahead, two small peaks could be seen framing the road they travelled. Roland signalled a halt.

"I smell water."

Declan sniffed the air.

"Yes, there is water ahead I think. Could it be the Sea of Galilee? That would be a story to tell!"

Roland kicked his horse in the flanks and moved off at a trot. As they reached the saddle between the two hills he halted again. Far below, the moonlight shone off a huge expanse of water. It could only be the Sea of Galilee. He started forward, but pulled up sharply. He was no longer looking at the sea ahead, but gazed at the ground to his front.

"Declan, dear God, look at this." Declan reined in beside him and looked out over a huge field dotted with splashes of white that seemed to glow in the moonlight. It was a field covered in bones—the bones of horses and men.

"What is this?" Declan whispered, afraid that to speak too loudly might rouse the spirits of so many dead.

"Look at these hills, Dec. Tuck told us about this place." As he recalled the friar's tale, he could picture it in his mind. "The Christian army camped there behind us. Saladin's army spread out down the slope, blocking the road leading to the lake. The Christians were out of water and mad with thirst. Then the Saracens started brush fires that choked the men. In their desperation, they charged—again and again, but could not break through to the water. In the end they died in battle or were taken prisoner and, if they were Templars, beheaded. This place is Hattin," he gestured at the two low peaks, "and those are the horns."

For long minutes, the two young knights sat their horses and pictured the carnage that had happened here. Four years past, the Christian army had fought and died on this dusty plain. Now all that was left were the bones of the fallen. From here Saladin had marched to take Jerusalem and the fates had conspired to bring them to this same field.

Roland did not share his friend's belief in ghosts, but the field of Hattin gave him a chill in his bones. Declan broke the spell.

"It will be dawn soon. No cover here. We need to find a place to hide."

Roland grunted his agreement and spurred his horse off the road toward the south. They would ride until they found a place to conceal them through the day. The next night they would head southwest until they found the army that had left these bones to rot into the earth.

***

The land to the southwest was much the same as that they had covered over the past two nights. Rolling hills, some high and rocky, others covered with low scrub trees came one after another. They fell into a rhythm in their travels, riding swiftly along roads between the few villages, then dismounting and leading their mounts on goat trails around any place inhabited.

To their relief, they encountered no armed patrols. Saladin was focused on the coast and the Crusader army and was not wasting resources guarding areas in his rear that should have been secure.

As dawn approached on the seventh night of their journey, they topped a ridge and found what they had been sent to find. There, in a long valley that dropped away to the northwest, an army was gathered. Silently, the two dismounted and led their horses back down the reverse slope to concealment and crawled back to the top of the ridge.

The soft glow from banked fires that had burned low during the night stretched out of sight around a bend in the valley. White tents covered both sides of the defile and hundreds of horses milled about in pens. Even at this hour, some troops could be seen beginning their morning routine. This was Saladin's army and, from the looks of it, it had been swollen with fresh troops since his withdrawal from Acre.

"We need to get to cover before it's full light," Declan said.

"Somewhere we can keep a close watch," Roland agreed. They eased themselves back from the crest of the ridge and found a rock outcropping that offered visibility into the valley below as well as concealment. Thirty paces behind was a small stand of olive trees with a little grass for the horses that hadn't been cropped clean by the goats. Once their mounts were secure, they crawled back to the overlook and settled in to take shifts sleeping and watching the enemy.

For the next several hours, the army came to life. Everywhere preparations for battle were evident. Archers in long ranks practiced sending shaft after shaft into targets across a field. Horses were saddled, and mounted warriors wheeled and manoeuvred in intricate patterns under the command of their leaders. Infantry troops stood in line to have their swords and lances sharpened at an armourer's wheel. More significantly, tents all over the valley were being struck and piled into a long line of carts. This was an army preparing to move—an army marching to battle.

After a time, Roland edged back from their lookout and motioned Declan to follow. When they had crawled back to the safety of the trees, Roland assessed what they had seen.

"Saladin has been reinforced. If he had an army like this six months ago, he would have swept us from Acre and into the sea." Declan nodded.

"They are moving—and not toward Jerusalem. They will be in position to attack with our army on the move. It's what the King feared."

"Aye, the King must know of this and quickly. He could be on the march south by now. If Saladin strikes with our army strung out along the coast road…" He did not need to finish the thought

Declan grunted. "It could be another Hattin."

They had seen enough. It was time to go. In the thicket of trees they waited for nightfall and considered their plans.

"Back the way we came?" asked Declan.

Roland shook his head.

"That way could take us at least five nights and by then it might be too late. Besides, we will not know exactly where either army will be by the time we get back to the coast."

"Then what shall we do?"

Roland was silent for a long moment.

"Saladin has scouts. They will know where our army is and will be leading their own in that direction. We must shadow them until we get near the coast, then try to slip through their lines. It's the only way to reach the King before the trap is sprung. We must go west."

Declan sighed and nodded.

"Like it or not, west it must be."

Roland smiled. One thing his Irish friend was not, was faint of heart.

"At full dark, we go."

***

As the day progressed, the army in the valley finished breaking camp, shook itself out into a thick column of march, and gradually moved off until only supply wagons remained in the valley. When the last hint of twilight faded, Roland and

Declan left behind the grove of olive trees to begin their own journey to the sea.

Moving as silently as possible, they headed down the ridgeline that followed the valley to the northwest. As they moved, Roland noted that there was no glow in the sky ahead of them. Their enemy was making a cold camp for the night to conceal their location from any who might be watching. They were unaware of the two Crusader knights who moved quietly along the ridgeline above them.

Traveling at night was difficult and slow, but before the first hint of dawn appeared in the east they were well beyond the leading units of Saladin's main force. Ahead, there would be an advance guard of cavalry scouting the army's path to the coast, which could not be far.

Getting through that screen would be much more difficult than shadowing the main force from afar and no place would be entirely safe from discovery. The two young knights led their mounts down the backside of the ridge as the sky grew lighter. There they found a small spring that was sufficient to refresh their horses.

Roland leaned against a gnarled tree trunk as he watched the horses drink. He was exhausted and could see by the dull look in Declan's eyes that the Irishman was as tired as he. They were covered with the accumulated dust and grime of hard riding in strange country and had long since run out of the rations they carried. There had been nothing to eat for two days.

"The coast must be near I think," Declan said as he splashed a handful of spring water on his lined face. Roland nodded, almost too tired to speak.

"I have been figuring the distances in my head. I think the sea is less than a day's ride from here. With luck we can make it through the patrols and reach the coast by dawn. I will be able to tell if our army has passed or not. If the tracks are there, we ride south. If no tracks, we turn north."

"Either way," Declan said, "I'm ready to be back among our own. You are more born to this 'scouting' business than I!"

As the sun rose further, they led their horses further back into the trees away from the spring. Such a place could attract visitors and they did not want to be discovered in daylight. They settled down to wait until dark. The day seemed to last an eternity, but finally the sun dipped below the ridge and shadows began to thicken. As they readied their horses, Roland spoke.

"We go on foot and lead the horses until we are well clear of close-in patrols around the army. Then we mount and ride west as if we own this land. Perhaps these filthy robes will be convincing from a distance, but if we are challenged, we must split up and run. One of us must get through. Agreed?"

As Roland moved to untie his mount, Declan grasped his arm.

"I'm glad we found you on the road to York, you dog-eatin' Dane. You are a true friend. Don't let the Saracens catch you!" Declan O'Duinne, like most Irish, was not given to hiding his emotions. Roland had a lump in his own throat.

"As I recall, I found *you* on the road to York and you almost skewered me. For all that, you are my true friend. May God help us both get through."

In single file, they led the horses out of the trees and onto the goat path that ran along the ridge.

Capture

Two dark figures moved quietly along a narrow path high on a ridge overlooking the valley below. A bright moon was rising over the horizon, its light so strong it cast a faint shadow that followed them as they trudged along. It made finding their way easy, but Roland wished fervently that there was no moon this night—of all nights. In this moonlight he felt exposed to any eyes that might be watching.

For two hours they walked. In the valley below, there were glimpses of small groups of riders, but with no fires in the enemy camp, it was hard to tell if they were merely local patrols near the army or the advanced scouts probing toward the coast. It was time to mount and ride. If they waited longer, they could not get clear of the enemy cavalry before dawn came again.

Wearily they climbed into the saddle and clucked to their tough little mounts. In the light of the full moon, the horses had no trouble finding their way along the twisting paths in the high ground, but in time, the long ridgeline ended and the trail west led down into a confusing set of hills and valleys bathed in the soft glow from above. Nothing could be seen moving below as they eased down the slope.

Reaching the bottom, they came upon a wide road. It was covered in a fine dust that gleamed like silver in the moonlight. The road headed west, but forked just ahead where the valley was cleft by another ridge. One branch led southwest and one more directly west. Keeping their horses to the flanks of the road, they considered which branch to take. Perhaps it was his imagination, but Roland thought he caught a faint scent of salt on the air. *So close.*

Then there was no longer time to ponder. Both riders turned in their saddles at the same time to the rumble of hooves on the road behind them. A large mounted patrol came around a bend not a quarter of a mile behind them. The riders were coming fast, but did not shout out alarms when they saw the two mounted men stopped by the road ahead. Perhaps they thought the two were from another patrol, but Roland did not hesitate. In a few moments the riders would be on them and any pretence would be futile. They had to run.

"We split now, Declan," Roland shouted. "Take the right fork and ride like the devil. I'll see you at the sea!" With that, both men dug their heels into the flanks of their horses and tore down the centre of the shining road. No alarm needed to sound nor any command given when the two riders broke into a gallop. The men in the patrol instantly spurred their mounts in hot pursuit.

As the road forked, Roland tugged his reins to the left and took the branch that headed southwest. He caught a final glimpse of Declan, his body low over his horse's neck, flying down the other road before he was lost behind the ridgeline. His friend had the Irish way with horses, and he prayed that skill would get him through.

His own horse was game, despite the miles it had travelled and the poor rations it had survived on the past few days. As the road twisted through the serpentine valley, Roland couldn't tell if his pursuers were gaining or falling back, the drumming of his horse's hooves masking any sound from behind.

Ahead, the valley seemed to be broadening and once more he sensed a touch of sea air in the wind rushing by him. He chanced a quick look over his shoulder and saw that the riders were still there, though no closer. When he turned back, his heart sank. Armed riders blocked the road ahead.

He reined in his horse and looked frantically for some way out of the trap, but the sides of the valley were far too steep for a horse and rider to manage. He leapt off onto the fringe of the road and reached for the longbow that was still slung over his shoulder.

I'll not go down without a fight.

The horse skittered away and with it his quiver of arrows. He dropped his bow and was reaching for his sword when his head exploded in a bright flash of sparks that faded into darkness.

The leader of the patrol dismounted and looked at the crumpled man on the ground. He had hit him with the flat of his sword. The general was always pleased with captives and he hoped he had not killed this one. He nudged him with a boot and got a groan in return. The leader smiled and called one of his men forward.

"Throw him over a horse and take him to the General." As the man moved to obey, the leader reached down and picked up the bow from the dust of the road. It was of an odd design. "And take this with you," he said, tossing the longbow to his man.

***

Roland opened his eyes and the sunlight seemed to cut like a blade through his head. He groaned and tried to inspect the damage to his skull, but his hands were tied behind him. His mouth was gritty with sand and his lips were cracked and swollen. He lay on his side outside a white tent. When he tried to sit up, the pain in his head returned with a vengeance and he lay back down.

"You...wake up. Wake up!"

Someone was speaking to him in broken English. He opened his eyes again, just as a man kicked him in the ribs. He gritted his teeth and tried not to cry out. Rough hands grabbed him and pulled him upright just as a short but commanding-looking man came through the flap of the tent. His face was round and his features would appear jovial if not for fierce dark eyes set very deep beneath his brow. His robes were of the finest fabrics and the sword at his belt looked well used and well cared for. There was no mistaking a man born to command. He turned to the man who had kicked Roland and spoke calmly in Arabic.

"He ask if you English," the man translated.

Roland nodded. "Aye, lord—English."

The commander nodded and spoke a single word of inquiry to his interpreter.

"Spy?"

Roland shook his head. "Scout, lord, like your own men who caught me." His voice was barely a croak. The commander smiled when the reply was translated and spoke at some length. He then turned and reached back inside the tent flap as the interpreter spoke.

"He say, you not very excellent scout. You…captured."

As the man spoke, Roland saw that the commander had retrieved his longbow from the tent. He turned it over in his hands and spoke through his interpreter.

"I have seen this weapon—at Acre. You are archer?"

"Aye, lord."

The commander nodded before he heard the translation of Roland's answer—as though he had already made a decision.

He gave crisp instructions to his man and handed him the longbow. The man used it to prod his captive toward a string of horses tethered near the tent. Roland did not understand what the commander's orders had been, but he had heard him speak a name that filled him with dread—Salah al-Din—*Saladin*.

***

It was dawn when a lone rider emerged from low hills onto the coastal plain. The horse he rode stumbled and nearly fell, worn out from hard use. The rider dismounted, and led the exhausted beast to a small stream where they both drank greedily until the rider pulled the horse away.

"Not too much, me lovely," the man whispered.

He led his mount across a dusty landscape covered with small bushes and patchy grass. He allowed it to graze for a bit then pressed on. In time he came to the sea and looked north and south. There was no evidence that an army had passed this way. He looked south where other valleys opened onto the plain. His companion would come from that direction if he had won through to the coast. For a long time he stood watching and waiting, but nothing moved to the south. He shook his head.

Declan O'Duinne turned north and began to walk.

* * *

Roland's hands were retied in front before he was ordered to mount the horse. Once in the saddle, a rope was snaked beneath the horse's belly and tied to each of his ankles. There could be no sudden leap for freedom with him thus bound. The man who received the commander's orders grasped the pony's reins and led them through the camp.

As they rode, Roland wondered at the fate of Declan. He had not seen his companion in the Saracen camp. He prayed to God that his Irish friend had made good his escape. He tried to not think on the alternatives.

The roads were jammed with troops and the going was slow, but after several hours they passed beyond the rear guard of the army and reached an open road. With his hands bound in front, Roland was able to examine his injured head. There was an impressive knot and some crusted blood in his hair, but it seemed his skull had withstood the blow from the scimitar.

For two long days, they travelled swiftly along roads that were mostly empty, save for the occasional courier carrying messages from the army back toward Jerusalem. Five times each day, his captor halted, laid out a small mat and prayed, bowing and rising while reciting in Arabic. During those times, Roland was pulled from the horse and securely bound to whatever was at hand.

Twice each day, the man gave him some flat bread to eat from his own bag of provisions and, blessedly, water, which he gulped down. The liquid seemed to restore some of his strength and he watched carefully for opportunities to escape, but his guard was ever watchful, even during his prayers.

Near the end of the second day, they began to pass through villages where the inhabitants gawked at the man tied to the horse. As the sun was setting, they came to a broad valley that rose to a rolling highland. On those heights was a walled city. It could be no other—Jerusalem—the object of so much longing and bloodshed.

Roland studied the place as they drew nearer. The highest point within the walls was capped by a magnificent temple with a striking dome. Roland wondered if this was the Temple of Solomon that some of the Crusaders had told him of, or some shrine built by the Muslims. Somewhere in the maze of streets below that hill was the Church of the Holy Sepulchre, built over the tomb where Jesus had lain awaiting resurrection. It was a holy city indeed.

At the opposite end of the city, higher walls and towers marked what had to be a citadel of some sort. His captor seemed to be headed in that direction. As they rode on, he noticed that atop the city walls an army of labourers were hard at work repairing damage to the defences. At the base of the wall, another huge throng was digging out the dry moat that kept siege engines at bay.

Among the thousands who laboured were many with ragged tunics that still showed the cross—perhaps prisoners taken when the city fell to Saladin. Whoever commanded at Jerusalem was leaving nothing to chance with a Crusader army approaching.

His year before the walls of Acre had taught Roland much about the strength of fortifications and his heart sank at the sight of Jerusalem. These walls looked thicker and taller than those at Acre, and an army of slave labour was making them stronger still. To even launch an assault, King Richard would have to fight his way through the army he had so recently spied upon and would then face the task of breaching these walls or starving out the city.

He knew the King wanted this final victory badly. He had staked his warrior's reputation on it—and would not care what the butcher's bill might be to have it. But the King's iron will could not change the reality of what he was seeing.

This place will never be ours.

The realization hit him hard. Regaining Jerusalem was the whole purpose of all this effort, all this blood. A part of him grasped why men would be moved to fight and die to possess this land, but he had been at Acre. He had seen Hattin. Possession of this holy land now seemed more a curse to him than a blessing.

As night fell, they made their way through increasingly crowded streets to an arched gate in the north wall. A few blocks into the city, they came to another archway that led to the high citadel he had seen from afar. His captor halted in a courtyard and gave curt instructions to two soldiers who untied Roland's ankles and dragged him from the horse. One man grasped each of his arms and pulled him through a narrow door into a gloomy hallway and then down a series of stone steps.

A jailer rose from a bench and seemed to take a mental inventory of his cell space before opening one of the heavy wooden doors and motioning to the two men. Without a word, they shoved him inside. The door slammed shut and a bolt was slid into place with a clank of finality.

Inside was near complete darkness, but Roland could hear others stirring in the gloom. His eyes slowly adjusted, but he started when he felt a gentle tap on his shoulder. He turned quickly and could just make out the shape of a tall thin man with a long beard standing before him.

"I am Sir Harry Percival," a voice came out of the darkness, "and who are you?"

Roland could not believe he was hearing English spoken in this god-forsaken place.

"Roland Inness…uh…Sir Roland Inness, my lord."

"English! God be praised!" The man clapped him on the shoulder and Roland thought for a moment he was going to wrap his arms around him. Then the old knight stepped back.

"Forgive me Sir Roland, I am not thanking God that you were captured—no, it's just that I've had no one to speak the mother tongue to since Sir Edward lost his wits. But please, tell what news of the outside? We know a Christian host must be near or they would not be working us to death repairing these walls!"

The man gently took Roland by the arm and led him across the cell to an unoccupied corner. In the dimness he saw almost a dozen other men curled up on the floor or leaning against the walls. He could understand the man's thirst for tidings from outside his prison and told him what he knew.

"Sir, Acre has fallen to us. I am not at liberty to say where King Richard will lead the army next."

"Ah, yes, quite right," the knight said, then pulled Roland close and whispered urgently in his ear. "These walls hear things. Can't let 'em know the plan!" The knight's hushed warning was followed by an odd cackling laugh that was cut short by a rasping cough. Roland instinctively recoiled a little.

This man is both sick and a bit mad.

The knight got control of his hacking cough and resumed speaking.

"We heard King Henry had passed on—great king Henry was—but Richard, now there is a man to make the mountains tremble! You know the Saracen mothers hereabout scare their children with tales of King Richard? They call him 'Melek Ric' and tell the little ones that he will get them if they misbehave! So our new King scares both young and old among the enemy!"

The older knight paused for a moment, but only to catch his breath.

"I have been a prisoner four years, Sir Roland—ever since the city fell to Saladin. I have waited long in these cells, but my prayers have finally been answered. Melek Rick will surely restore this city of God to us, praise the Lord."

Roland stayed silent. He did not have the heart to tell the man that deliverance would not come from the English king. Jerusalem was lost to them.

***

For ten days the Crusader host remained at Acre as King Richard fumed over delays in organizing the march south. None of the promised ransom from Saladin had been delivered, the Pisans were refusing to continue the campaign without higher wages, and the Germans had left in a huff.

And the French...oh, the French. Philip haggled with Richard over every item of plunder from the city and, once he had taken his pound of flesh, had the gall to announce that he was ill and returning to Paris! Richard was aghast. Ill? God's breath! Everyone in this pestilential land was ill. This was a trick! At their final meeting, Richard confronted his detested rival.

"You swore an oath, man, and now you leave after one battle? The Pope should excommunicate you as an oath-breaker!"

"Really, Richard? I? An oath-breaker? Shall we talk about your promise to marry my sister? Broken! Shall we dwell perhaps on the oaths of loyalty you took to your late lamented father? I think good King Henry would call you an oath-breaker—if you had not hounded him to his death!"

"Enough, you perfidious Frank! Go, if you must. We will triumph without you and have no need to share the glory. But mark me well, Philip—in Burgundy we pledged to meddle not with each other's lands and possessions while this Crusade was being fought. If I find you are trifling with my lands in Normandy, or Poitou, or anywhere on the continent, I will come for you. I will march into Paris and pursue you to the Rhine as need be! Mark it well, Philip!"

The King of France smiled.

"Why Richard, you should not get so choleric. Your lands are safe from me. I would never take advantage while you are engaged on God's work. And as for glory, you would grasp it all yourself—whether I stay or go. So I go. Bon chance on taking Jerusalem." The French monarch took his leave, with Richard muttering curses in his wake.

***

Outside the palace of the Templars that served as quarters for the King of France, servants and courtiers scurried about sorting and packing all of the things that would need to be loaded onto ships by morning so that their sovereign could sail for home at first light. The Bishop of Beauvais entered the King's chambers in haste and addressed Philip breathlessly.

"Your grace, a messenger has arrived from Paris. The news is promising. John's ambitions grow and our men are well placed to put much of the island in his hands." The Bishop handed the King the written report he had received just moments before from his second–in–command. Philip read it with interest.

"Richard worries about his lands in France, cousin. He does not realize the real danger is closer to home. With just the right nudge, the Midlands will rise for John and Richard will lose control of England itself." The King smiled. "Your men have exceeded all of my expectations, lord Bishop. Well done!"

***

At last the Crusader army was ready. With the loss of the Germans and most of the Frankish contingent, it was a diminished force that marched out through the gates of Acre. The army took the coastal road toward Jaffa, more than a hundred miles to the south.

Richard had the Templars as the advance guard, the English mounted knights following closely behind and the Hospitallers were his rear guard. Between came the small French contingent that Philip had left behind, the English foot, the Pisan crossbowmen and the supply carts.

The column assembled and moved out each day at dawn and marched until noon when it halted for a midday meal and to wait out the heat of the day. The march resumed late in the afternoon and continued until twilight. Richard had learned from King Guy's mistakes at Hattin. He would not have his army exhausted and thirsty when battle came.

With this routine, the army covered forty miles in the first three days of the march. With no delays, they would be at the gates of Jaffa in a week. But this progress did not go unobserved. From dawn until dusk, Saladin's scouts could be seen in the hills to the east. It served to remind the men that the enemy could strike at any time.

Given the order of march, Friar Tuck found it a simple thing to drift to the rear of the Templar ranks and take up company with Sir Roger and Sir Robin as the column trudged along. The missing young knights were the main topic of conversation and the fate of the two hung heavily on the minds of the three men.

"They're resourceful lads, Roger," Tuck offered. "They may have gone to ground for a bit. I shouldn't give up hope."

"Oh, I'll not give up hope, Father, but they are at least three days overdue. It cannot be good news. If they are lost, how will I face Catherine…or Millie ?"

No one had a reply that would comfort the Norman knight. For an hour they rode in silence, until a courier rode up to the group at a full gallop.

"Sir Roger de Laval—the King requests your presence!" Sir Roger looked at his companions, then laid his heels into the flanks of Bucephalus. Uninvited, Sir Robin and Tuck followed behind. When they reached the King's position, they saw that he had dismounted and was down on one knee. Sir Roger leapt from his saddle and hurried through the cluster of guards who surrounded Richard. There he saw the King bending over a man who lay on the sand. It was Declan O'Duinne.

He was alive, though in shockingly bad shape. His fair complexion was an angry red, with the skin peeling off in strips. The King was dribbling water from his own water skin into the young knight's mouth. After a bit he coughed and abruptly sat up.

"My horse died."

The King exchanged glances with Sir Roger.

"I've been walking. Need to get to the King. Warn him."

"You're here lad, tell me your warning," the King said gently.

Declan's eyes seemed to focus for the first time and he started when he saw the King leaning over him.

"Your grace, the Saracens…have a great host…they lay in wait, five days march south of here," he blurted. "I've come as quick as I could."

"You did well, Sir Declan. Praise God you survived to bring us this news. You may have saved the army."

Declan caught sight of Sir Roger and staggered to his feet. The King had to steady him. He looked at his master and asked the question his master wanted to ask him.

"Where is Roland?"

Saladin

The sharp clanging of metal announced a new dawn in the dungeons of Jerusalem. Roland awoke from a troubled sleep. There had been dreams of pursuit, close enough to reality to leave him breathing hard when he came awake. He looked around the dreary cell. A bit of morning light came through a tiny opening high on the east wall, and for the first time he got a better look at his fellow prisoners.

They were an odd lot. Several had the tattered remains of knightly garments, including the man who had engaged him the night before. Others appeared to be of more local origins.

Sir Harry was up and vigorously walking in place in one corner of the cell.

"Best to get the blood flowing first thing!" he declared.

Despite his manic energy, the man looked old and forlorn in the morning light. His beard hung to near his waist and was flecked with grey. His hair was a filthy tangle and the tunic he wore was so thin and faded that his sun-browned skin could be seen through it.

The door was flung open and his cell mates rose groaning and began to shuffle forward. Waiting outside were a half dozen heavily-armed guards. At the centre of the outer chamber was a bucket of foul water with a ladle that each man drank greedily from. Next to the bucket, a guard passed out a single piece of rank flat bread.

Roland drank along with the rest and forced down the mouldy bread. He was going to need all of his strength to survive this place. Sir Harry, who had gone just ahead of him in the line, nodded and smiled when he saw his new companion copying the rest of the men.

No time was allowed for lingering as the line of scarecrow prisoners was marched up the steps and into the courtyard of the citadel. There they stood blinking in the bright morning light as other prisoners flowed in from other parts of the citadel. Once all of the cells had been emptied, a curt command was issued and the entire group was herded out into the street. Sharp-eyed guards with spears made certain that no one got out of line, and several soldiers armed with crossbows were positioned to bring down any man who tried a dash for freedom.

It did not take long to reach their destination. A section of wall near the north gate had not been fully restored to its required height and skilled stone masons were overseeing the repair. The prisoners were sorted out into groups and began the back-breaking task of carrying stones from the street below to the top of the wall, there to be chiselled, mortared and placed by the masons. Along the way guards with whips stood by should any man falter.

Compared to the men who worked beside him, Roland was strong and healthy. His fellow prisoners, worn down by long days of toil and poor food, shuffled slowly forward with their loads, their faces a study in resignation.

Will I look like that in a year's time? The thought was chilling. He had expected to be questioned and then executed as a spy when they reached the city, but the prospect of endless captivity now seemed even more dreadful.

All through the morning the labour went on as the late August sun rose slowly, turning the exposed wall and the courtyard below into an oven. Men staggered in the heat, but feared to stop and draw the attention of the guards.

With each trip from the street below up the ramps to the wall, Roland studied his surroundings. At the top, as he unloaded his burden, he took a moment to look over the wall at the surrounding country. He did not know how or when, but he prayed a chance would come for him to escape this place. If it did, he would be ready.

On his return trip he carefully studied the streets below, but within the walls Jerusalem was a crowded tangle of buildings. He could not see more than a few hundred feet in any direction. No way to get the lay of things inside the walls of the city.

It was midafternoon when the monotonous repetition of the labour was interrupted by a messenger who handed a paper to the chief guard. The man looked around and pointed a finger at Roland, barking a command in Arabic. Two guards snatched him out of the line and hustled him back down the street toward the citadel.

When they passed through the archway into the courtyard, two additional guards took possession of him and stood waiting at the bottom of the stone steps that led up to the higher levels of the fortress. Roland steeled himself for whatever was to come. The wait wasn't long.

Two men, who by their dress were senior officers, came hurrying down the steps just as grooms appeared in the courtyard with horses. The officers mounted and gave a hand signal to the guards who bound Roland's hands in front and hoisted him up on one of the horses. One officer grabbed the reins and led the prisoner's mount out through the archway with the other man following behind. They rode the short distance to the northern gate before passing out of the city.

Are they taking me to be executed? The stray thought of the morning now took on a much more immediate importance. But why would they take the trouble of taking him out of the city to kill him? He would know soon enough. In the meantime, he searched in vain for an opportunity to escape.

The riders turned off the main road a mile from the gate and made for a rocky hillside. A shaded pavilion had been erected there and a large group of men clustered around it. The officer who had been in the rear now galloped ahead and reined in before the crowd, leaping from his horse in a fluid motion. Despite his fear, Roland could not help but admire the man's skill. *Good rider—but I've seen better.* The image of Millie de Laval on her bay mare, her hair flying behind her, had come unbidden to his mind.

His guard led Roland's mount to the front of the pavilion and, rather than wait to be dragged down from his horse, he swung his leg over and leapt nimbly to the ground. Hands went to the hilts of swords throughout the crowd at this display and his guard leapt down and cuffed him sharply. He staggered but did not go down. If they were going to behead him like a Templar, he would show them how an Englishman faced death.

"Khalass!" The command came from somewhere under the awning of the pavilion and the men around him froze. He watched as a man of middle years emerged from the shade. He was not large in stature, but his manner left no doubt that he was the senior man in this group. His bearing would have marked him as a leader in any group. The man made a gesture with his hand and guards dragged Roland forward. The Saracen leader spoke quietly to a man beside him who turned to the captive.

"You are an English archer?"

This was not what he had expected.

"Aye, I'm an English knight...and a bowman."

The translator repeated Roland's answer in his own tongue and waited for a response from his master. When it came, he gestured behind him, then spoke.

"The Sultan wants to know if this is your bow?" A man appeared holding his longbow. Roland nodded.

"Aye."

Hearing a defiant tone in the captive's voice, one of the officers who had delivered him stepped forward and struck Roland, knocking him to his knees. Then the Sultan spoke sharply and the man retreated. The interpreter spoke, and the words were his own.

"You are before the Sultan Salah al-Din. You must show respect!"

Roland looked up at the man who loomed over him. The lines around his eyes marked him as a man well beyond his youth, but his close-cropped black beard showed no grey. His face had a weary sadness to it, but his eyes shone with an intensity and intelligence he had only seen once before—in the eyes of his own King Richard. Something in those eyes spoke of both gentleness and an iron will. This was not a man that "Melek Ric" would frighten off.

"The Sultan has heard that this weapon can kill at a great distance—can penetrate armour. He wishes to see its power in the hands of one trained to it. You will show what this bow can do."

To his shock, Roland was handed his longbow as well as his own quiver of arrows, no doubt retrieved from his pony when he was captured. He stood and a guard stepped forward to cut his bonds. He chafed his wrists to restore the blood, then grasped the top of the bow and began to bend, securing it with the deft placement of ankle and calf. He leaned his weight onto it until he was able to slide the string over the notch.

As he reached down for his quiver, he caught motion out of the corner of his eye and saw half a dozen crossbowmen with their weapons trained on him. He realized that if he so much as turned in the direction of the Sultan they would cut him down in an instant. He straightened, but did not nock the arrow to the string. The interpreter spoke again.

"We have had our finest Parthian bowmen try this weapon. They complain that it is too crude and stiff and not accurate, but the Sultan has had reports to the contrary—from Acre. We have targets. You will show us."

For the first time, Roland noticed that the pavilion had been set on something of a plateau and that there was a long flat stretch along the ridgeline. Far down the way he saw men standing near a straw target. The distance was perhaps one hundred and fifty yards. Nearer, there was a pole driven into the ground. From it was hung a set of the scaled armour the Saracens favoured.

As he was gauging the task before him the crowd parted and a fierce looking man with billowing pantaloons and a peaked cap stepped forward. He was carrying the recurved bow used by the Parthian cavalry. The man nocked an arrow and, with hardly any effort to aim, loosed it at the target. It hit, dead centre. The Parthian archer's fierce expression did not change, but he gestured for Roland to follow suit.

Roland looked about him. Saladin had him fixed in an unblinking gaze. This was not a royal archery tournament with a golden arrow as a prize. He knew naught if to best the

Parthian would bring a reprieve or instant death. Taking up his arrow he drew the longbow and sighted.

Might as well show them what good English yew can do!

He let fly and his arrow landed within an inch of the Parthian's. Without hesitating, he motioned to the men down range to move the target back. They waited until they received a signal from the Parthian, then complied, moving the target another fifty yards out.

The Parthian stepped forward, wetted his finger to gauge the wind and elevated his recurve bow at a sharp angle. It was not enough. His shot was online, but fell thirty yards short. There was an anxious murmuring in the crowd, though the Parthian seemed unmoved.

Roland stepped forward and drew the bowstring back almost to his ear, gauged the distance and calmly sent his arrow into the centre of the target. While the crowd was still murmuring over this shot, he sorted through his quiver and took up a shaft with a bodkin head. Turning, he loosed it at the armour hanging on the pole about twenty yards away. With an audible ringing sound, the arrow pierced the armour and imbedded itself almost to the fletching.

Over his shoulder he heard the Parthian utter a curse, and there was an anxious buzz coming from the crowd. He turned and the crossbowmen tensed. A guard approached. Roland casually unstrung the bow and handed it to the man. Saladin broke the silence and spoke through his interpreter.

"How is such a bow made?"

"It cannot be made in this land, lord," Roland answered. "It is the yew that gives it its power, and you have no such wood in this country."

Saladin waited for his interpreter to translate and then nodded. He spoke once more.

"It is good that you cannot find the wood here to make more. We have seen what you can do with but a few of these bows at Acre. Your king was foolish to not bring more. Thanks be to Allah."

When the interpreter had finished, Saladin gestured and Roland's guard quickly stepped forward and rebound his hands.

The demonstration was done and the great Muslim general stepped back into the shade of the pavilion.

As they dragged Roland toward the horses, he looked back at the Parthian who was now holding his longbow. The man held it in a wide grip and brought it down with tremendous force across his knee. He was a powerful man, but the longbow did not break. The Parthian cursed and tried again, but the yew only gave a little and did not crack. In disgust, he threw it on the ground and walked away with an angry stride.

One of the men in the Sultan's party picked up the weapon from the dust and carried it away into the crowd of onlookers. At that moment Roland knew that whatever became of his longbow, he would not see it again. He could make others. There were four good yew staves curing back at Shipbrook, but this had been his first—the weapon his father had helped him fashion. That bow had changed the course of his life, for good and ill. It was lost to him now. It felt like a death.

And perhaps his own death was near. Would he be executed now that his demonstration of the longbow was done? It wasn't until he they reached the citadel and he was herded back into the narrow passageway that led to the dungeons that he knew the answer. He would live—for now. But what sort of life would this be?

Worse than death.

Flight to Shipbrook

Darkness fell over Chester as two figures hurried along the southern wall of the city. They crouched as they moved so that none below could see them silhouetted against the evening sky. In the streets of the city armed patrols were clearing the anxious crowds that had gathered. Here and there, knots of Earl Ranulf's men were being marched, under guard, to the castle. With remarkable ease, William de Ferrers had secured the greatest English city in the west of the country for himself. Throughout the town, his men sought the two people who now scurried along in the shadows.

"Where are you taking me?" hissed the Earl of Chester.

Millicent turned and whispered back.

"The gates are all held by de Ferrers men and they will have posted patrols on the road to London—if Lady Constance did as I expect. If she told them I was with you, which is likely, I fear they will be watching the road to Shipbrook as well."

"So we are trapped?"

"My lord, I hope they have not thought of the Dee. It flows from here right by my home and if we can secure a boat we could be there by morning. I know a way down to the Shipgate. There are many boats tied up there."

The Earl contemplated this plan and nodded.

"I used to fish on the Dee as a boy. I know how to handle a boat. How shall we procure one?"

Millicent looked at him as though he were a slow child.

"My lord, we *steal* one!"

"Ah, of course. That would be best," he agreed.

By now it was full dark, but Millicent could see patrols still searching for them by torchlight. In several places men had begun searching the city's walls and towers, and ahead she saw a large force stationed at the bridge over the Dee. The few travellers arriving at the city gates were being closely searched and no one was being allowed to leave.

The Shipgate where she was leading the Earl served the city merchants, traders and fishermen who plied the waters of the Dee. It opened onto a short canal that led from docks inside the walls to the river, just a bit downstream from the bridge. Thankfully so, for with de Ferrers' men occupying the bridge they would never get a boat past it. Even so, the canal from the Shipgate to the river was easily watched from there. They would have need of stealth and speed to make good their escape.

As she knew from her many scouting forays, the steps that led down to the primary docks of the Shipgate were inside the walls. When they reached the steps, she saw that someone had thought about this gate as a possible bolt hole. There were two guards lounging nearby keeping an eye on the narrow lanes that approached through the merchant storage houses to the water. Millicent had hoped it would not be watched, but was not surprised that it was. The Earl hung his head and his shoulders sagged.

"They have cut us off. It looks like the game is up."

Millicent turned to the man and tried to keep a snarl out of her voice.

"My lord, I have been troubled by the poor state of repair of your city walls, but now I am thankful that you neglected them. There are boats aplenty tied up outside the walls and I know a way to get there. Follow me!"

Millicent moved a few yards further along the wall walk to a place she had noted before. Here was one of the several crumbled sections of the wall. She picked her way down the broken stones and came to a six foot drop. Below was the top of a rubble pile sloping down into the dry moat.

"You are taller, my lord. I think it best you go first and help me."

Earl Ranulf seemed pleased to feel useful and nodded. Gingerly he sat on the ragged lip of the wall, planted his hands and lowered himself as far as he could before dropping the last few feet. He stumbled a bit on the broken stones, but quickly regained his footing and climbed back to the top of the pile.

"Come along, my dear. I'll catch you," he whispered.

Millicent sat on the edge of the wall and slipped over the side. The Earl caught her at the waist and eased her down beside him.

Not very ladylike, she mused.

As quietly as possible, they made their way down the slope and into a tangle of briars that had overgrown the moat. The barbs tore at their clothes, but neither seemed to notice as they moved toward the shabby piers that lined the canal outside the Shipgate. River men often secured their boats here to avoid the fees charged for docking within the walls. Above them, they could see torches approaching the spot where they had climbed down. They were still a step ahead of their pursuers.

Finally they reached the end of the tangle of growth that hid their movements. Ahead of them was a strip of bare trampled earth that marked the path watermen used to pass from the rickety looking piers through a narrow arched passage that flanked the wider arch of the Shipgate itself. Barely a hundred yards further loomed the bridge over the Dee with its guards and lookouts.

"My lord," Millicent whispered. "Can you swim?"

"Swim? No—why should I have to swim?"

"My lord, I expect there are archers on that bridge. If they see us, we will be in range. If we can get to a boat and cling to the gunwales, they will have a poor target to shoot for. The current in the canal isn't much, but the tide is falling in the estuary, so it is moving toward the river. Once we reach the Dee and are out of range, we can climb aboard. Can you do that?"

By now the ruler of Cheshire had given up any pretence of being in charge of events. He gave a sharp nod of his head.

"If I must, I can!"

Millicent studied the row of piers. A torch sputtered on each side of the Shipgate giving barely enough light to see. Some of the docks were empty. Some had large barges tied up. Off to the right she saw a small boat with oar locks tugging at the line that secured it to a pier that seemed ready to collapse from rot. She nudged the Earl and pointed to the boat. He nodded.

"We must move quickly and stay low. Enter the water carefully—no splashing. The boat is near shore. Just wade in and grab a gunwale. I will slip the line and push us into the canal. Ready?"

The Earl nodded once more and they slipped quietly out of the underbrush, creeping toward the canal. Millicent made for the rotting dock and began picking her way carefully out over the water to where the line secured the boat. Reaching it she untied the knot and, holding the boat steady, motioned for the Earl to slip into the canal. He started gingerly forward into the dark water.

"You there!" a shout came from above them on the bridge. "Halt!"

Millicent jumped off the edge of the dock and into the murky water. She could hear shouting from the bridge and from behind her as well. The guards who had been lounging around the inner docks were now alerted and coming their way. For a moment she felt panic as her soaked dress pulled her down, but she had secured a hard grip on the side of the craft after her plunge and she was able to keep her head above the dark water. A few feet away, the Earl struggled to make headway as the boat began to drift away.

"My lord, take my hand!" She stretched out as far as she could and the Earl lurched forward, fear in his eyes, as his feet lost the bottom. Millicent grabbed his wrist and pulled him beside her. Gasping, he clung to the side of the boat for dear life. The girl began to kick her legs furiously. Slowly the small boat gained momentum, but they were still fifty yards from where the canal entered the river.

Millicent could hear the thud of running feet along the barren path that ran along the canal. A spear landed in the water just behind them. Shouts were still coming from the bridge high above. She heard an evil buzzing sound as the first arrow flew overhead—uncomfortably close. A hail of shafts followed, striking the wooden deck of the boat with sickening *thunks*. Protected by its hull, they slid through the water.

At last she felt the nose of the craft begin to turn to the right and knew they were entering the northwesterly flow of the Dee. She began to kick her legs harder to drive the little boat further out into the main channel and away from any archers on the banks. Slowly the urgent shouts from de Ferrers' men faded away behind them.

"I think we can get out of the water now, my lord," she said, and managed to heave herself up and over the side of the boat. The Earl struggled a bit, but gave her a look of warning as she reached to help him. He had had his fill of helplessness for one night and managed to drag himself aboard.

Millicent scanned the banks ahead. A half-moon had risen behind them and visibility was good, which was a mixed blessing. She could see where they were going, but pursuers could see them as well—for pursued they would surely be. She expected that pursuit to be on land for she doubted de Ferrer's men would dare follow them in the dark down an unfamiliar river.

She knew forests grew right down to the river through here and later, marshy ground and reed beds limited access to the banks for anyone seeking them. There were a few places where farmers had cleared the land to allow their cattle to come down to drink. They would have to stay clear of any such places until they were almost to where the Dee emptied into its estuary. There was a final ford there. It was the place that Shipbrook had been built to watch over. There they could come ashore. There they would be safe.

She turned back to the Earl. He sat forlornly on a rough bench with his head in his hands as water drained from his soaked clothes. He had the look of a man whose world had been turned upside down. Then, his head came up and he reached beneath the bench to draw out an oar, affixing it to the lock and doing the same with the other. Wordlessly, he began to pull on the oars and the little boat quickly gained speed. Millicent watched him in the moonlight, but could not make out the expression on his face.

Perhaps there is more to this man than I thought.

After rowing silently for a time, the Earl spoke—but did not stop his strokes.

"Lady…eh…Millicent is it?"

"Aye, my lord."

"How far to Shipbrook?"

"Not far, my lord—perhaps an hour to the ford and then another to walk to the keep."

"Will we get there before de Ferrers?"

"I think we will, my lord. I doubt he or his men know exactly where it is located. They will have to find someone in your service who knows the way and that will take time. The road passes through deep forest for most of the way and this moon will be of no help there. They will not be able to spur their horses. Yes, we should beat them, but not by a great deal."

"And what shall we do when he arrives? Can the keep be defended?"

Millie thought for a moment on that.

"Sir Alwyn, my father's Master of the Sword, will have to judge that. If he says Shipbrook can be held, he will hold it."

The Earl sat silently for a bit, absorbing the information, then spoke.

"I know your Sir Alwyn and I would not like to be the one to oppose him, but de Ferrers will come in strength when he comes. I fear even Sir Alwyn cannot stop the man."

Millicent could not gainsay the Earl's logic, but did not want to dwell on what awaited them at Shipbrook.

"My lord," she asked. "What part does the Earl of Derby's son play in all of this? Malachy seemed to be acting as an agent for the French, but, as we saw, he is under de Ferrers' command. What can his game be?"

Earl Ranulf gave a half laugh and half snarl.

"I never liked William de Ferrers—ever since we were boys. He was greedy and a bully and cheated at games. I rather liked his father, Earl Robert, but he judged poorly in leaving this strutting cock to rule Derbyshire while he went crusading. It does not surprise me that William would covet Cheshire, but I would not have thought him clever enough or man enough to risk taking it." As he spoke he continued to pull strongly on the oars. The little boat shot forward with each stroke.

"No, this was not a plan de Ferrers could have hatched alone. Perhaps this Father Malachy is an agent of the French king, and perhaps Sir William is as well, but I'm not so sure. He would not be the first nobleman on this island to cosy up to Philip, but why discredit Constance, who would be a potential ally? No, I think this plan was aimed at me—and I see the hand of someone much closer than King Philip at work here."

"Who do you mean, my lord?"

"Prince John, my dear. Who besides de Ferrers stands to gain by eliminating me? John has been parading around the country making promises and acting as though he is already the monarch. He has told me and others that Richard will not survive the Crusade, and that we should look to our own interests. But he knows that I am loyal to the King to the end. I can only believe that he plans to seize power and is moving against any who oppose him."

Millicent listened as the Earl carefully played out the logic of the plot that had sent them fleeing for their lives. Once again she had to reevaluate this man. Earl Ranulf was neither a coward nor a dolt. He was not a natural leader. He was indecisive. But he was a man who stood by his loyalties. And that counted for much with the de Lavals. After a long silence, the Earl spoke again.

"So what are we to do, beyond avoiding my arrest?"

Millicent did not hesitate.

"We must get to the Queen. She has to know that you are no traitor." She saw Ranulf shake his head in the moonlight.

"Ah, my dear, this stroke was well timed. The Queen left over a month ago for Normandy to watch over Richard's interests there. Who knows when she will be back in England? Getting to her will not be easy now I'm a hunted man, and even if I can get to Rouen, why should she believe my innocence? The damned letter Constance signed will carry more weight with the Queen than my word."

Millicent hesitated for a long moment before replying.

"Aye, my lord. She may not take your word, but I believe she would take mine."

"Yours? Why on earth would the Queen take your word on a matter such as this?"

"Forgive me, my lord, but I must confess—I am an agent of the Queen. She asked me to go to Chester and to keep her informed of events in your household."

Earl Ranulf stopped pulling on the oars. Millicent was glad she could not see the man's face. She knew her own was red.

"You were a *spy*...for the *Queen*?" he sputtered.

"Aye. I've called myself a scout, but spy is close enough to the truth. My lord, I did not want this. The Queen..."

The Earl shook his head incredulously.

"Good God! Spies, conniving priests...what else have I missed?" The man's voice was bordering on despair.

Millicent felt her cheeks flush.

"My lord, you've missed much, but you are no traitor. I have spied on you and I am sorry for that, but I am also bound by my father's oath. Our first loyalty is to you, my lord, which is why I came to you and did not seek the Queen when I heard of this treason. It is why I am in this boat. I know that you are no traitor and the Queen will believe it, if it comes from me."

The Earl was silent for long moments as he took in this latest turn of events. He began to pull on the oars once more. After a while, he spoke.

"Miss...Lady Millicent...I understand you had no choice in this. A request from the Queen is as good as a command, though I doubt her grace would approve of how you've handled your duties this night. As you say, you could have left me and fled, but you did not. Were it not for you, I would currently be locked up in my own dungeon. I am in your debt."

"My lord, you and your father have been good to my family. You owe us no debt."

"Ah, girl, it is debts that bind us together. And now we must find a way to get to Eleanor."

Millicent watched the oar blades as they rose and fell, shining into the black water.

"I wish my father were here now."

The Earl managed a rueful laugh.

"So do I, my dear, so do I!"

***

A rider reined in his horse hard as he entered the gate of Chester Castle, sparks flying from the cobbles as the horse tried to stop. William de Ferrers broke away from a small group in the courtyard to get the news.

"No sign of them on the road to London, my lord."

De Ferrers nodded. He had half expected this. There had also been no sign of the fugitives on the roads north or west. An earlier report now began to take on more significance. His men had seen a boat being stolen from the docks outside the city walls. Not an unusual occurrence, but all the same...

It had been too dark to identify the thieves, though one of his men thought that he had seen a girl. Could it be the de Laval girl? The boat had drifted out into the river and headed downstream—and the Dee flowed westerly toward the de Laval lands. He turned back to the rider.

"Leave two men to watch the London road. Keep patrols on the roads to Manchester. Take the rest to meet our men on the west road. Tell them to be prepared to ride hard." The rider raised his arm in acknowledgement of his orders and spurred away.

"Malachy!"

The priest quickly came to his side.

"I am convinced the girl has stolen a boat and is taking Ranulf to her family's keep west of here. Find someone in the Earl's household who knows the way—and quickly."

Malachy made a slight bow.

"I shall have a guide by the time you assemble your men, my lord."

"See that you do! I hold you responsible for this, priest. Having Ranulf at liberty threatens everything. You should have eliminated that girl!"

Malachy bowed and turned away. He would have no problem using his powers of persuasion to find a guide—willing or otherwise to take them to Shipbrook.

That damned girl! He had to concede de Ferrers was right. He should have strangled her in her bed. He simply had not imagined she would cause this much trouble.

I will not make that mistake again.

***

"My lord, we are here." Millicent pointed toward the right bank of the river where there was a break in the wall of reeds that lined the shoreline. A muddy path led away into the darkness. "It's the ford."

Earl Ranulf shipped his left oar and pulled hard on the right. The bow of the boat slid onto the low muddy bank and came to rest. The Earl secured the oars and climbed over the bow, pulling the small craft up and out of the current. Millicent scrambled over the bench and took the Earl's outstretched hand as she hopped on to the spongy ground.

"Follow me, lord. It's not far."

She headed up the familiar path. It had been down this same trail that the Welsh raider Bleddyn had led her as a captive more than a year ago. He had taken her deep into Wales—to the trackless forest of Clocaenog and kept her as hostage there. Were it not for her father and Roland Inness, she would likely still be there. Would that Sir Roger and Roland were here to help her now, but they were a world away. She would have to make do.

Hezekiah's Tunnel

ork details had already returned from their labours when Roland was cast back into his cell. Sir Harry welcomed him back to his confinement. The old knight seemed to have no curiosity about where the guards had taken his young cell mate for the better part of the afternoon, but, as always, he was full of rumours.

"There is going to be a great battle in but a few days—or so say the guards when they think I cannot hear!" Sir Harry imparted this new titbit with his usual relish, but having given the news, he turned morose. "I fear it may be the end for us."

"Why do you say that, Sir Harry?"

The old knight shook his head.

"I have lived long in this land and have seen too much. Should Saladin win this battle and drive our King back across the sea, we will rot here. If he loses, he will likely have us killed—if he cannot use us to deter Richard from attacking the city. Either way, we are doomed." He paused, overcome with gloom, then brightened. "If I was a younger man, I would make good an escape!"

One word in the knight's discourse banished all others from Roland's ears.

"Escape? How could you escape this place, Sir Harry?" Roland waited for an answer, half afraid that the old knight had lost his wits during his long captivity and would suggest some fantasy rather than a real plan.

Sir Harry Percival looked around the cell and led Roland to a dark corner. He spoke now in a whisper.

"I know a way to get free of here and even to get outside the walls, but to what end? The land swarms with the enemy and they would catch me before I was out of sight of the city."

"They wouldn't catch me, Sir Harry," Roland said with conviction. "And if you are with me, I could get you through as well."

Sir Harry shook his head sadly.

"I am too old and too weak, Sir Roland. I would slow you down and we would both fall back into the hands of the enemy." Roland started to protest, but Sir Harry held up a hand to silence him.

"Truth be told, I am wed to this place, even if it be as a prisoner. I have had the joy of living in this city for over twenty years. I could not bear the thought of never seeing Jerusalem again...could not bear it. And perhaps Saladin may neglect to execute the lot of us, even if the city is falling. King Richard could yet take this place and free us."

Roland looked at the old knight. It was time for him to know the truth.

"Sir Harry, the King cannot take this place. I have seen Saladin's army. I've seen the strength of these walls and I know the strength of our own army. If King Richard does not receive reinforcements, there is no way he can take Jerusalem—and there have been no reinforcements for months. I doubt he could even fight his way through the hills to lay siege to the city. If you stay, there will be no rescue."

Sir Harry took a moment to digest this news. He sighed and shook his head.

"Even so, Sir Roland, I was at Hattin. I marched out with the others to destroy Saladin and save the Holy City. Almost all of my comrades died there. I should have died along with them, but fate held a different plan for me. I was one of the few who made it back from that field of death. I fought to defend Jerusalem—and failed once more. I cannot abandon her again, my young friend." The knight spoke with quiet resolve.

"You have not fallen under the spell of the Holy City and that is good for one so young. I will show you the way out, but I will not follow. Jerusalem holds my heart hostage."

Roland looked down at the old knight who now slumped in the corner of the cell. He could not understand the passions that ruled so many in this land, but they were real enough. He spoke gently to his companion.

"As you wish, Sir Harry, and God be with you. Will you tell me the way?"

Sir Harry's head snapped up and some of the old mad gleam came back into his eye.

"This is an ancient place and it has many secrets, Sir Roland. I know things about Jerusalem its current masters have not yet learned. I have been a prisoner in these dungeons for over four years and I know the habits of our captors. I have watched the guards and have seen them grow lax. That is essential to the first part of the plan."

"How mean you, Sir Harry?"

"During the hottest hours of the day, the guards who watch us on the walls retreat into the shade. What the guards do not know is that under our feet is a vast cavern. It's where Solomon quarried the stone for the Temple—and I know where there is a hidden entrance. If we wait until the guards are seeking shelter from the sun, we might just slip away and reach that place before they even know we are gone. They may not miss us until they muster at the end of the day."

"Where does this cavern lead?"

Sir Harry smiled almost giddily. "Out, boy, out! It runs from Herod's Gate, near where we work on the wall, under the city to the foot of the Temple Mount. There it ends."

"But that would lead us to the centre of the city. How would that help?"

"Ah, here is what few know. Solomon's quarry has a fissure at the far end that connects to Hezekiah's tunnel under the city."

"Hezekiah's tunnel? What is that?"

The old man paused for a moment to recall the old story.

"Hezekiah was King of Judah and made his capital here, as David had done before him. When the King of Assyria swore to seize the city, Hezekiah cut a tunnel through the bedrock to bring water within the walls from the Spring of Gihon, which lies to the east. The spring is the only reliable water supply for miles around. There is a low redoubt around the spring itself and usually a guard, but the guard is watching out into the valley and not back into the tunnel. With luck, we can dispatch the sentry and have you over the wall unseen. Then it becomes a matter of avoiding the patrols."

For all the mad gleam in Sir Harry's eyes, Roland thought the escape plan seemed sound enough, though fraught with peril as any escape would be. He had one burning question.

"When?"

Sir Harry grinned at him.

"No profit in delaying. If the battle the guards speak of happens soon, we could all have our heads lifted at any time, so I say we go tomorrow."

Roland nodded.

"Tomorrow it is."

***

The Crusader column had just resumed its late afternoon march south along the coast after sheltering from the hottest part of the day when Friar Tuck spurred up to Sir Roger, Declan and Sir Robin. They were less than one day's march from where Declan had seen Saladin's army gathering and tensions were high in the ranks of the army. The young Irish knight had recovered most of his strength with rest, food and water and the three rode near the head of the English contingent. They were used to Tuck's daily visits and valued the bits of information that he always seemed to glean through his Templar connections.

"Well met, Sir Friar," Sir Robin called as the monk reined in his horse. "What news have ye?"

The look on the jovial priest's face would have answered the question even if he had not spoken.

"Bad news, my friends. Indeed, evil news. Ride out with me."

The three knights followed the friar as he rode well out of earshot of any in the passing column.

He halted and turned to the men, a pained look on his face.

"Richard has slaughtered the hostages at Acre. At the King's order, they were led out of the city and cut down two days after we marched out."

For a moment the three sat their mounts silently, aghast at what the priest had reported.

"Merciful God, what madness is this?" Sir Roger finally asked in an anguished voice. "Why would he do it?"

Tuck shook his head and sighed.

"It is said that Saladin failed to meet his promises. The True Cross was not produced nor the Christian prisoners, or any of the gold. It is said that the King wished to show he could not be trifled with." He paused,, a look of disgust on his face.

"There was rejoicing among the Templars and prayers of thanksgiving at the news. That is the kind of madness we are dealing with. It is the kind of madness I had my fill of five years past when I left this place behind. It is as though this land brings it forth." The monk spit on the ground, as if the land itself had offended him.

Sir Robin looked as though he might be ill.

"There were hundreds of hostages, perhaps more than a thousand. I cannot fathom it."

"Not only will this be a stain on our honour, but no city in this land will ever surrender to us again," Sir Roger added. "They will fight to the last man!"

"When news of this spreads, thousands will flock to Saladin's banners," Sir Robin said.

"And they will revenge themselves on whatever Christian prisoners they now hold..." said Declan, his voice filled with despair. They had openly hoped that Roland was a prisoner and not killed. Now even that faint hope seemed fruitless.

"What are we to do?" asked Sir Robin.

Sir Roger slammed his fist into the palm of his hand in anger. "We cannot desert the army in the field, but...we shall *not* be party to the slaughter of captives. We shall *not* befoul our own honour. And...we shall get ourselves back to England at the first opportunity."

"And never follow this King across the water again!" added Sir Robin.

"Never," said Sir Roger.

"Never," agreed Declan.

Friar Tuck nodded. "Amen to that."

***

Saladin sat his horse and watched impassively as his infantry marched past. At last he had the forces he needed to take on the invaders in a pitched battle—and this battle would be one of annihilation. He called for a messenger and the man reined in his horse a respectful distance away.

Only an hour before, word had come to him of the slaughter of his people in Acre. It made his blood boil to think of it. He had been late in meeting his payments, it was true, but this—this was madness! Had he not spared the Christian defenders when he captured Jerusalem? Now he must respond, in a way that this English king will understand. He motioned the messenger forward.

"Take word to the commander of the Jerusalem garrison. The Christian prisoners are to be put to the sword—at once."

***

The sun was high in the sky over Jerusalem as the exhausted labourers hauled stone up the wooden ramps from the street below to the top of the damaged northern wall. The August heat had been building relentlessly since sunrise and the air shimmered above the cobblestones.

As the sun reached its zenith, the guards edged back into the small pockets of shade offered by overhanging balconies and rooftops. They watched the prisoners at work, but with no great vigilance. No one had escaped from them in memory and they did not expect this day to be any different.

With each trip up the ramps, Roland noted the position of the guards closely. By a little past noon, he saw them huddled in the shade to escape the blindingly hot sun. The time was growing near.

As he dropped his load of stone in the pile for the masons, he gazed out at the land beyond the walls. The pavilion of Saladin was gone from the ridge north of the city. The Sultan had surely gone to join his army for the rumoured assault on the Crusaders marching south along the coast.

In the night, Sir Harry had coached him carefully on the location of the secret passageway into Solomon's quarry. To reach it they would have to cross twenty feet of open ground from the far edge of the stone pile to a narrow alley.

If the guards noticed them, it would then be a footrace and Roland was doubtful Sir Harry could win such a contest. But, come what may, he must have the knight to show him the way underground. No amount of coaching could help him in that dark labyrinth.

As he made his way down the ramp for another load he saw Sir Harry lingering by the rock pile. He appeared to be repositioning an awkward stone to lift, but Roland recognized it as the signal they had agreed upon. As he neared the bottom of the ramp, he watched the old knight simply turn and walk slowly across the open ground into a narrow alleyway. No alarm was raised. Roland paused for a moment to glance around. The guards were not watching and none of the other prisoners seemed to have noticed Sir Harry's exit.

As he reached the far side of the stone pile he took a deep breath and simply kept walking, following in Sir Harry's footsteps. With a dozen agonizingly slow steps he reached the alley where the knight waited for him with a broad smile.

"I said they were lax, did I not!" he whispered. Roland nodded and fell in behind the man as he turned and walked as quickly as his old legs would carry him away from the walls and the guards. The alley split and Sir Harry went left. He had only gone a few yards down this path when he stopped and stroked his chin, a slightly perplexed look on his face.

"Umm...should be hereabouts, but where is the infernal door?"

All of Roland's fears about the old man's sanity came rushing back. If they could not find the entrance to the cavern quickly, someone was bound to spy them and alert the guards. They were covered in white dust from the stonework. There was no mistaking the two for casual strollers.

"Ah...there 'tis!" The old knight pointed a little way ahead at a small wooden door that sat at an angle between the edge of the alley and the wall of a building. Sir Harry bent down and gave a tug on the iron handle. The door did not budge.

"Seems stuck," he announced and tried pulling upwards with both hands, his skinny leg braced against the building. Still no movement. Roland could not stand by any longer.

"Sir Harry, let me have a go." As the old knight stepped back, Roland stepped forward and pulled tentatively on the handle. There was some give in the wood, but it was securely fastened. Time was running out. At any moment a local resident would turn a corner and spy the two men bent over the door.

Roland grasped the handle with both hands and heaved back violently. There was a distinct cracking sound as somewhere the frame began to give way. He heaved again and stumbled to the other side of the alley as half the door ripped loose in his hand.

Sir Harry slapped him on the back and immediately lowered himself into the dark recess. Roland followed, being careful to set the broken half of the door back in place. It was very dark as rough steps led downward. Roland stumbled into Sir Harry who had stopped only a few feet below him.

"They keep flint and torches about here," he said, no longer bothering to whisper. Both men felt around in the dark and Roland's hand touched a rough wooden staff. The bulge of bound rags at the end was sticky with pitch. It was the torch. Sir Harry let out a quiet shout as he found the set of flint and steel that had been placed in a niche in the wall. After a few quick strikes, the torch flared and gave off a dim, smouldering light. It was enough to guide their steps.

Sooner than expected, the narrow passage carved out of stone began to expand around them. Fortunately, as the torch continued to burn, it grew brighter and now Roland could see that the ceiling was not carved at all, but was the natural top of a cavern.

"This is it, lad—Solomon's quarry!" Sir Harry stopped and swung the torch from side to side showing that the space had not only expanded overhead, but on all sides. The cavern was of such a size that the light from the torch could not fully illuminate the far reaches of the place.

They were at the bottom of the carved steps and there was a path ahead through a jumble of stone. These were blocks cut from the bedrock of the cave. Sir Harry moved forward confidently, leading the way. Distracted by the echoes and shadows thrown off by the torch, Roland hardly noticed how long it took to reach the far side of the cavern, but soon the space began to close in once more.

"This is the crack that leads to our exit, Sir Roland. Mind your head, for it gets a bit tight through this part."

And indeed it did. As they moved forward, the walls drew close enough to reach with outstretched arms and the ceiling was now only six feet over head. For a long time they followed this narrow crevice that wound through the darkness. Roland had been in a few caves back on Kinder Scout when he was a boy, but the size of this place and the distance they had come began to weigh on him. He did not like having this huge mass of stone over his head.

Finally, he caught the sound of running water ahead and within a few moments they emerged onto a small ledge above a stone ditch. The ditch was only three feet across, and the water was clear enough to see that the bottom was less than a foot deep. Sir Harry beamed at him through the torch light.

"Hezekiah's Tunnel, my boy! Wasn't sure I could find it all these years later."

Roland took in a quick breath. If his guide had lost their way down here and the torch had burned out, they would have been doomed to an unpleasant death in the dark.

"How long since you've come this way Sir Harry?"

"Oh, eighteen years or so I'd reckon. I was hardly more than a boy when me and some of me lads came exploring through here. It's a good thing stone don't move!"

Good thing, indeed, Roland thought.

"It's about a half mile up through this channel to the redoubt where the water emerges from the spring. If the torch fails us, just keep to the up slope. The passage branches as it descends, but not as it passes up toward the spring. No chance of getting lost now."

Sir Harry stepped off into the water that came up to his calves and began sloshing up the ditch. Roland stepped in and followed.

Arsuf

Tension was high in the Crusader ranks as they broke camp for the morning march south. Richard had issued his orders the night before. The Templars would lead followed by the English knights. Knights loyal to the King of Jerusalem as well as the small French contingent would take up the middle section of the column, with the rear guard made up of the Knights Hospitaller. The infantry would march inland to screen the mounted formations as much as possible from Saladin's archers.

The King's instructions were clear and unbending. He was determined to force Saladin to hurl his main force at the column to stop their progress toward Jaffa. Only then would he order his entire army to close with and destroy the Saracens. Until he personally gave the order, the mounted formations in the column were not to turn and assault the enemy, no matter what sort of injury they may suffer at the hands of the foe. He had learned from the accounts of Hattin. He would not have his forces goaded into piecemeal attacks and cut to ribbons.

The Crusader force did not have to wait long for their discipline to be tested. Hardly had they shaken out into line of march, when swarms of mounted archers emerged from the surrounding hills and began sending a steady stream of arrows into their ranks. Crossbowmen with the infantry did their best to keep the archers at bay, but the swift horsemen made difficult targets.

The mounted Crusaders made easier targets as they had to ride slowly to keep pace with the foot soldiers on their flank. Many shafts glanced off the armoured knights and their armoured mounts, but some found gaps and men and horses began to go down.

Sir Roger rode next to Declan and just behind Sir Robin. All three held their shields high on their left side as they rode. Within the hour the shields bristled with imbedded shafts. As the morning wore on, the casualties mounted, but the ranks held and the column continued to the south toward the small village of Arsuf, where they had planned to halt for the midday meal.

There would be no stopping for food now with the enemy nipping at their flanks. The King, worried that there would be a breakdown in discipline, rode with his bodyguard down the length of the column and back again, determined to maintain control. He had just returned to the head of the column when his rear guard broke.

The plight of the Hospitallers had been especially severe as they were beset both to the east and from the north as they brought up the tail of the Crusader column. It was all these fierce warriors could do to hold their ranks and not turn on their tormentors as the English king had ordered. But as another of their number fell with an arrow striking his eye, a ripple ran through their ranks.

With no order given, broadswords were drawn and lances were lowered. Once started, there was no stopping the surge of fury that gripped these men who had endured so much. In twos and threes, then in a full ragged contingent, they turned their mounts to the east and charged at the enemy.

It was what Saladin had been waiting for. As the Hospitallers raced after the Parthian bowmen, the Sultan sent his heavy cavalry crashing out of the valleys and ravines where they had been lying in wait. If they could cut off the Hospitallers and crush them, they could then turn on a weakened Crusader force and gain their vengeance for Acre.

In the middle of the column, Sir Roger felt a distant rumble and knew it for what it was—the thunder of charging warhorses. A shudder ran up the flank of Bucephalus and the great charger's nostrils flared. He knew it as well. Sir Roger turned to Declan.

"Prepare yourself, Sir Declan. The Hospitallers have broken and all hell is about to be unleashed." He had barely finished when Richard and his guard came racing past to assess the situation to the rear. The King's face looked grim.

"Is it to be another Hattin?" Declan asked his master. "I've seen the bones of that field. I don't fancy adding mine to their number."

Sir Roger drew his broadsword.

"Richard may be a bastard, lad, but there is no better commander in the field than he. He will salvage things if they can be salvaged."

From the rear of the column where the fighting had grown fierce, the King's trumpeter began to blast out a signal to the rest of the Crusader force. All along the way, swords were drawn and lances lowered. Great warhorses turned to the east and began to advance.

Sir Roger, Sir Declan and Sir Robin rode side-by-side as the charge began to gather speed. From the valley to their front a huge wave of Muslim heavy cavalry emerged and bore down on them. Both forces closed and the sandy soil of the coastal plane flew beneath the galloping hooves of their horses.

"Stay close!" Sir Roger shouted above the din. Then thousands of pounds of horseflesh and steel met with a sound oddly like the crackling of lightning.

***

The water was cold but no more so than many a stream he had waded in as a boy hunting crayfish on Kinder Scout. The passageway ran fairly straight with only an occasional bend. Roland could see the clear marks of chisels on the walls where men, a thousand or more years before, had carved out this tunnel. With each step he felt his gloom lift. If he could win free of this place, he would stick to ridgelines and animal tracks and would make for the coast. But one thing troubled him— how could he leave Sir Harry behind?

As they trudged through the water, he rehearsed various arguments to use on the old knight that would convince him to leave his beloved Jerusalem. But he knew his companion was a man of iron will. He had to be to have survived Hattin and four years in Saladin's dungeons. Roland doubted any argument would sway him.

His thoughts were brought to an abrupt halt as Sir Harry pulled up short in front of him. Without a word, the knight plunged the torch into the water and all was instantly dark.

For a moment Roland felt a surge of panic, but as his eyes adjusted he could make out the faint outline of the man in front of him. For there to be any light in this narrow passage meant that they were near the spring and the exit. Sir Harry moved forward more carefully now, and soon the passageway began to widen. Ahead, Roland saw a shaft of light and stone steps leading upwards.

"The Spring of Gihon," Sir Harry whispered to him.

Freedom! Roland thought.

The water channel broadened as it entered the light. Roland touched Sir Harry on the arm and took the lead. If there was to be a fight at the top of those stairs, it would be his fight.

Carefully, the two men edged up the steps that led from the tunnel to the top of the redoubt that protected the spring. All was silent except for the melody of a songbird perched somewhere outside the wall. Then the sound of metal on metal reached their ears. As they reached the top of the steps, Roland peered over the edge.

Sir Harry's prediction was close to the truth. There were two guards instead of one, but both were standing together and casually watching activity outside of the walls. Surprise would be his only weapon against these men, but perhaps it would be enough. Roland motioned for Sir Harry to stay where he was and began to stalk silently toward the two men who were engaged in an animated conversation.

They never saw him coming. As he drew near, he broke into a slow trot, then to a full run and barrelled into the man on the right with his shoulder. The man fell, the breath knocked from him. Roland picked up the man's spear that still leaned against the wall and without hesitating, brought the shaft down on the second guard who was just starting to overcome his shock. The man was out before he hit the stone parapet.

Turning back to the first guard, a swift blow from the spear shaft rendered him senseless as well. Sir Harry had been hurrying forward, but the work was done before he arrived.

"Well done, lad. Well done indeed! I could never have moved that fast, even in my younger days."

Roland was breathing hard, his blood still up from the fight.

"Sir Harry...I must be over the wall, and soon. Will ye not come with me?" He had to make a final plea.

Sir Harry gazed back from the redoubt to the higher walls of Jerusalem. It was the first time he had seen them from the outside in four years. He smiled gently at Roland and shook his head.

"I think I will go over the wall, but I'll not follow ye. Ye need to be getting back to the King, and I...well I would fancy a stroll across the Valley of Kedron below and up to the Mount of Olives yonder. I always liked the view of the city from there."

"They'll catch you."

"Aye, I expect they will, but do not trouble yerself, Sir Roland. I am content. Get yerself back to England, lad—and stay there!"

Roland surprised the old knight when he stepped forward and hugged him.

"I owe you my freedom, Sir Harry. I won't forget. Now, we must be gone!"

He picked up a short sword dropped by one of the guards and thrust it in his belt. Then he led the older man to the top of the wall and found a spot where the hillside was fairly level at the base. With care he helped Sir Harry over the rampart and lowered him to within a few feet of the ground before releasing his grip.

For Roland the drop was almost ten feet, but he landed lightly. When he turned he saw that Sir Harry had already begun wandering down the slope toward the valley. He gave the old man a wave, but his companion never turned to acknowledge the farewell.

He took a deep breath. He was free, but had forty miles of enemy territory to cover before he would be safe. He turned toward the setting sun and headed west.

Pursuit

Lady Catherine de Laval awoke from a fitful sleep. Strange dreams had been troubling her as they did most nights, but it was not a dream that drew her awake. Someone was pounding on the door to her chambers. She arose quickly, threw on a robe and opened the door. It was one of the young men-at-arms and he was breathless.

"My lady, Lady Millicent is here! She's brung the Earl! They are in the courtyard. She sent me to fetch you." Lady Catherine had not waited for the boy to finish. She hurried down the spiral stone steps to the great hall and out the entrance to the courtyard. Coming up the steps to meet her were a bedraggled daughter and her liege lord, Ranulf, Earl of Chester—who looked equally dishevelled. This could only be serious trouble.

She wanted to race down the steps to embrace Millie, but the girl was hanging back, respectful of the man she accompanied. She gave the girl a searching look, but turned to the Earl and curtsied.

"My Lord Ranulf, you are most welcome at Shipbrook, please come inside." She held out her hand and the Earl took it.

"Lady Catherine, I am grateful for your welcome, but I fear you may come to regret it."

"Never, my lord—but let's get you some dry clothes while you tell me what brings you here." By now the entire household had been aroused and servants had gathered in the hall. Lady Catherine ordered one to fetch some dry clothes from Sir Alwyn for the Earl. Her husband's things would have been impossibly

222

large for the man. Another servant had already added wood to the fireplace and was stoking it back to life.

The Earl dropped, exhausted, onto a small couch that had been pulled near to the fire. Millicent followed close behind and now Sir Alwyn joined the group, having posted guards at the gate and walls. The Earl looked at the anxious faces surrounding him.

"I was here once, you know—as a lad. Your husband took me down to the ford at the Dee. Showed me hills to the west where the raiders come from."

Lady Catherine smiled. "I remember your visit well, my lord. You should come more often, but perhaps under pleasanter circumstances. Please tell us what the trouble is."

"How shall I begin?" He spread his hands as if in supplication.

"My lady, your daughter saved my head from the chopping block this night, for I was being led like a lamb to slaughter and saw it not. I will not belabour the details, but my dim-witted wife has been persuaded to sign a document addressed to the King of France seeking his aid on behalf of her son—*against King Richard*. It was to prevent just such an alliance that King Henry had me marry her when Geoffrey died. I was supposed to control the infernal woman! None will believe that I was ignorant of this plot!"

Catherine took in the Earl's anguished recounting of the events that had driven him to her doorstep. He looked like a thoroughly beaten man.

"I believe you, my lord, but I can see that others might not. If this document be proof of treason by Lady Constance, you are right to fear being implicated—but why have you not seized this message? Why are you here?"

The Earl sighed and shook his head. He turned to Millicent.

"You tell it my dear."

Millicent turned to Lady Catherine and her mother nodded.

"It was the priest, Mother, the one I saw inspecting the defences of the city when he first arrived. I kept watch on him and overheard him persuading the Lady that her son was in danger from King Richard and Prince John. Father Malachy offered the protection of the French as though he was an agent of King Philip, but it now appears he is in league with Sir William de Ferrers." Lady Catherine cut in.

"De Ferrers? How does the ruler of Derbyshire play in all of this?"

"Sir William and his men took the city by surprise at dusk and he now holds it. We saw the priest deliver the treasonous document to him. He has the document, Lady Constance, and the city under his control and seeks the Earl. It cannot be long before he guesses where we have fled. He could be here within hours and he will come in strength."

Earl Ranulf roused himself to take up the thread of the story.

"De Ferrers is ambitious enough to covet my lands, but not man enough to have launched this brazen attack on me—not on his own. He must have real power behind him. Perhaps it is the French king, but I think that power comes from Prince John."

It was now Sir Alwyn's turn to speak up.

"William de Ferrers is a treacherous man and a coward. We might be out here on the frontier, but word does reach us as to which way the wind is blowing. It is hardly a secret that John covets the throne and any nobles that are loyal to Richard are an obstacle to him. It would seem you are in his way, my lord, and perhaps de Ferrers and this charge of treason are his instruments for eliminating you."

Millicent looked at Sir Alwyn. "How stand our defences Alwyn?"

"Sound, Millie, but designed to repel a few Welsh raiders, not a Norman host. You say he comes in strength—what strength?"

Millicent did a mental assessment of the knights and men at arms that she had seen as they fled the city. Some would be left behind to secure the place, but the rest...

"Far more than a few Welsh raiders, I fear."

Alwyn nodded. "Then we must gather what we can and get the Earl out of Sir William's reach." He turned to Lady Catherine.

"I am sorry, my lady, but we must abandon Shipbrook."

Lady Catherine de Laval did not flinch. She looked at the Earl, her daughter, and back to Sir Alwyn.

"Give the order."

***

The road to Shipbrook was hardly more than a rough trail through the dense forests that flanked Chester to the northwest and the going had been infuriatingly slow. At least one knight had lost his mount with a broken foreleg trying to follow the path in the darkness. But at last the woods gave way to fields and pastureland and the road became clearly visible in the bright moonlight.

It had taken de Ferrers almost four hours to assemble his troops and make the journey to this god-forsaken outpost on the frontier, but now Shipbrook lay before them. He could see torches illuminating the towers and the small curtain walls of the place. He summoned one of his knights to his side.

"Take men and prepare a ram. We may have to break down the gate." He called Father Malachy forward.

"Hail them. Offer a reward to give up the Earl. Tell them that all who harbour traitors will be slain on the spot."

Malachy nodded and had his horse approach the gate at a slow walk. He felt an odd tingling in his body as he came within the glow of the flickering torches. *Was there an archer hidden on the wall about to loose a bolt into him?* He reined in when he was fifty paces from the gate.

"Hello, the castle!"

Silence.

"Hello, the castle!" he shouted again. "We come to arrest the traitor Ranulf. Give him up and your lives and property will be spared. Resist and all will die!" He waited as the silence grew longer. Then he knew. He turned his gaze from the gate and began to search the ground nearby. It was difficult in the dim light, but the signs were clear enough. He pulled his horse's head around and spurred back to where his master waited.

"They've gone, my lord."

"Gone?"

"Aye, my lord. But they cannot be far ahead of us. Tracks lead off west."

Sir William cursed. The loose end that was the Earl of Chester was proving difficult to tie up. He slapped his gloves on his thigh in exasperation.

"How much farther west can there be from this place? The Irish Sea must be nearby. Are they trying to escape over the water?"

Malachy shook his head.

"I doubt they would have had time to arrange for a boat, my lord. The tracks lead west from the gate. They might turn northeast to reach the road to Manchester, but we've men watching that route." He signalled for their guide to be brought forward. It was one of the Earl's men who had laughed at Millicent's impudence but a few hours earlier as she tried to warn the Earl of danger.

"What is west of here, man?" the priest asked sharply.

The young nobleman was quaking but managed to reply.

"Wales, my lord, just over the Dee. Shipbrook guards a ford near here."

Malachy turned to de Ferrers.

"I'll wager they've crossed the ford. They expect we won't follow them over the frontier."

"Then we must not waste more time." De Ferrers turned to the knight beside him and gestured toward the pitiful young nobleman who had betrayed his liege lord.

"Have *him* torch the place," he said pointing to the gate of Shipbrook.

"Burn it. Burn it all."

***

The departure from Shipbrook had been swift and wrenching for all who called it home, little knowing if they would ever return. There had been no time for careful planning. They had little choice but to flee west into Wales. South would lead them into the force coming from Chester and the roads north and east towards Manchester would be watched by now.

Millicent had thrown together a small bundle of her riding clothes, then sprinted for the stables where grooms were saddling their horses. She tied her kit to the back of the bay mare's saddle and scurried up a ladder to the hay loft. There, lying across the rafters, were four long yew staves, left to cure until they would be fashioned into longbows. They had been selected and cut by Roland Inness, to be finished when he returned from Crusade. Millicent gathered them up and scrambled back down the ladder.

Sir Alwyn was mounting his own horse when he saw her strapping the lengths of wood to the side of her saddle and smiled.

"He'll be proud you thought of those, Millie. And we may all have a need for more longbows before this is done." Millie returned his smile.

"Hope for the best and prepare for the worst my father always said." She mounted her bay and followed Alwyn out into the courtyard where her mother and the Earl were waiting with their few men-at-arms. Through the gate, servants, cooks, grooms and others were streaming out to disperse into the countryside. Lady Catherine took a long, last look around at her home and gave the signal to ride. As they passed through the gate, Millicent was determined to do as her father had done and did not look back.

The path to the ford was known to them all and they reached it quickly. Catherine, the Earl and Millicent had just splashed ashore on the far bank of the Dee when they heard shouts from across the river. Sir Alwyn, who had placed himself at the rear of the party came splashing up the bank and reined up next to Catherine.

"My lady, they are not far behind and closing fast. I will hold them at the ford for as long as possible. Get yourself and the Earl as far away from here as you can. I'll be along."

Lady Catherine looked at the gnarled face of Alwyn Madawc in the bright moonlight. She had known him as long as she had known her own husband. She started to protest, but he cut her off.

"Cathy, get on with ye. Ye know I'm right."

Still she found she could not turn her horse and leave this man behind. She felt a soft hand on her arm and turned to see her daughter. Millicent's tears glistened in the confounded moonlight.

"We must go, Mother. Alwyn is right. If we stay, all will be lost and Father will have nothing to come home to."

Lady Catherine slumped in resignation. She turned to Alwyn and reached between the horses to touch his shoulder, then she turned her horse's head to the west. She looked at Millicent.

"Where shall we go, daughter?"

Millicent turned her favourite mare's head to the west as well—toward Wales.

"Follow me, Mother. I've been this way before."

Even in the dark, the trail was fairly clear leading into the low hills of Wales. Millicent had been brought this way by Bleddyn and his men. It was a trail that had been used for a thousand years for trade and war between the ancient tribes that inhabited the opposite banks of the Dee. Further west, the trail split with branches turning north and south. They would have till then to decide where they were bound.

Their group was now reduced to only the three and Millicent led the way, with Lady Catherine and the Earl following. She kept a steady pace to put distance between them and their enemies. She prayed that Alwyn could hold de Ferrers for a while and then follow this same trail to find them.

It was well past midnight when they topped a rise and she stopped to give their horses a rest. From here they could look back across the valley of the Dee. The river was a silver line of moonlight surrounded by darkness below, but far to the north flames lit the night sky. Mother and daughter knew what those flames meant, but said nothing.

***

William de Ferrers sat his horse among the tall reeds on the northern bank of the Dee and sent a dozen of his armoured knights on their warhorses to clear the ford. His men were in high spirits. They had taken Chester with scarcely a fight. Off to the east there was a glow in the sky where the castle of Shipbrook was being consumed by flames. For the men who

228

had followed William de Ferrers from Derbyshire, this had been a lark—more of a fox hunt than a battle.

That changed as their chargers reached the shallows on the far side of the Dee and began to climb the muddy bank. They had seen nothing as they splashed toward the far shore, but now a madman with a wicked battle axe came from the darkness and the reeds and fell upon them.

The first man was dead before he slipped from the saddle, the axe taking him in the neck between helmet and mail. Knee deep in water, Alwyn Madawc pivoted and rammed the broad side of the axe into the head of a horse who promptly threw his rider. The man, in full mail, sank beneath the brown water and did not come back up.

On the bank behind the Welshman, half a dozen men-at-arms emerged from the reeds and formed a hedgehog of spears guarding the exit from the ford. After two more men went down, the others turned and fled back across the river.

Alwyn grabbed the reins of a panicked warhorse whose rider was no more and led the beast up the bank. He turned to his men with a grin.

"There are no men in Derbyshire, only women!" he hooted. As he stood there leaning on his bloody axe a strange thought came to him.

I do know one true man from Derbyshire. I could make good use of Roland Inness and his longbow just now.

On the far bank he could hear William de Ferrers cursing his men as bootless cowards. Now a larger host entered the river. Fully twenty knights trailed by men-at-arms with lances came on—this time with considerably more caution. When they reached midstream, they came to a halt. Alwyn stood at the muddy exit from the ford with his bloody axe at the ready.

"Come on, ye Derbyshire sheep," he muttered. "I'm in the mood for shearing!"

There was an odd hissing sound that came from the ranks in the river and Alwyn Madawc knew that sound. It took a split second for the bolts loosed by a half dozen crossbows to strike him. He staggered backwards but did not fall. Some of the bolts deflected from his mail, but one found an exposed point just below his neck. He raised his axe and tried to roar his defiance, but no sound came forth. The man who had fled Wales so many years before fell back on the muddy bank and died there on his native soil.

***

A cold rain fell at dawn on three riders as they made their way up a narrow path through a cleft in the hills. For a day and a night their enemies had pursued them closely, gaining little ground, but leaving them no time to rest. Once, the riders de Ferrers had sent to hunt them down got close enough to be seen only a ridgeline away. But the mounts of the Earl and the ladies of Shipbrook were well-bred and their enemies could not close the distance.

The gusting rain chilled them, but was a blessing. Someone in the group behind had tracking skills and they had not been able to throw them off the trail. Now their tracks would be lost in the downpour. It gave them new hope.

At the top of the cleft they stopped to rest the horses and found a little shelter under a rocky outcrop. As they huddled out of the rain, Millicent broke their exhausted silence.

"My lord, if I recall this place correctly, there is a well-used trail in the next valley that crosses our path heading north towards the sea and south along the border." She stopped and waited for a response.

None came immediately, as the Earl of Chester sat in a miserable heap on the ground and tried to control his shivering. Lady Catherine glanced at her daughter and spoke patiently to the young man on the ground.

"My lord, we must have a plan. Till now, west was the only path we could take. Now we must choose."

The Earl's head snapped up and he clambered to his feet, embarrassed that he had shown more weakness than the two ladies who stood before him. His voice quavered with the cold, but there was certainty in his words.

"We cannot go south. John has the other Marcher Lords in his pocket and is himself the Earl of Gloucester. They control all the lands that lie between us and the ports in the south of

England, and you can be sure that by now the word will have gone out to arrest me for treason. We cannot go south, ladies."

"West leads further into Wales and through the Clocaenog forest," Millicent said. "I would have no wish to chance that place again, even though Bleddyn is now dead." The Earl nodded at that.

"Nothing but brigands and wilderness further west. If we turn north, I would reckon it to be less than twenty miles to the coast and there is a small port there—Rhyl I think it's called— that might have what we seek. We would be passing through the region of Gwynedd to get there. The lords of that place were bitter enemies of my father and his father before him. We are not likely to find friends in those parts, but they will not be searching for us either. I think north is our best hope."

"Then north it is, my lord," said Millicent. She turned toward her horse and froze. Through the pelting rain she saw a line of armed men moving quietly toward them. The sounds of their approach had been masked by the downpour and they now cut off any chance escape.

She heard a quiet command and through the line of silent men stepped a tall figure clad in a mail shirt. He wore a long cloak that shed the rain and was too fine a garment for any brigand or cattle thief. He was young, but looked well accustomed to command. A broadsword hung at his waist. Millicent took an involuntary step backwards.

The tall warrior stopped beside the bay mare and gave the horse a long look. He stepped over and ran his hands along the yew staves strapped to the mare's flanks and said something to the men in the ranks. For the first time, Millicent noticed that over half of his men had bows in their hands or slung over their shoulders. They were *longbows.*

Finishing his inspection of the staves, the man spoke in Welsh, his voice firm, but not threatening.

"Pwy ydych chi?

Millicent knew enough Welsh to understand him.

Who are you, he'd asked.

Jaffa

Roger de Laval dipped a piece of cloth in the steaming kettle of water suspended over the campfire and gently began to clean the long nasty wound that ran along Declan O'Duinne's left side. In the chaos of the battle, a Saracen infantryman had managed to drive a short spear up under his mail shirt. Had the blow been at a slightly different angle, the spear point would have gone in under his ribs and pierced his heart. As it was, there was a deep furrow in the skin and muscle that would be long in healing and leave a truly impressive scar. It hurt like the devil and Declan clenched his teeth to keep from crying out as his master worked on him.

Sir Roger grimaced as he worked. An angry black bruise ran down one arm where his mail had stopped an enemy sword. Across the way, Robin of Loxley was using the same kettle of water to clean his own wounds. They were minor, but might fester if left untended.

After a while he arose groaning and probed with his fingers along one thigh. The examination made him wince. His horse had gone down in the carnage and fallen on his right leg. It was Declan O'Duinne who'd leapt off his own mount and stood over the trapped knight until he could pull himself free. It was while the Irish knight was climbing back on his horse that the enemy spearman struck. In the next instant, the man died under Sir Robin's blade.

"Is it always like this?" asked the knight from Loxley.

Of the three, only Sir Roger had been in a set piece battle between two armies in the field. The older knight grunted.

"Yes—and no. Every battle is different, but all are chaos."

"I hope I never see another," said Sir Robin.

"Nor I," added Declan. "A man could get killed."

"I have seen my share, but if I ever see another, I swear it will be on English soil," said Sir Roger, "not in some far off place like this—though God forbid England shall ever see the like."

"I will join you in that entreaty to God, brother Roger." The three men around the fire turned to see Friar Tuck join them. The man moved slowly, favouring some unseen injury of his own. He stopped within the dancing firelight and lifted his eyes upward, saying a silent prayer for the peace of England and sending it heavenward along with the sparks that flew into the night sky. He crossed himself when he was finished and squatted by the fire.

"The scouts report that the slaughter of Saladin's army exceeds our own and that he has withdrawn into the hills toward Jerusalem. They also say the Sultan has destroyed the fortress at Jaffa, stone by stone, to keep it out of our hands. We will not have to fight to take what's left."

"Will the King pursue Saladin to Jerusalem?" Sir Roger put the question bluntly to the priest.

The friar poked a stick at the coals in the fire and was silent for a moment.

"Oh he wants to, he does. His blood is up. It was a very close-run thing today. Our brethren in the Hospitallers were nearly the death of us all and it was only the King's order to launch the entire army into the fight that kept them from being cut off and butchered. That was Saladin's plan and it nearly worked. Richard knows how close we came to disaster, but he is also flushed with his victory. He wants Jerusalem badly and cannot face the thought of failing."

"So we will go," said Declan

"I think we will—unless he can be persuaded not to."

"Can we take the place, Tuck?" asked Sir Roger.

"I think you know the answer to that, my friend," Tuck replied. "You are an old soldier. What do you see?"

"I see the King has left troops behind to secure Acre. He will need more to garrison Jaffa if it is rebuilt. News of his slaughter of the prisoners will be spreading. It will enflame the region and bring reinforcements to Saladin. We have received no new troops in months and no more are coming, I think." The big Norman knight paused, looking out into the darkness beyond the fire's glow.

"Richard may want what he wants, but unless there is a miracle, he can't have it—though we may all die before he sees that."

Tuck continued to poke his stick in the shimmering red coals of the fire.

"You said we would need a miracle to take Jerusalem, but is this not the land of miracles?" he asked.

"I've seen none since my arrival," offered Sir Robin.

"Nor I," agreed Declan.

Tuck threw his stick onto the fire and it flamed up.

"Then perhaps the miracle we need is not the taking of Jerusalem, but the opening of the King's eyes."

***

For days, the Crusader encampment outside the ruins of Jaffa buzzed with activity. Richard had ordered the rebuilding of the city walls and work was already underway. Fresh supplies, though no reinforcements, had been landed at the port and the Christian forces busied themselves with the thousand tasks of an army that had been on the march for weeks and had fought a pitched battle.

Horses were given grain to rebuild their muscle and stamina. Physicians made the rounds tending to wounds that were not healing. Gashed mail was repaired and weapons of all kinds cleaned, repaired and sharpened.

The King sent out urgent messages to the Pope and the crowned heads of Europe entreating them to send fresh troops to aid his cause. All knew that, even if these requests were heeded, it would be half a year before help would arrive.

But the King pressed on with preparations to advance on Jerusalem. The heavy siege engines that had finally battered a breach in the walls of Acre had been disassembled and brought by sea to the port at Jaffa. Engineers split their time between supervising the rebuilding of the city walls and organizing the supply train for the march on the Holy City.

Back in the hills, Muslim cavalry still patrolled, keeping a wary eye on what the Crusaders were up to. No doubt Saladin would know about any move toward Jerusalem before the army had broken camp. To counter this, Richard had sent heavy cavalry up the several roads that led east from the coast to probe the defences and to hinder Saladin's scouts. Not a day passed without dead and wounded on both sides.

A league inland, Sir Robin of Loxley led a patrol of heavy cavalry on the deepest probe yet up the Jerusalem road. All morning the swift Muslim horsemen had stayed just ahead of his mounted knights. As the patrol rounded a bend, they found archers and infantry blocking their way.

Sir Robin ordered a halt and studied the forces arrayed across the narrow valley floor. The King had made it clear he did not want these probes to turn into major skirmishes and it would take at least that to break through this roadblock. It seemed their probe was done for this day.

He stood up in his stirrups and was about to order a withdrawal when a shout came from behind him. When he turned, he saw that a lone figure had leapt from the concealment of the scrub growth on the steep side of the valley between his position and the enemy roadblock. The man was running full out toward them as arrows from the enemy archers began falling around him.

A nervous man at his side drew his sword. Sir Robin reached over and kept him from raising it. The runner had outdistanced the range of the bowmen trying to bring him down and was but fifty feet away when Sir Robin leapt from his horse and ran to meet him.

"As God is my witness, I think I am seeing a ghost!"

Roland Inness grinned between cracked lips as he fell into the man's arms.

***

Sir Robin released his men when they reached the outposts of the Crusader camp, but did not report to the King as he had been ordered. Richard could wait. He made straight for the small English contingent and arrived just as Sir Roger and Declan were gathering for an afternoon meal. They were circled about the gruel pot and did not see the man mounted behind their friend.

"Just in time for a bowl, Loxley!" called Sir Roger.

"I'd have one as well," came a new voice. Sir Roger and the others turned as Roland slid down from behind Sir Robin. The big Norman knight dropped his bowl in shock and Declan just hurled his to the side and ran to greet his lost friend. After an awkward embrace he held Roland out at arm's length.

"Gad, Roland, I had ye certain dead when ye didn't turn up on the beach. Where in the name of all that's holy have ye been?"

By now the others had gathered around to slap him on the back. Sir Roger turned away so that the others would not see his eyes well up.

"It's a long story, Dec, and I will tell it till yer all sick of hearing, but I need to get me to the King. I have information he needs to know."

"Aye, lad," said Sir Roger, thrusting a bowl into Roland's hand. "But have a bit of this to get yer strength back. Ye look like ye need it."

Roland hesitated but a second, then scooped his hand into the gruel and ate greedily. It had been near three days since his last meagre meal. The knight stood and looked at the dirty and battered face of his former squire. It had aged much since he first saw the boy on the road to York. It was a man's face now. It gave him a twinge of sadness.

When the last dregs of the bowl were consumed, Sir Robin beckoned for him to follow and they made their way through the tents toward the King's headquarters. When they arrived, the King's guard recognized Sir Robin and motioned him to pass, but stopped Roland.

"He's with me, lads, and he's just returned from a special mission for the King. I'd let him pass," said Sir Robin casually. The two guards at the entrance glanced at each other and nodded. Sir Robin grabbed Roland by the arm and led him inside. The tent was huge with a number of tables set up, some with maps, others with the remains of the noon meal. A few high nobles milled about inside, but none stood near where the King sat pouring over a scroll. The monarch looked to be in a foul mood and they found it convenient to avoid him at such times. Sir Robin approached and cleared his throat. Richard looked up with a furrowed brow.

"Loxley, what is your report? Are they still moving inland?"

"Aye, your grace. We pushed a few miles farther up the main road, but were stopped by heavy infantry."

The King nodded absently, then seemed to see Sir Robin's companion for the first time.

"Who is this?"

Roland bowed.

"Sir Roland of Kinder Scout, your grace—returned from my mission. Forgive my lateness and my appearance, but I thought it urgent to report what I've seen."

"Kinder Scout, you say?" For a moment the King struggled to place the young man who stood before him. Then it came to him.

"De Laval's squire. I knighted you for holding the breach at Acre! Good God, we all thought you dead when the Irish lad came back." As the King rose, he glanced at the few noblemen still present.

"Clear the room," he said, by way of dismissal, and they all made haste to exit the tent. He placed a hand on Roland's shoulder. "Tell me what you've seen, Sir Roland."

How to tell it?

"Your grace, Sir Declan and I scouted the forces of Saladin before they marched from Jerusalem to lay a trap for you at Arsuf. Thankfully, he made it out in time to bring you warning."

The King nodded.

"Sir Declan's warning was well timed. We were ready when Saladin attacked, and still we were almost overwhelmed. I hate to think of the outcome had we been surprised. But all this we know. Tell me what I don't know."

"Your grace, I was captured when Sir Declan escaped. I was carried back to Jerusalem and imprisoned. Along with many other Christian prisoners, we were put to work strengthening the defences of the city."

The King's eyebrows shot up.

"You have been inside Jerusalem?"

"Aye, lord."

For a moment the King had a wistful look on his face.

"Was it beautiful?"

"Aye, your grace. Very beautiful, but strong."

The King's manner turned serious.

"You are a young man, Sir Roland, but you were at Acre. You saw what it took to breach the walls there. Can it be done in Jerusalem?"

Roland had not expected the King to ask his opinion, and now he hesitated. Would this most warlike of kings scoff at what he had to say?

"Your grace, any fortress can be taken with enough troops and time, but the defences of Jerusalem are much stouter than those at Acre, and, in truth, we had to starve that city out to win it. With respect, I do not think we have the men to fight our way to the city and besiege it or the time to starve it into submission. I saw new troops arriving daily to strengthen the Saracen army. Saladin will only grow stronger in time. Can we say the same, your grace?"

The King scowled, but held his tongue. He began to pace in front of the two knights, slamming a huge fist into his palm as he walked. Finally he stopped and looked at the weary young man before him.

"Do you not think God will lead us to victory, Sir Roland—despite what you have seen?"

Roland thought for a moment to tell the King that he had been brought before Saladin and had seen no hint of surrender in him. No doubt the Sultan also thought his cause favoured by God—but a more potent recollection came to him.

"Your grace, in my scouting I chanced upon the field of Hattin. I have seen the bones of those who thought God would give them victory. I would trust to what we can do without his help. It does not seem to be something we can rely on."

At this the King gave a faint smile.

"I'll ask the bishops that hover around me what they think of that!" he said. "I've come to expect my advisors to always agree with me, which is gratifying, but rarely helpful. It surprises me when a man will tell me what I do not wish to hear. You have my thanks for that, Sir Roland. I think you've learned much from your master. Sir Roger was never one to mince words. Now get yerself back to camp and get some rest. It looks like you need it."

With that dismissal, Roland and Sir Robin left the King and made their way back toward Sir Roger's cook fire. As they approached, Friar Tuck rushed forward to greet them.

"Roland! I just got the news of your deliverance. I have prayed that you still lived, and as you can see, my prayers are very potent! Welcome back, lad."

"Father! I thank you for your prayers. They were sorely needed."

"You have no idea, my son! At first, I prayed you had been captured and not killed, but events put an end to that particular prayer," the friar said, with genuine sadness in his voice.

"Events, Father? What events."

Declan stepped forward.

"Roland, the King had the prisoners at Acre slaughtered. Perhaps he thought to frighten Saladin—who knows? But we feared that the Christian prisoners in his hands must have paid a sore price for that folly."

Roland's face turned pale beneath the grime that covered it.

"My God, this will not frighten Saladin. He will have them all executed—of that I have no doubt." He turned to Tuck.

"Father, will you say one of your potent prayers for those men and one for the man who saved my life—a prayer for Sir Harry Percival?"

The friar nodded and raised his eyes to heaven.

***

As dawn greeted a new day in Jerusalem, a ragged column of Christian prisoners was marched out to the square in the citadel. Swords were drawn and the bloody work of carrying out the Sultan's orders began. Outside the walls, a cavalry patrol moved unhurriedly along the road that ran over the flank of the Mount of Olives and out to the Judean desert. No enemy would likely approach the city from that desolate quarter, but orders were orders.

They paid no attention to the tattered old man who waved at them near the top of the hill as they passed. Just another old beggar on the highway. The faded cross on his ragged tunic was no longer visible from a distance.

***

Three days passed as Roland slowly regained his strength. Despite his ordeal, he could not just lie around and do nothing. He began to busy himself with the basic duties of a squire, duties that he and Declan had gravely neglected since being pressed into the King's service.

He might no longer be a squire, but still served Roger de Laval until his master chose to release him. Besides, it always calmed him to brush the grey coat of Bucephalus. He was in the paddock ministering to the big warhorse when Declan burst in.

"The King wants to see us—and Sir Roger—now!"

Roland gave him a questioning look. The Irishman shrugged, but the pained look on his face spoke for them all. Summons from the King rarely ended well.

For this occasion they dressed in the best clothes they could find among the faded garments in camp. Roland's view of the King had changed irrevocably since he learned of the execution of the Acre prisoners. He could never again summon up awe and admiration for the man, but Richard was still king—for all his flaws. Once more Sir Roger advised caution.

"The last time the man wanted something from the two of ye, one almost died of thirst and t'other found hisself in a dungeon. As for me, I've not seen my wife or child in a year and half. The King must be obeyed, but for mercy sake, do not volunteer for anything!"

Roland cinched up his sword belt as Sir Roger finished speaking.

"No need to warn me, my lord. I will be on my guard, as I know Declan will—though from what, I cannot fathom."

Together the three knights from Shipbrook trudged off through the dusty campground toward the King's tent. It was pitched overlooking the sea—the better to catch what little breeze there was.

The sun had dropped near the western horizon when they arrived. They were escorted in by one of the guards. No one stopped Roland this time. The King was alone and greeted them warmly.

"Ah, Sir Roger and his brave lads, can I offer you some wine? A shipment just arrived from Cyprus." The men nodded and the King poured the goblets himself. He raised his and offered a toast.

"A pox on this infernal place!"

They hesitated, then raised their glasses.

"A pox!" they toasted, with enough fervour that the King arched an eyebrow.

"You will be wondering why I have called you here."

"Aye, your grace," Sir Roger answered for them.

"I have work for you all—critical work. Do ye stand ready?"

None hesitated. They were boxed in and knew it.

"Aye, lord," they said in unison.

"Good! Good!" the King smiled broadly and clapped Sir Roger hard on the shoulder. Then his expression turned serious.

"Gentlemen, I have sworn to take the Holy City, but the French have deserted me, as have the Germans. Absent a miracle, a siege will fail, as Sir Roland here has so clearly pointed out to me. So what am I to do?"

He let the question hang in the air for a moment, but expected no reply from the men before him.

"I will confide to you that I have opened secret talks with Saladin. The man knows he cannot defeat me in battle. Arsuf proved that. But he also seems to share Sir Roland's belief that Jerusalem will not yield to a siege. It seems we have reached a stalemate, but I must not leave here having gained nothing. In the end, I must strike a bargain that will justify the blood and treasure we have expended here and get myself back to England. There is trouble afoot there."

"Trouble, your grace?" Sir Roger asked.

"Aye, my little brother seems to have lost his wits, but all will be set to rights upon my return. In the meantime, I have important work for men such as you."

He turned to the two younger knights.

"Sir Roland and Sir Declan, you have each shown courage and resourcefulness in my service. I have a message that must be delivered to the Queen, but it seems my messengers have recently fallen prone to "accidents" and have failed to arrive. I trust that you two can avoid such a fate. So I would have you take ship at the first opportunity and seek out the Queen in London. My message is for her ears only and must get through."

"What is the message, your grace?" asked Roland.

"Tell the Queen that I shall depart these lands no later than midsummer next and will return to England by Christ's Mass. She will know what to do with that information—but take heed, there are many who would also profit from knowing my plans, so be on your guard."

"Aye, lord," said Roland.

"Aye, lord," said Declan

The King turned to the older knight.

"Sir Roger, my old warhorse! I know where your heart would lead you, but I beg you to stay with me a bit longer. For me to strike a bargain with Saladin, I must remain a threat to him and it is our heavy cavalry he fears. You are the best leader of heavy cavalry in my army. I am giving you command over the English mounted knights. Many are of higher rank than you, but you will act with my full authority. I intend to press the Saracens and force them to bargain with me. I know ye long to get back home, but your King needs you here."

Sir Roger could only bow his head as they were dismissed. When they exited the tent they saw Sir Robin and Friar Tuck standing beside the guards.

"Summoned?" asked Sir Roger.

"Aye," said Tuck. "It seems a day for summons."

As the three knights from Shipbrook headed back to their camp, Sir Robin and Tuck disappeared into the King's tent. The King rose to greet the new arrivals.

"Ah, Sir Robin and Father Augustine, can I offer you some wine? A shipment just arrived from Cyprus."

***

That night five men gathered around a sputtering campfire as a strong desert wind blew sand and sparks about. No one looked happy.

"It is not right, my lord. Not right," said Roland shaking his head. "I made an oath and now must break it at the King's command. What shall I say to Lady Catherine?"

Sir Roger de Laval snorted.

"Ah, she will not be happy with you for coming home without me, but she will be furious with me for staying here. We must all take our medicine in our own time."

Friar Tuck threw a small piece of driftwood on the fire.

"The Templar Grand Master volunteered my services to the King. Apparently he feels I lack the proper zeal for slaying Saracens—and in that he is more correct than he knows. Still, it irks me."

He and Sir Robin had returned to camp only a short time after the three men from Shipbrook. They had also been given a mission—to take the same message to the Queen, but to seek her out in Normandy. The King was not sure where the Queen would be in three months and was taking no chances.

"I must confess, I am happy to be going home, but this business has left me with a bad taste. A lot of good men are going to die here so the King can save face." He quickly looked up at Sir Roger. "Present company excepted, I'm sure."

Sir Roger looked across the fire at the young knight from Loxley and smiled.

"I wish I were that sure! But you and the Friar, as well as my young lads here, are as likely to be heading into danger as those who stay behind. Someone is making the King's messengers disappear. See that you don't join them."

A gust of wind blew a swirl of sparks into the sky.

"Amen to that," said Friar Tuck and crossed himself.

Homeward

The sun was well up in the eastern sky as the men gathered on the beach near Jaffa to say their farewells. Roland and Declan had secured their gear in the small boat that would take them out to their ship, and Sir Robin and Friar Tuck had done the same in another boat hauled ashore a few yards down the beach. The leave-taking was strained. Tuck turned to Roland and broke the awkward silence that had fallen over the group.

"Master Inness, mayhap we will meet again—under pleasanter circumstances I pray."

"I would take that as my great good fortune," said Roland as he grasped the monk's beefy hand.

"As would I. Ye recall the priory where yer kin are sheltered, lad?" the monk asked.

"Aye, Father. I'll get me there as soon as my business is done. It's time the Inness' were a family again."

As Roland finished his farewell with Tuck, Sir Robin stepped forward and offered his hand.

"Sir Roland, I hope we'll cross paths again," he said. "Chester is not so far from Nottinghamshire and I've not had the opportunity to challenge you to a rematch with longbows."

"I would be delighted to take that challenge, Sir Robin, but as you may have heard, I lost my own bow to Saladin."

"Aye, I heard that and I think it a shame that the best archer in England should be bowless." He slipped his own longbow

244

off his shoulder and handed it to Roland, then leaned in and whispered. *"I have a man, a Dane to be precise, who knows the craft. I've put away two dozen of these back in Loxley manor for...uncertain times. I'll not miss this one."*

Roland took the bow in his hands. It was rough, like his own and perhaps an inch or two longer. It was no beauty, but he had seen it used by a great bowman. It would serve him well until he could craft his own. He would keep safe the knowledge of Sir Robin's secret cache of longbows.

Times were always uncertain.

"My thanks, Sir Robin, and a safe journey to you."

While Tuck and Sir Robin had been saying their farewells to Roland, Declan had been taking his leave of Sir Roger. As the knight and the friar turned away, the Norman knight took Roland aside.

"Son, it's an ill thing the King has done here. I know you and Declan have proven yerselves—more than once, but the men of Shipbrook came here together. By rights, we should go home together."

"Aye, my lord. I pledged to Lady Catherine that I would watch your back. Now I feel I am betraying you, and her." As he spoke he fought the lump growing in his throat. "My lord, you have been...to me, you have been..."

Sir Roger stopped him.

"I know, lad. I know. No need to speak of it. It was a good day when you tried to filch that mutton back on the road to York—for both of us. I know yer own father would be proud of you." Sir Roger's voice had grown husky as he spoke, but he gathered himself.

"Now, be on your toes, and as soon as duty allows, get to Shipbrook. Get to Catherine and Millie. Tell them I live and not to fear. For though Saladin himself was to bar my path, I ..."

Now it was Roland's turn to help his master get past his emotions.

"I will, lord. You know I will."

"Then God go with you, Roland Inness, and look for me one day at the gates of Shipbrook." With that, the big Norman knight stepped back. In his place stepped Declan O'Duinne.

"Ready?"

"Aye."

The words had all been said. Roland and Declan walked down the beach to where a Genoese boatman waited. They shoved off and rowed out to where the Christian fleet lay at anchor. The ship they approached was as familiar to them as any home they had ever had. It was the *Sprite*—assigned to convey them back to England.

"Welcome aboard, lads—or should I address you as Sir Roland and Sir Declan." Master Sparks shouted this down from the sterncastle as the two started to climb up the side. Both men grinned as they hauled themselves over the rail and onto the deck.

"I see word travels, even out to the fleet, Master Sparks. It is good to see you," said Roland. A voice broke in from behind them.

"Just 'cause yer now new-minted knights does not mean ye can laze around me deck on this voyage, young sirs."

It was Boda, who spoke.

"I'm glad to see you too, Master Boda," Roland replied.

The anchor was weighed and the *Sprite* caught the offshore wind to get underway. Roland and Declan stood on the sterncastle next to Master Sparks and looked shoreward. Sir Robin and Tuck had taken their own boat out to the fleet and were no longer in sight. A lone figure was left standing on the beach and Roland waved to Sir Roger de Laval until he disappeared from view.

When will I see him again?

***

The *Sprite* made better time heading home than on the outward-bound voyage. Master Sparks dropped anchor once more on the coast of Crete to replenish their water supply and again in Sardinia. They thoughtfully skirted Sicily. While Richard had tamed Tancred, in theory, they did not want to tempt fate by putting in there.

As they passed the coast of Calabria, Roland thought of Isabella and wondered if she had found contentment—and a man. Master Sparks offered to put in at the river town where she had left them to make inquiries, but Roland would not countenance a delay.

Luck was with them when they reached the Pillars of Hercules. This time a steady breeze was blowing out into the Atlantic, and though galleys sallied forth from both sides of the strait, none could match the speed of the *Sprite* in a good wind. They fell behind as the ship cleared the narrow waterway and veered to the north for the run up the coast of Iberia and into the Bay of Biscay. Ten days later, a cry came from the lookout.

"Land to port!"

Roland and Declan rushed to the forecastle and peered into the distance. Boda stepped up beside them. The low hills of Cornwall were just emerging over the horizon.

"There she is, lads, England."

Master Sparks called from the sterncastle where he manned the steering oar. "Have ye decided where ye wish to land, gentlemen?"

They had. It was not one of the channel ports or any of the many anchorages along the southern coast of the island. These would all be closely watched. It was a place that no one hoping to intercept messengers from the King would expect. Roland absently touched the silver yew tree amulet at his neck.

"Master Sparks, set a course for the west coast," he said. "We are making for the mouth of the River Dee."

They were going home.

Historical Note

The history of the Third Crusade is well documented and forms the backdrop for the continuing saga of Roland Inness and his companions in *Warbow*. While I have tried to stay true to that history in this novel, *Warbow* is not intended to be a rigorous work of historical fiction. The presence of Friar Tuck and Sir Robin of Loxley as characters in this story will hopefully alert readers that there is as much myth as history in the Saga of Roland Inness.

There are a number of historical characters who appear in *Warbow*. King Richard, Queen Eleanor, King Philip of France and Saladin are, of course, major players during this period. I have used a number of actual English nobles as significant characters in Roland's story. Ranulf, Earl of Chester, his wife Lady Constance and most notably my villain, Sir William de Ferrers, are real, but their motives and actions as they relate to this story are entirely fictional.

I suspect Sir William was no more or less villainous than any of his fellow earls of that period. Robert, Earl of Derby, was also real and did die at the siege of Acre, but his name was William, like his son. To avoid confusion between the two, I gave William the elder the name of his own father—Robert, the Second Earl of Derby.

Several interesting story elements in *Warbow* are historically accurate. King Philip's white hunting falcon did escape while he was landing and did go over to the enemy. Philip tried, unsuccessfully, to negotiate its return. Hezekiah's tunnel and Solomon's Quarry still exist today and can be visited if you are in Jerusalem. The tunnel was constructed as described in the book, but whether there is a connecting passage from Solomon's Quarry to the tunnel is another matter entirely.

And yes, Richard did order the death of about fifteen hundred hostages at Acre when Saladin was late with his ransom. Some suggest that he did so because he could not afford to leave troops behind to guard them when he marched south, but regardless, it has been a stain on Richard's reputation ever since.

I did make use of excellent historical works to provide the proper flavour needed to bring this tale to life. In particular, I would recommend *Warriors of God* by James Reston, Jr. and *Dungeon, Fire and Sword* by John J. Robinson as great places to get insight into Richard of England, Saladin, the Knights Templar and the complex politics of the time.

Warbow is the second of four novels in The Saga of Roland Inness. It takes Roland Inness from England to the Holy Land for the Third Crusade and back to England where he will seek to settle accounts for his father's murder and find a place for himself in a restive land where kings, princes and nobles all manoeuvre for power.

To learn more about The Saga of Roland Inness and the author, visit www.waynegrantbooks.com.

ABOUT THE AUTHOR

Wayne Grant grew up in a tiny cotton town in rural Louisiana where hunting, fishing and farming are a way of life. Between chopping cotton, dove hunting and Little League ball he developed a love of great adventure stories like Call It Courage and Kidnapped.

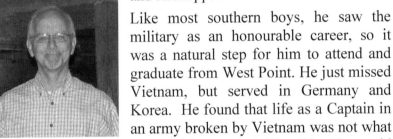

Like most southern boys, he saw the military as an honourable career, so it was a natural step for him to attend and graduate from West Point. He just missed Vietnam, but served in Germany and Korea. He found that life as a Captain in an army broken by Vietnam was not what he wanted and returned to Louisiana and civilian life. He would later serve for four years as a senior official in the Pentagon and had the honour of playing a small part in the rebuilding of a great U.S. Army.

Through it all he retained his love of great adventure writing and when he had two sons he began telling them stories before bedtime. Those stories became his first novel, *Longbow*.

The remaining novels in The Saga of Roland Inness, **The Broken Realm** and **The Ransomed Crown** are now available on Amazon. The author is now working on a fifth Roland Inness story.

77365005R00146

Made in the USA
Middletown, DE
20 June 2018